Re

Doms of the FBI #7

Michele Zurlo

www.michelezurloauthor.com

Doms of the FBI: Re/Captured
Copyright © February 2017 by Michele Zurlo
ISBN: 978-1-942414-31-5

All rights reserved. This copy is intended for the original purchaser of this e-book ONLY. No part of this e-book may be reproduced, stored in or introduced into a retrieval system, or transmitted, in any form, or by any means (electronic, mechanical, photocopying, recording, or otherwise), without the prior written permission from the copyright owner and Lost Goddess Publishing LLC. Please do not participate in or encourage piracy of copyrighted materials in violation of the author's rights. Purchase only authorized editions.

Editor: Nicoline Tiernan
Cover Artist: Anne Kay

Published by Lost Goddess Publishing LLC
www.michelezurloauthor.com

This e-book is a work of fiction. While reference might be made to actual historical events or existing locations, the names, characters, places and incidents are either the product of the author's imagination or are used fictitiously, and any resemblance to actual persons, living or dead, business establishments, events, or locales is entirely coincidental.

Warning: This e-book contains sexually explicit scenes and adult language and may be considered offensive to some readers. It is not meant for underage readers.

DISCLAIMER: Education and training are necessary in order to learn safe BDSM practices. Lost Goddess Publishing LLC is not responsible for any loss, harm, injury or death resulting from use of the information contained in any of its titles. This is a work of fiction, and license has been taken with regard to BDSM practices.

Reading Order
Re/Bound
Re/Paired
Re/Claimed
Re/Defined
Re/Leased*
Re/Viewed
Re/Captured

*Re/Leased is also a prequel to the SAFE Security series

Acknowledgments

Thanks to Karen for her keen eye and enthusiasm.

As always, thanks to the person who is my editor and partner in so many crimes—my wife.

Blurb:

When a day helping out at Legal Aid puts Katrina in the crosshairs of a serial killer bent on sending his version of romantic gifts, life starts to spiral out of control. Not only is she trying to plan her wedding, but work and home life are increasingly hectic.

Keith has doubts about Kat and the reasons she keeps postponing the wedding, so he sets out to recapture her heart. Meanwhile, the serial killer's obsession with Katrina only grows—threatening her entire family.

Sacrifices must be made, but can love help them survive the fallout?

Warnings: BDSM, anal sex, D/s

 Chapter 1

Katrina Legato hustled down the wide hall, heels clicking on the polished marble and echoing her resolute attitude. Shoulders back and head held high, she downed the last of her coffee and tossed the paper cup into the recycling bin outside the door of Judge Osman's courtroom. The heavy wooden double doors were open, signaling that court was not yet in session. She sailed through them and to her place at the prosecutor's table.

This morning's business would be quick, just the entering of pleas and hearing judgments on motions. After this, her day at work was over, but the hard parts were just beginning. Now that she was a parent, taking half a personal day meant kid business. Today Angelina, her 6-year-old adopted daughter, had an appointment with her therapist. Angie's fits and tantrums had diminished greatly in the two years since she'd come to live with Katrina and her fiancé, Keith, but they weren't gone.

Taking a pile of files and a legal pad from her bag, Katrina made sure she had everything she needed for the morning to proceed without surprises.

"Morning, Trina."

Katrina threw a smile at Alvina Lindholm, a co-worker and friend, as the woman slid into the chair next to her. "Hey, Vina. How are you?"

"I was doing great, but then I heard Osman's in a pissy mood. Things may not go our way today." Vina grimaced, which did little to mar the beauty of her face. Vina was one of those women who had perfect hair no matter how windy it was and perfect skin no matter how many loaded potato skins she ate. She wore no makeup and seemed unaware of her physical perfection. Over the past two years since she'd started working at the DOJ with Katrina, the two had become good friends.

Michele Zurlo

Katrina refused to let that news spoil her day. The morning was supposed to be the easy part. She finished riffling through her papers and sat down. "He's gearing up to run for Court of Appeals."

"Again?" Vina added. "He keeps losing."

Osman had joined the minority party in his district, so the votes weren't there. "Judges shouldn't have to be affiliated with a political party. That's just wrong." As someone who planned to run one day, it irritated Katrina that she would have to declare her political beliefs, but it was the only way to get funding for the inevitable campaign.

"All rise."

Vina and Katrina got to their feet as Judge Osman entered the courtroom. He was a fair judge, and he was a stickler for following procedure and the letter of the law. In the five years she'd been with the DOJ, Katrina had never found him to be unreasonable or moody.

Today proved to be no exception. They moved through the morning, finalizing pleas and deals for sentencing, without hitting a snag. After her final case finished, Judge Osman threw his curveball.

"Before we adjourn, I have one final piece of business."

Katrina paused, notepad in hand, and waited. Her mind was already on picking up Angelina from kindergarten.

"Ms. Legato and Ms. Lindholm, Legal Aid has a tremendous backlog. I'm assigning you each thirty cases."

With her plate already full, Katrina didn't want to take on more. She stood. "Your Honor, with all due respect, we're not defense attorneys."

"You have enough experience on the prosecutorial side to know what you need to do. You're both bright and efficient. I have faith that you'll be fine." He lifted his gavel.

Vina stood next. "Your Honor, I think what my esteemed colleague means is that we both have our hands full already and won't be able to give these cases the attention they deserve."

"Right now, nobody is giving them any attention. Report to Legal Aid this afternoon."

Katrina lifted a hand. "I have personal business this afternoon."

"Not anymore."

If this had been a doctor appointment for herself, Katrina would have no trouble canceling, but this was for Angelina. "Your Honor, it concerns my daughter who has special needs. I can't reschedule." Katrina almost never played the special needs' card. She'd spent a lot of time and effort fighting so that Angelina wasn't treated differently from her peers.

Judge Osman had four children of his own, and he was running on a platform of putting families first. Refusing—on record—to let Katrina attend to her child's needs would give his opponent easy ammunition. He hesitated. "Tomorrow morning. First thing." He banged the gavel before either of them could issue a further objection.

Vina turned to Katrina, eyes wide. "I've never heard of a judge assigning a prosecutor to help out at Legal Aid."

"Maybe he's looking to distinguish himself?" The other problem was that Katrina and Vina both specialized in prosecuting white collar crimes. Most of their defendants did not qualify for state-provided legal help. "This is going to suck. We have to let Alder know as soon as possible."

They hurried upstairs to the DOJ offices to find that the news had reached Elizabeth Alder, their immediate boss, already. Statuesque and imposing, she met Katrina and Vina at the door to her office. "I know. There's nothing we can do about it."

"Thirty cases," Vina said. "That's insane."

Alder didn't appear impressed. "Not for Legal Aid. Perhaps it's good for you to see what the other side is like. It'll help you appreciate the resources we have here."

Katrina already appreciated the resources available to the DOJ. After college, she'd toyed with the idea of taking a job at Legal Aid, but the pay was nothing, she didn't have a burning desire to live with her parents for the rest of her life, and most judges came from the prosecutorial side. She checked the time. "I have to go. If you need anything, leave a message. I won't have my cell on for most of the afternoon."

Corey, Angelina's four-year-old brother, was with her parents, and they could take care of any emergency should it arise. Three days a week, they provided free day care. Corey loved preschool and school-based day care, but he loved his grandparents even more. Katrina knew she was fortunate to have parents willing to pitch in and help out, especially because she and Keith often needed assistance outside of normal day care hours. Keith's parents, both practicing alcoholics, weren't part of their lives, though they did send birthday and holiday cards.

Her cell rang as she approached her car in the parking garage, the chimes indicating the caller. "Keith, I'm leaving now."

"I'm running late," he said. "Sorry. Can you get Angie, and I'll meet you there?"

Michele Zurlo

This was not unexpected. As one of the best FBI agents to ever exist—Katrina was not at all biased—Keith's schedule was never as exact or reliable as hers. Bad guys tended to go out of their way not to cooperate. "Sure, no problem. Is everything okay?" She meant specifically in regard to him and his general health and wellbeing. His line of work put him in some dangerous situations.

"Yeah. I'll be there. Don't worry." Someone said something in the background, and he responded. "Kat, I have to go. I love you."

Keith was the only one who called her Kat. The rest of her family and friends shortened her name to Trina. A wave of love washed over her. Those simple words coming from him never failed to make her knees weak. "I love you too. See you soon."

She'd met Keith thirteen years ago when her older brother, Malcolm, had been home on leave from the Marines. He'd brought his new best friend home to meet his family, and Katrina had promptly fallen in love. Handsome didn't begin to describe the 6'2, blond-haired, green-eyed man. He exuded sex and danger, two qualities that made every woman who crossed his path weak in the knees. Keith's badass look wasn't for show, either. He'd looked like the kind of man who spent his days making criminals quake in their boots and his evenings using women and tossing them aside—and that's exactly who he'd been.

Back then, Keith hadn't appeared to notice her in a romantic way. As the years passed, he'd become part of the family. Her parents had treated him like a third son, and even extended relatives had invited him to events like they did the rest of the Legatos. Keith had prohibited himself from looking at Katrina as anything but a sister, and Malcolm had also placed that restriction on his best friend. He'd known exactly how Keith treated women, and he hadn't wanted his sister's heart shattered. She and her mother had been the only women Keith had allowed into his heart, and he'd put them in a box that he stowed safely on a pedestal. Breaking through that barrier had been difficult, and it had taken her eleven years to make a move.

She made it to the school just before Angelina's scheduled lunch period, and she sighed. Angelina did not react well when her schedule was disrupted, and she was even less thrilled when she missed her favorite class—recess. "I hope you had morning recess," Katrina mumbled as she approached the building. Shrieks, the happy kind, carried from the playground on the side of the building.

In the office, they smiled politely. Katrina knew they didn't like her, not since she'd threatened to sue when they balked at making accommodations for Angelina's needs. They'd argued that it was too early, and that they preferred to wait until second grade. Katrina had come armed with the law and Keith, who could be scary under normal circumstances. Put his little Angie into the mix, and his bearing hinted at lethal tendencies.

"Can I go get her?" The school had a policy of making parents wait in the office for their children. "It might be easier."

"Of course, Mrs. Rossetti." The secretary's saccharine smile widened. "I'll let Mrs. Tully know you're coming down."

Katrina arrived at the cul-de-sac that housed three kindergarten classrooms in time to hear Angelina's protest. "I don't want to go."

Peeking into the classroom door, she spied Angelina sitting on the carpet in the corner of the room, arms and legs crossed and epic defiance written across her face.

When she got like that, she looked so much like Keith that Katrina had to stop her heart from melting. Angelina and Corey were the biological children of Keith's older sister, Savannah. Savannah had abused Keith when he was a child, beating him bloody on a regular basis. Though nothing had been proven, both Angelina's behaviors and Keith's certainty pointed toward Angelina having suffered similarly. Katrina's heart went out to the little girl.

Mrs. Tully motioned Katrina forward, giving permission to enter. If the office staff and administration was cool toward Katrina, Angelina's teacher was the opposite. Warm and compassionate, she'd bonded with Angelina from the start.

Katrina knelt next to Angelina and Mrs. Tully. "Hey, there, Angie. It's time to go."

Angelina's bottom lip trembled, and she tugged at the end of her dark brown ponytail. "Is Daddy coming?"

"He's going to meet us there."

She looked up, her round, chocolate eyes tear bright. "Did he catch a bad guy?"

Unsure of Keith's progress or even what case he was working on today, Katrina lifted her shoulders. "If not, then he's getting closer." Holding out a hand, she invited Angelina to get up. "Come on, Angie. Let's get your things."

Angelina looked to Mrs. Tully. "Will you read my story tomorrow?"

"Of course." Mrs. Tully smiled. "We'll do it special for you." She set a hand on Katrina's shoulder. "I have to get the class ready for lunch. Take your time."

They didn't have time, but forcing Angelina would lead to a meltdown. Katrina rubbed Angelina's back. "Baby, let's go see Daddy."

Michele Zurlo

From the start, Angelina had favored Keith. The two had a special bond forged from factors Angelina didn't understand—but she definitely felt it.

Angelina put her hand in Katrina's, and they left without further incident. In the car, Angelina ate her lunch while sharing observations and shooting questions at Katrina. "Kyle S. took the truck I was playing with, and I used my words."

They'd been working with her on controlling her anger. Katrina peeked into the rearview mirror to smile at Angelina. "That's great. I'm proud of you. Did he give it back?"

She thought for a moment. "He told Mrs. Tully that I said a bad word."

Katrina swallowed. When Angelina had first come to them, she'd possessed a vocabulary that had included colorful swears and creative slurs Katrina had to Google in order to understand. Breaking her of the habit had proven difficult because it also meant guarding their own language. "Did you say a bad word?"

"No. I told him to give me back the damn toy. I didn't say fucking toy. That would have been a bad word." Angelina munched a carrot stick and looked out the window at the passing scenery. "Mrs. Tully said for Kyle S. to give back the toy, and she said I shouldn't say damn. I told her that Daddy and you say it, and she said then it was a word for at home."

Katrina pulled into the therapist's parking lot, scanning for Keith's black SUV. "Actually, that's an adult word. I'd like if you didn't say it anymore."

Angelina sighed. "Mommy, I'm doing my best, okay? I was thinking the F word, but I didn't say it."

"Thank you for that." She stifled the urge to laugh. Sometimes Angelina came up with such wise and mature responses, and they sounded strange coming from a child's mouth.

"Are you still proud of me?"

She spotted Keith leaning against the back of his car, and her heart beat faster. His white dress shirt delineated his broad shoulders and muscular chest, and his slacks pulled tight around his powerful thighs. Katrina's pussy woke up as well, and she pulled into an empty spot two spaces away. "Of course. You used your words." In the past, Angelina had hit, cried, and thrown tantrums when she was upset, frustrated, or angry.

"Daddy!" Angelina unlatched her seatbelt as Keith opened her door. Once the path was clear, she launched herself from the car, trusting Keith to catch her. He always did.

Katrina emerged to find the man of her dreams listening intently as Angelina related the woe of having to miss afternoon recess.

"We'll take Corey to the park after dinner." His reassurance mollified Angelina, and he leaned down to greet Katrina with a kiss. "Everything go okay?"

That was code for *please let her not have thrown a fit*. This was the first therapy appointment since Angelina had started school, and they hadn't been sure of her reaction. "It was fine. She ate lunch in the car."

Keith's expression remained impassive, which wasn't a new look for him. She'd grown used to watching for micro-expressions. "Did you eat?"

"No time."

"Want a carrot, Mommy?" Angelina shoved a carrot at Katrina. "I have three more."

"Thanks." Katrina accepted the gift. "We should get inside."

Keith parked his free hand on the small of Katrina's back and guided her into the building. She shivered at the contact and the possessiveness of his touch. In the waiting room, he set Angelina on the floor and leaned closer to Katrina. "We can stop off and get something when we leave here." His breath feathered against the sensitive skin on her neck, and her nipples hardened. He might as well have ordered her to remove her clothes. "Damn, you smell so good."

Her body swayed toward his, and his arm came around her waist.

"Tonight," he promised. "When the kids go to sleep."

"Tonight," she agreed.

The therapy sessions consisted of Angelina spending time with a therapist while Keith and Katrina met with a counselor who helped them navigate parental problems, and then the trio met up for a group session. At first, they'd attended sessions weekly, but now they were down to once a month.

They watched Angelina disappear into a room with Dr. Walter, and they followed Ravi into the room across the hall. Finding a counselor who worked for both of them had been difficult. They'd gone through six so far, each unsuitable for one reason or another—one had spent the time giggling at everything Keith said even though he hadn't said anything particularly jocular, another had been terrified of him, a third had railed at Katrina for being a submissive, two had moved to other jobs, and the last one had been convinced that their relationship was abusive.

Ravi seemed to understand them the best so far. They'd been with him for almost a year. His office was tiny, but comfortable. They settled into their spots, Ravi in his chair, while Keith and Katrina sat on the sofa.

"How are things?" He smiled widely, his teeth extra white against the darkness of his lips.

Keith threaded his fingers through Katrina's. "Excellent. The wedding is in two months, and Angie is excited to be the flower girl. She's come so far in such a short time."

"Children are resilient," Ravi agreed. "How have things been at home? Any meltdowns?"

"Three months," Katrina said. "It's been three months. Today a kid took her toy, and she told him to give the damn thing back. A year ago, she would have dropped the F-bomb and punched him."

Keith pressed his lips together and looked at his lap.

She knew exactly what he was thinking. Angelina had been expelled from three different preschools. "It's an improvement."

"I don't disagree."

"Then what?"

"I signed you up for a Tae Kwan Do class."

Katrina started. "Me? Why?" She'd learned the basics of self-defense years ago, and she'd used those skills in the real world.

"You and Angie. It's a mother-child class. I would have signed up, but I'm too experienced for a beginner class."

She knew he'd waited until they were on neutral ground to tell her that. They'd argued over the kinds of extracurricular activities Angelina should do. Katrina was in favor of traditional sports like soccer and lacrosse, while Keith kept suggesting one form of martial arts after another.

"Are you fucking kidding me? We finally got her not to lash out as her first reaction to a negative emotion, and you want to teach her to fight?"

"I want her to learn the situations under which you should and shouldn't fight. They teach more than just kicking and punching, Kat. They teach problem solving." He tightened his grip on her hand, not allowing her to pull away. "Since her last meltdown I've been letting her blow off steam on my punching bag. I told her anytime she feels like she's getting upset or mad, she could use it, and she has been. That's why she hasn't been melting down. She needs a way to productively funnel her aggression."

Keith and Katrina didn't have a 24/7 dynamic, but that didn't mean Keith's dominant tendencies ever went away. This was the heart of who he was, and while Katrina loved that about him, it also drove her crazy.

Looking for a way to productively funnel her anger, Katrina narrowed her eyes at Keith. "You signed us up for a class without asking me first."

"I've been asking you for a year. You keep saying no."

"And I'll keep saying no." Her volume rose, and she channeled her inner prosecutor. "She doesn't need violence in her life. She's been through too much already." She pulled harder, yanking her hand from his grip.

He shifted, parking his arm on the couch behind her and crowding into her personal space. "Kat, she may not consciously remember anything, but stuff happened. If she doesn't have an outlet, she's going to look for other ways to numb the pain—drugs, alcohol, sex."

She crossed her arms and huffed. "You'd know." Low blow, she knew, but he did know. He'd become an alcoholic, drinking his way through his teen years, and his appetite for sex was significant.

"I do know, and I'd rather her learn empowerment and self-defense than have her bottle it up. For fuck's sake, I still have a hard time showing any kind of emotion or reaction. My first instinct is always to bury it. I don't want that for Angie."

Tears pricked at Katrina's eyes. She didn't want that life for Angelina or Keith. Once she'd cracked his shell, he'd begun showing more emotion, but most of that was related to protectiveness or sex. Because he'd evolved so much with her, she often forgot that he waged a daily battle with darkness. She twisted to face him and set her palm against his cheek. "I don't want that for either of you."

The steel in his eyes softened, though his dominant stance didn't. "Take the class. It's six weeks."

In addition to understanding how much this meant to Keith, she could see his point. Still she couldn't lose the nagging feeling that the class might traumatize Angelina. She let her hand slip from Keith's cheek to his shoulder. "Ravi, what do you think? Will a class like this be good for Angelina or will it harm her?"

Ravi uncrossed his legs and spread his hands. "It depends on how you approach it. If you frame it as empowerment and exercise, she will probably enjoy it. Taking it together is a good bonding experience, and the two of you need that."

Katrina winced. While Keith and Angelina had immediately bonded, that hadn't been the case for her and Angelina.

Keith slid his arm around her shoulders and pulled her closer. "Kat, it takes time. She distrusts women more than men. That's why we got her a male therapist." They'd tried to find a male teacher, but unfortunately men were actively discouraged from teaching lower grades due to society's unreasonable fear of males who nurture. Only female teachers were available in all the area schools.

"Okay. I'll do it, but if she hates it, we will quit. I'm not going to force her to go to an activity she hates. That would be the opposite of bonding."

The next morning, Katrina woke early to a silent house. She slid out of bed and tiptoed to the shower. Warm water slid down her body, seducing her into lingering even after she'd washed and shaved. She stood there, enjoying the gentle sluice. With her eyes closed, the sensation and the sound urged her mind to wander.

Last night Keith had not lived up to his promise of mind-blowing sex. After all was said and done, they'd fallen in bed too tired for more than a quickie. She'd enjoyed it, but she also knew the full extent of his capabilities. Today she was worried about the task Judge Osman had assigned. It had been years since she'd practiced defensive law. What if she screwed up or forgot something important?

The shower door opened, pulling her from her musings. Keith flashed a sinful smile. "Good morning, my gorgeous sub."

She allowed her gaze to roam down his sinewy and naked body. "Good morning, Master. I see you're fully awake."

With a sexy chuckle, he stepped into the spray and closed the door. "I locked our bedroom door and the bathroom door. Kitty Kat, gimme a kiss."

Rising to her toes, she slipped her arms around his neck and brushed her lips against his. Though he'd commanded her to kiss him, he took over, thrusting his tongue into her mouth to deepen it. She mewed as she surrendered to his mastery. He stabbed his tongue into her mouth, fucking it with small strokes as one hand grasped her wet backside and the other palmed her breast. Her bones melted, and cream rushed to her pussy. When she was breathless, he broke off, biting a path of hot, sucking kisses down her neck. She moaned as he bit into the fleshy part of her shoulder.

"Last night was too fast." His voice vibrated against the hollow of her neck.

"Yes." Right now she would agree to anything he said.

He dipped his head and sucked her nipple into his mouth, a hard pull that she felt all the way to her clit. She clung to him, digging her nails into his shoulders, anchors to keep her from drifting away. Loving the pain, he moaned and released her nipple. "Touch yourself, Kitty Kat."

Obediently she slid one hand between her legs, and he went back to torturing her breasts. Their combined efforts brought her to the brink. "Master, please may I come?"

"Yes."

With that permission, she surrendered to the tension, letting those gentle waves overtake her. Keith abandoned her breasts to hold her while she quaked with the aftereffects of her climax.

"You're so fucking beautiful, Kitty Kat. I love watching you come."

Her eyes fluttered open, and she smiled softly. "Can I touch you, Master? Maybe suck your cock?"

"Another time." He seared her with another kiss, and then he turned her to face the wall. "Brace yourself, Kitty Kat. I'm going to get rough. Come if you can."

She widened her stance and arched her back, assuming the familiar shower-sex position. He slid the tip of his cock along her opening, teasing her swollen tissues before stabbing home. Katrina's breath caught as she savored the way he felt inside, and then she squeezed her vaginal walls.

He groaned as he withdrew and thrust deep. "Vixen."

"Yes, Master."

"Keep doing that."

"Yes, Master."

As promised, he set a furious pace. Katrina timed her squeezes with his thrust, eliciting groans of increasing magnitude from her lover. The small orgasm from masturbating returned, throbbing harder and harder until an even larger climax robbed her of control. She gagged herself by biting her arm to keep from crying out too loudly.

Keith thrust a few more times, and then he buried his face in her neck to muffle his shout as hot semen bathed her insides. He held her until they'd both recovered enough to stand independently. Once upon a time, she'd refused to call him by title. He'd used it to put distance between them, but now using it brought them closer together. He cherished her and respected her autonomy, but he also owned her heart and soul.

He rinsed her body, laughing wickedly when he got to her pussy and she flinched under the force of the water.

"You're evil." She pushed his hand with the shower head away.

"You love it." He smacked a kiss on her mons.

Michele Zurlo

Stroking his head, she urged it toward her pussy. "Maybe you should just use your tongue."

His eyelids shuttered his mossy green eyes, but she knew what he was thinking, and discipline was on the menu. An insistent pounding on the bedroom door saved her. "Tonight," he promised. "You're mine."

She opened the shower door and glanced back. "I'm always yours."

"Better believe it," he muttered as he shoved his head under the spray.

Katrina wrapped herself in a towel and hurried to the bedroom door, thankful that Keith had remembered to lock it.

Re/Captured

Chapter 2

"We need more paralegals." Vina paged through a thick file. "I can't possibly look up all the precedents and statues I need in order to adequately address these cases."

Katrina agreed, but her smile didn't fade. "Yeah, this sucks. It gives me a new appreciation for what public defenders do."

Vina frustration morphed to bafflement. "Why isn't this stressing you out? I would have thought you'd have lost it by now."

Unable to access the place where her anxiety resided, Katrina continued scanning the files of the cases she'd been assigned. "I'm categorizing them by what needs to be done. Some of these are a matter of filing paperwork. Others will need trial prep."

"No trial prep." Markus Brooks, who was immediately in charge of the extra help that had been assigned to Legal Aid, issued the order in a rumbling baritone that Katrina felt more than heard. He stood over them, his linebacker build backing up his edict. "Get as many pleas as you can. We can move deals through fairly quickly, but trials cost time and money."

Living with a Dom had taught Katrina when people were firm in their orders and where there was wiggle room. She sensed that Markus was all bark and no bite. Leaning back, she tapped the tip of her pen on the file she was reading. "The law guarantees everyone a fair trial. If we push them through the system, then innocent people will end up with convictions."

Markus regarded her through heavy-lidded eyes. "Ms. Legato, Legal Aid is no place for idealism. If the State believed that everyone deserved a fair trial, then we'd have more staff than the prosecutor's office instead of half."

Her smile didn't diminish. "Well, I'm here now."

"You're here for a day. Close as many as you can. You're due in court in a half hour." He pointed, the sweep of his finger taking in Katrina, Vina, and two other lawyers who'd been pressed into service. "You'll get five, maybe ten minutes to speak to your clients before trial. Get them to plead it out, and you'll save a bundle of time and money." With that pronouncement, he left.

Michele Zurlo

Katrina thought about Keith and what he'd planned for them that evening. Since they both had the day off tomorrow, they could sleep in until seven, when the kid alarm went off.

"Earth to Trina." Vina snapped her fingers in front of Katrina's face, jerking her from her musings. "Did you have mind-blowing sex last night? Is that why you're so unfazed?"

"Regular sex last night," Katrina corrected. "Mind-blowing sex this morning."

Vina rolled her eyes. "I need a man like yours—nice to look at, devoted, and energetic. Are there more where he came from?"

Glancing at the clock, Katrina collated her stacks of files. Most of Keith's friends were in serious relationships. "I got the floor model, cleaned him up, and polished his rough edges. Believe me, it was not a quick process. I knew him for eleven years before we got together. He's my brother's best friend, so I had over a decade to work on him."

Following Katrina out the door, Vina sighed. "I can't put that kind of time into a man. I need one who's already polished."

"Good luck with that." If she wasn't willing to put time and effort into a relationship, then she wasn't going to find anything worth having. Perfect men were a myth, and she wasn't inclined to share Keith's negatives. When you loved someone, you loved them—flaws and all.

The cases moved along fairly quickly. One defendant after another pled guilty in exchange for a reduced sentence. Most of them didn't even notice that she wasn't the same attorney who had represented them for their arraignment. It was disheartening for her, and she could only imagine what it was like for the people being ground into dust by the system. These were cases that would have never crossed her desk because Katrina only handled Federal level white collar crimes—fraud and money laundering—and these encompassed a variety of cases backlogging the Public Corruption and Violent Crimes divisions.

"Hey."

Attention focused on memorizing as much as she could about the next case before the judge called the court to order, Katrina heard the word, but it didn't quite register. This next case was going to be complicated. The defendant was charged with using his position as a township trustee to pay for an apartment for his mistress. If she were prosecuting this case, she would have had weeks to study the evidence and question witnesses. This whole "ten minutes between clients" pace didn't guarantee justice for anyone, especially considering that this one was a jury trial. She hadn't been present for the choosing of the jurors.

"Kat."

At the sound of her name, Katrina perked up. She glanced over her shoulder to find Keith standing on the other side of the railing that separated the spectator viewing area from where the players sat. She swiveled in her seat. "Hi. I didn't know you had court today." He wore a suit and tie to work every day, changing into other clothes when there was a need, which was why he kept a bag with jeans, fresh shirts, and a backup tie in the back of his SUV.

"I didn't know you were a defense attorney."

After their counseling session, they'd talked to Angelina's therapist. By the time they'd arrived home and settled into the normal routine, she'd completely forgotten about the assignment. "It slipped my mind. Yesterday Judge Osman decided that Legal Aid needed to clear out some of the backlog, so he assigned me, Vina, and a couple others to help out. It's just today."

He frowned. "That's unusual."

It was very out of the ordinary. "But not unprecedented. He's getting ready to announce a run for Appellate, and he thinks this kind of interagency cooperation will look good on his record."

Keith's brow wrinkled in a cynical expression that looked a lot like his bored/pissed expression, but Katrina knew him well enough so that she could distinguish the difference. "You're doing the cooperating. You should run."

A judgeship was in her master plan. She grinned. "It could be fun." Then she gestured to the file on her table. "I really need to read this."

"Sure. We'll talk later." He turned and ran into a petite woman. Grabbing her arm, he steadied her. "Sorry."

When he went to pass her, she reached out and snagged his hand. "Keith Rossetti? Is that you?"

Katrina's attention should have been on the contents of the file in front of her, but it was mostly on the skinny blonde whose talons were still wrapped around Keith's hand. The woman was attractive in a bouncy, plastic kind of way.

He peered down at her, but his back was turned, so Katrina couldn't see his face, not that he'd crack a real expression with someone he barely knew.

"You don't remember me?" The woman huffed, affected a pouty smile, and put a hand to her heart, drawing attention to the plunging neckline of her dress. She'd chosen to wear the bare minimum for her day in court.

"You're not someone I've arrested." He responded in a flat tone.

Michele Zurlo

Her high-pitched giggle carried far enough to attract attention in the immediate vicinity. She smacked his arm playfully. "No, you naughty man, but handcuffs were involved."

Katrina rolled her eyes and gave up trying to focus on the facts in front of her. Keith peeked over his shoulder to see her openly observing.

He coughed. "Sorry. I don't recall."

He brushed past her, but she snagged his wrist, digging her nails in and yanking hard. Katrina held her breath. No matter how amusing the situation had been, it wasn't now. Keith did not respond well to people who put their hands on him like that. He turned back, the foreboding in his bearing and the menacing firmness of his eyebrows making it clear that altering his course was entirely due to his decision.

It amazed Katrina how much emotion Keith could communicate with the slightest arch of his golden eyebrows.

The woman shrank back, but she didn't release Keith's arm. "Sorry, Sir. It's me—Shyann Hauck. We dated for almost six months about four years ago. I remember we spent a lot of time in that dungeon in your basement."

Keith frowned, and Katrina knew he was searching his memory for the name. If it didn't ring a bell for him, it definitely did for her. Shyann Hauck was the girlfriend whose lifestyle the trustee had been bankrolling. She was here to testify as to the gifts she received, a witness for the prosecution.

Some of the menace left Keith's expression, and he removed her hand from his wrist. "We didn't date, Shyann."

That hand went back to her chest. Keith's gaze didn't follow it. "Maybe we stayed in more than we went out, but it was a relationship."

He responded by not changing one iota of his forbidding demeanor. Katrina struggled not to laugh. Before she'd come along, Keith's track record with women had been worse than dismal. He'd treated his girlfriends abysmally. The first day of their relationship, he'd tried it with Katrina, but she'd put an immediate stop to it. Rather than feel jealous, Katrina felt sorry for the woman. She must not have had much self-esteem if she'd thought she was in a relationship with him. He'd most likely viewed her as a submissive plaything with a recurring role.

She swatted the air. "Doesn't matter. You were always a lot of fun." She angled her head to better flirt. "I'm single again."

"I'm not." He lifted his chin. "Have a good day." His attention flashed to Katrina, and his eyes asked a question that demanded an answer. Katrina lifted a shoulder to indicate that the past was better off when left in the past. He visibly relaxed, and then he exited the courtroom.

Shyann sat down where she was, her legs appearing weak and rubbery. Sadness flickered over her features briefly before acceptance took its place. Katrina felt sorry for the woman, but not enough to go easy on her once she took the stand.

"Ms. Hauck, you stated in your testimony that Mr. Breitenberg paid your rent. Do you have receipts or cancelled checks showing that the money came from Mr. Breitenberg?"

She favored the jury with a pouty smile. "He gave me cash, and I put it into my bank account."

"So the checks all came from you?"

"I got money orders, not checks. But the money came from him."

"Did other men give you cash?"

She lifted a shoulder. "Sometimes."

"How often?"

She giggled. "When they came over."

Katrina studied the jury to see if anyone had caught the implication of what Ms. Hauck had said. "How many other men gave you cash?"

"I didn't keep track."

Turning to Ms. Hauck, she spread her palms. "Estimate. Every week, how many men would you say came to your apartment and gave you money?"

"Like three or two." Shyann rolled her eyes.

"About how much did they give you when they came over?" Katrina wasn't aiming to get the woman to admit to prostitution, but she wanted the jury to draw that conclusion in order to discredit the witness. "Estimate."

"Like fifty or a hundred. Sometimes two or three hundred."

"So eight or twelve men, in addition to Mr. Breitenberg, came over every month to give you between fifty and three hundred dollars? That's—what?—between four hundred and thirty-six hundred dollars each month?"

"Objection." Luciano Weber, a colleague of Katrina's from DOJ, finally caught on to what she was doing. "Ms. Hauck's other income is not relevant."

Katrina turned to the judge. "Your Honor, if Ms. Hauck gained income from all of these different sources, then she cannot honestly testify that she received almost four hundred thousand dollars from Mr. Breitenberg alone."

Michele Zurlo

The judge nodded. "Overruled."

By the time the jury filed out fifteen minutes later, Katrina was confident that she'd raised reasonable doubt. She was also certain that the defendant was guilty, and part of her hoped to lose this case. The trial had taken a total of thirty minutes.

The moment the judge called for a recess so they could all prepare for the changeover to the next case, Katrina found Keith leaning over the railing and loudly whispering. "Hey—you're not mad, are you?"

In the midst of searching for the next file, she paused and looked up. "Why would I be mad?"

"That...woman."

"No, of course not. I feel sorry for her."

He blinked. "Why?"

She decreased the distance to lessen the likelihood of being overheard. "Because she submitted to you, and you don't even remember her."

He glanced away, guilty of the crime. "I'm not like that anymore."

She set a comforting hand on his arm. "I know."

He closed his hand over hers. "Kat? Are you defending the next case?"

"Yes. Why?"

His lush, kissable lips thinned. "It's mine."

A stone dropped in the pit of her stomach. One of the great things about their working relationship was that they were never on opposite sides. They'd worked together on many investigations, marrying arguments and evidence to create airtight cases.

She'd read the briefs. This wasn't one on which they'd collaborated. "I don't think there's a conflict of interest, but I will inform the judge of our relationship."

First she went to Yessenia Cremin, the prosecuting attorney. The two had met, but because Cremin worked primarily with Violent Crimes, their meetings had been brief and superficial. "Hi, Katrina Legato for the defense."

Yessenia tossed her long brown hair over her shoulder, the tight curls bouncing as they went. She flashed a tepid smile. "Yessenia Cremin. I think we've met, though. Didn't you used to work in WCCU?"

"Still do. I was assigned to help at Legal Aid today."

Yessenia's brows lifted and fell in sympathy. "I started out in Legal Aid. It's brutal. What can I do for you, Katrina?"

"In the interest of full disclosure, you should know that I'm engaged to one of your witnesses."

That got her attention. She stood up straighter. "Which one?"

"Keith Rossetti."

Her mouth pursed as she thought. "I don't think he'll give an inch, even for you."

"He wouldn't, but the defendant might use that as grounds for a mistrial, argue that I didn't go after him enough." They were both approaching the situation as prosecutors, assuming the government would win. Katrina bit her lip. "I will, of course. Shall we run it by Judge Konopelski?"

It ended up not mattering. When Katrina returned to her table to prep for the case—minimally, as time allowed—she found a glaring mistake on the part of the prosecution.

Her client came in just then, led across the courtroom in handcuffs. He was an unassuming man—medium height, wavy brown hair, glasses that magnified his brown eyes, and a friendly smile. Even his nondescript brown pants and white shirt caused him to fade into the background.

Katrina stood to greet him. They'd met briefly that morning. "Good afternoon, Mr. Norris." She turned to the bailiff. "Please remove the handcuffs." The jury didn't need to see the client as a prisoner before they made up their mind that he should be one.

Mason Charles Norris, charged with first degree murder, shook her hand. "It's great to see you again, Katrina. You are definitely the prettiest attorney I've had yet."

Motions came before the hearing. Yessina motioned for the judge to consider reassigning the Norris case to another attorney due to the nature of Katrina's relationship with the arresting agent, which was denied.

Katrina stood to appeal to the judge for a different reason. "Your Honor, I'd like to ask for a continuance. I was assigned this case—and twenty-nine others—this morning. It involves Murder One, and I'd like more time to prepare."

"Sorry, counselor, but this case has already been postponed twice." Judge Konopelski sounded sympathetic but firm. "Denied." She banged her gavel.

"Thank you, Your Honor. Next, the chain of custody for the evidence is missing from my files, and it's not listed on the records turned over to Mr. Norris's defense even though it was requested." That was a standard document to include. As a prosecutor, she had included it even when it wasn't requested. "There's nothing to prove that the items entered into evidence have anything to do with Mr.

Michele Zurlo

Norris. Move for recess until the prosecution provides all documents having to do with Mr. Norris's case."

That wasn't so easily dismissed. Judge Konopelski peered at Katrina through thick glasses, and she did not look at all pleased. She riffled through the documents on her bench, nodding when she found what she needed. "Granted. Court will adjourn today. We'll reconvene Monday at three-thirty. Ms. Cremin, please make sure to comply with the defense's request by the end of business today." She banged her gavel, effectively ending Katrina's hectic day.

Mr. Norris took her hands and gushed. "You are incredible. It's like you actually know what you're doing. What a refreshing change from the incompetent fools I've suffered before now."

"Sorry to prolong this, Mr. Norris, but this gives me more time to look over everything. I'll come by to prep you for trial Monday." She disengaged and the bailiff removed the prisoner. He'd been unable to come up with bail money, so he was going to spend the weekend in jail.

Keith met her as she exited the courtroom. "Is Alder going to let you stay with this next week? I heard she had words with Judge Osman about reassigning two of her prosecutors. Alard was also not thrilled to lose two of her crew from Violent Crimes."

This was news to Katrina. "I've been buried in work all day. This is the first chance I've had to breathe. I have no idea what Monday will bring. However I do know that if I don't do my job correctly and to the best of my ability, justice will not be served." If Norris was guilty and was convicted, then she didn't want to leave it open for appeal. Since the case had been Keith's, she was certain Norris was guilty. Keith didn't cut corners. He was methodical and meticulous in everything he did.

"Are you going straight home?" He changed the subject lest they come close to discussing the case.

"No. I have some work I need to do on my regular cases before I leave today."

They had arrived at the elevators. She was going up, and he wasn't. "I'll see you at home by seven. I'll take the kids over to Malcolm's on Sunday so you can have some time to finish up whatever you need to do." He'd used his gentle Dom voice, so he'd issued an order that he expected would be followed. Then he brushed a kiss on her lips and left.

Chapter 3

Court adjourning early meant Keith could beat rush hour traffic. He surprised Angie by picking her up early from after school care. She leapt into his arms and squeezed him in a tight hug.

"Daddy, I'm so happy to see you."

"I'm happy to see you too, baby girl. How was your day?"

She wiggled to be set down, so he obliged. "Kyle S. said you weren't an FBI agent, so I punched him, and I had to sit with Mrs. Glyss at lunch."

He sighed internally but did not react outwardly. This is the main reason Kat hadn't wanted to put Angie in a martial arts class—she struggled with impulse control. "Angie, you can't go around hitting people. Did you apologize to Kyle?"

Her bottom lip quivered. "He won't talk to me anymore. He said I'm not a good friend."

Resisting the urge to enfold her in his embrace to protect her from the outside world, Keith crouched down to be at her level. "Do you think it's okay for one friend to hit another friend?"

She blinked a tear from her big brown eyes. "You hit Uncle Malcolm when he makes you mad, and you're still friends."

Coming out on top in a discussion with Angie was not always assured. He and Malcolm had a habit of calmly punching one another in the arm or thigh. It was a guy thing. They hadn't degenerated to a knock-down, drag-out fight since Keith had sobered up ten years ago.

"That's different, Angie. Uncle Malcolm and I learned combat together. We're sparring partners. We know what we're doing, and we know what to expect. Has Kyle ever hit you?"

She wiped away another tear. "No."

"Then he's not the kind of person who wants you to hit him either."

More waterworks, and they tugged at his heartstrings. She stuck her lower lip out and crossed her arms, finding refuge in anger just like he used to do. "But I hit him in the arm, just like you and Uncle Malcolm do."

21

Michele Zurlo

"Angie, Uncle Malcolm and I know how to properly punch and how to take a hit. Neither you nor Kyle have those skills, and even if you did, you need to have his permission. Even then, you should never punch someone in school." He gave into the urge to hug his little girl. She'd been through so much in her short life, and she was still developing coping mechanisms.

This incident further convinced him of the need to put her in Tae Kwan Do. Angie already knew violence. Now she needed to know how and when to use it.

After signing her out, he swung by the office to see if the principal was still there. Kat hadn't mentioned getting a call from school, and if Angie had hit someone, he expected to be notified. He found Mrs. Glyss chatting with the office admin.

She pasted on a smile when she saw him. "Mr. Rossetti, thank goodness it's Friday, right?"

He didn't see what the day of the week had to do with anything, so he ignored the pleasantry. "Mrs. Glyss, do you have a few minutes?"

Trapped, she indicated her office. "Right this way. Would you like Angelina to wait out here?"

"Sure." He pointed to a child-height bench. "Angie, sit there. I won't be long." She obediently sat.

Mrs. Glyss followed him into her office and closed the door behind them. "You're here about the hitting incident today?"

"I didn't get a call."

"The Smiths just left. I was just about to call Ms. Legato."

Keith waited patiently for the woman to continue. Why everyone thought that the female parent always had to deal with children, he'd never know.

She cleared her throat and looked down. He reminded himself not to treat this like an interrogation. Kat had warned him repeatedly that he was intimidating more often than he meant to be. The principal was around his age. She had kind eyes and a genuine love for children.

He made an effort to gentle his bearing. "Angie told me what happened. Some of her behaviors stem from her issues, but this one is my fault. It seems she was emulating the way her uncle and I approach disagreements. I've talked to her about this, and I'm confident she understands what she did wrong."

Mrs. Glyss grimaced. "I'm afraid the Smiths want either Angelina or Kyle moved to a different class. She's targeted him several times before, and they don't feel their son is safe in the same classroom."

Part of him understood the Smiths' point of view. If some kid kept hitting and swearing around his kid, he'd probably take steps to keep them apart. "Angie's going to be crushed. She thinks they're friends."

"So you agree to move Angie?"

Angelina had issues with bonding and attachment. Moving her away from her teacher would send her into a tailspin that would set her back months—even years. "Absolutely not."

"The Smiths plan to meet with a lawyer."

The stubborn part of Keith's nature teamed up with his need to face down all threats. He leaned forward and regarded Mrs. Glyss with a steady gaze. "Angie will not be moving classrooms. Please let the Smiths know that we're more than willing to meet with them and their lawyer regarding the interactions of two kindergarteners." He rose and left, his movements calm and deliberate.

In the outer office, he found Kyle sitting next to Angie. She rubbed his back, comforting the child as he cried. "I'm sorry, Kyle S. I thought friends punched friends when they got mad, but my daddy said they don't. I promise I won't do it again. I still want to be best friends."

Kyle, the boy in question, cried harder. His white blond hair didn't hide his red scalp, though his hands hid most of his red face. He and Angie were physical opposites in every way. Angie's coloring, thanks to her mixed-race heritage, was closer to dark honey. Kyle was tall and stocky, large enough to blend in with the second-graders, where Angie was thin and petite, easily the smallest in her class.

A woman with similar coloring handed Kyle a tissue. "Stop crying, Kyle. You should be happy she won't be bullying you anymore."

Angie's head snapped up, her big brown eyes tear-bright. "I'm not a bully. I don't let the other kids pick on Kyle just because he likes to always talk about fashion and Ariana Grande. I'm a bully-stopper."

Keith extracted his card from his pocket and handed it to Kyle's mother. "Mrs. Smith, please have your lawyer contact me at this number."

She took the card and looked at it. "Oh. You are an FBI agent. I told Kyle we don't have the FBI in Michigan."

Grimacing inside but stoic on the outside, Keith said, "The FBI is everywhere." He held his hand out to Angie. "Say goodbye to Kyle. It's time to go."

She whispered something to Kyle before getting up. Reluctantly she picked up her Tinkerbell backpack and took Keith's hand. On the way to the car, Keith praised her for standing up for herself. "Never put up with people talking smack about you."

"And I don't let them say things about Kyle either. Some of the boys make fun of him because he likes girl stuff, but I tell them that everybody is allowed to like what they want to like." She climbed into the car and buckled in.

Keith checked to make sure she was in correctly. "What did you say to him before we left?"

"I said that we would still be best friends even though his mom is making him move to another class."

Picking up Corey was far easier. Happy and affable, Corey was the kind of person everyone loved to be around. They arrived as the kids were putting on their shoes to spend time on the playground. Corey tore down the hall, a huge smile on his face as he barreled toward Keith's legs. Keith scooped him up and hugged him. "How was your day?"

A caregiver bearing Corey's backpack approached. "He had a great day. We just finished afternoon snack."

He signed out Corey, and in the car, Corey told them every single detail of his day. When he finished, Keith said, "I have a surprise for you two."

"I love surprises." Corey beamed.

"A sleepover with Grandma and Grandpa?" Angie breathed her guess, half hoping and half requesting.

"Yes. We're going to go home and pack a bag. Grandma went shopping today so she could make your favorite dinner." He loved how much they loved spending time with Kat's parents, and not just because it made getting a night alone with her that much easier.

Donna and Mario Legato had pretty much adopted him as their own the first time Malcolm had brought him home on leave from the Marines. He adored his future in-laws.

Mama L met them at the door, bestowing hugs on the kids and Keith. "Alex, Andrew, and Colin are in the backyard with M.J and Malcolm."

M.J.—short for Mario, Junior—was Malcolm and Kat's oldest brother. Alex and Andrew were his sons, aged seven and nine. Mal's kids, Colin and Zella, were the youngest. Colin was almost two, and Zella was only three months old. Angie and Corey adored all their cousins. They dropped their backpacks, which now contained overnight gear, and ran through the kitchen and out the back door.

Mama L beamed. "I love having a house full of grandkids."

"Is everybody staying the night?"

"Yes. All of my children are going on dates tonight. Mario went to the store to pick up a few things. Where are you taking Trina tonight?"

She walked as she talked, so Keith followed her though the living room to the kitchen.

"No idea. This was impromptu, so I haven't made reservations. I'll see what she's in the mood for." He planned to have dinner waiting for her when she arrived home, and they'd eat it naked, but nothing on Earth would induce him to share that with Mama L. Looking out the back door, he noted five kids running circles in the yard.

"You need a better plan than that," Mama L said. "Get carryout from that stone oven pizza place she likes, light a few candles, drink some sparkling cider. It's hard to keep the romance going when you have little ones, so you have to make extra effort. That's how Mario and I made it this long."

"Noted." They chatted for a while longer, and then Zella's cry came over the baby monitor.

Mama L pushed him out the back door. "Go. Say hello to M.J. and Malcolm. Once Mario gets home, I'm kicking you all out."

He poured himself an iced tea and joined his brothers-in-law-to-be on the patio. M.J. stood. "Keith, how are you?" The pair shook hands.

Malcolm eyed the iced tea. "That looks good."

Keith ignored the fishing expedition. If Mal wanted iced tea, he knew where to get it. He settled next to Malcolm and across from M.J. "It looks like we all had the same idea."

Katrina's brothers shared her dark hair, brown eyes, and olive complexion, but where she was feminine and pretty, they were guys. Women seemed to like them, so they had that going for them.

M.J. said, "Mom called me a half hour ago, asking if the boys wanted to stay the night. Jen had their bags packed before I got off the phone." M.J.'s wife, Jennifer, had recently gone back to work after taking time off to stay home with the kids. She was working as a teacher's aide so that her hours matched the boys'.

"Darcy is due for a night without the kids. The doctor finally gave us the all-clear." Malcolm's wife recently gave birth to their second child. Since both condoms and birth control had failed for them, she had insisted that Malcolm have a vasectomy. The all-clear had probably been for Malcolm, since he'd put off the operation as long as he could, and Darcy had finally put her foot down.

"Still sore?" M.J. snickered.

Malcolm didn't answer, but his expression warned his brother to continue the topic at his peril.

M.J. took the hint. "What about you and Trina?"

Michele Zurlo

"I'm going to grab a pizza on the way home. I'll light some candles and have a relaxing evening at home." He flashed a grin at Malcolm's growing discomfort. Where M.J. didn't read anything into the statement, Malcolm did. As a fellow Dom, Mal knew that "lighting candles" and "relaxing evening" were euphemisms for bondage, S&M, and D/s play. M.J. chose to remain clueless.

"I bet Jen would love that." M.J. stood. "I'd better get going if I'm going to run to the store and get the pizza. She'll probably want a salad too. Great idea."

He and Malcolm watched M.J. bid his kids farewell and disappear.

Keith turned to Malcolm. "Can I ask you something?"

"As long as it's not about my sister."

Temper flaring, Keith struggled against the urge to punch Malcolm on the thigh. "You know, as my best friend, it's your job to listen, commiserate, and offer advice. I get that there are lines, like you don't want to hear me talk about my fiancé's incredible tits, but we should be able to talk about a lot more than we do. I listen to whatever you need to say about you and Darcy."

Malcolm washed a hand over his face, probably trying to scrub away Keith's mention of his sister's boobs. Then he stole Keith's iced tea. "Fine. What did you do?"

"Kat was assigned to work defense today."

"What?" Malcolm interrupted. "She's a prosecutor. Who assigned her to work defense?"

"Osman. He assigned her and Vina to Legal Aid. Anyway, I was at the courthouse today, so when I saw her in there between hearings, I ducked in to say hi. When I went to leave, this woman grabs me. I didn't remember her, but I guess we used to go out." Keith winced. Before Katrina, he'd treated women horribly, using them for sex and treating them like objects. He'd used the D/s dynamic to keep an emotional distance, and he'd reveled in his dislike of women as a part of the species.

"Was she your...type?" Malcolm chose his words carefully. Keith had usually managed to find women who fit his preconceived notion of the disposable woman.

"Yes. I didn't doubt her story. I just didn't remember her. Still don't. Shyann something. Anyway, Kat overheard the whole thing."

Malcolm finished off the tea. "Trina isn't the jealous type. She knows you're devoted to her."

"It's not—" He shook his head, searching for the right words. "Shyann was a witness for the prosecution. It was a fraud case. I couldn't stay for the whole thing, but I caught Kat's cross. She went easy on her. I mean, she got her point across, but—I've seen her tear into a witness on cross. She doesn't usually pull her punches. Afterward I asked her if she was mad at me, but she said she felt sorry for Shyann. She said—" Keith took a tortured breath. "She said that Shyann submitted to me and I didn't remember her. She said it like it was a personal affront to her."

A kid flew out of nowhere and rammed into Malcolm's leg. Mal laughed and scooped up the bundle of energy. "Hey, buddy. Are you having fun with your cousins?"

Colin babbled something, but it was nothing Keith could decipher. Then he held up a plastic sand shovel, showing it to Malcolm from two sides.

Malcolm repositioned Colin's hold on the tool and pointed to the flat part. "Scoop with this side."

Seeing the two of them together, there was no doubt they were father and son. Colin was a miniature version of Malcolm, down to the cowlick on the crown of his head. The boy wiggled to get down, and he was off as soon as his feet touched the ground.

Malcolm turned back to Keith. "Knowing Trina, she probably did take it personally."

That didn't make Keith feel better. "She's already put off the wedding twice. Maybe she doesn't actually want to marry me." Voicing his deepest fears made Keith feel vulnerable, but he was safe with his best friend.

Without missing a beat, Malcolm waved dismissively. "She's wanted to marry you since she was eighteen. I know because I read her diary. And then right after that, I made you promise to stay away from my sister because you treated women like shit."

Kat wasn't the kind of person who would share her diary with her brother, no matter how close they were, and Malcolm wasn't the kind of person who would invade his sister's privacy like that. "Why would you have read her diary?"

Not at all apologetic, he folded his arms on the table and leaned forward. "We came home on leave around her eighteenth birthday, and I noticed her looking at you strangely. I mean, she's had a crush on you since the first time she met you, but this was different. Rather than confront her and make her cry, I read her diary to figure out if I had to beat the shit out of you or not."

Keith had kissed Kat as part of her present. He'd been too drunk to listen to the voice in his head warning him against such action. "I guess you didn't find the part where I kissed her." It was a logical conclusion based on the fact that Mal hadn't tried to beat the shit out of him.

Malcolm stared at Keith hard, dissecting him like a criminal. "You kissed her? Way back then?"

"Once. On her birthday." He leaned away. "You can't hit me. Angie got in trouble at school today because you and I set a bad example for how to solve disagreements."

Malcolm froze. "Really? Because it would feel really good right now to punch you. I have to defend my sister's honor."

"Which brings us back to my original point—do you think she really wants to marry me?"

"Yes, dumbass. She wants to marry you. Are you getting jitters? It's not bad, this being married gig. I quite enjoy it."

"No jitters. I wanted to marry her two years ago. She's the one who keeps putting me off, and after today—" He broke off, shaking his head. "What if she's marrying me because you all expect her to?" Her entire family, immediate and extended, had assumed they would get married. They'd greeted the announcement of their engagement as if they'd already been informed. And then Keith and Kat had adopted two children together. If they didn't get married, more hearts than just theirs would be broken.

"Dude, I know my sister. If Trina doesn't want to marry you, she won't."

Somehow Malcolm's assurances weren't enough. Keith knew without a doubt that she loved him, but he couldn't shake a nagging feeling that he was missing something important.

Chapter 4

The house was quiet when Katrina arrived home a full twenty minutes before seven. No patter of little feet greeted her. No laughter or loud chatter came from the direction of the living room or the kitchen. But the aroma of her favorite pizza filled the air, drawing her toward the kitchen. The pizza sat on a sheet pan, warming in the oven.

"Keith?"

He appeared from the other side, having come from the dining room. He'd changed out of his suit and into a plain cotton shirt and the sexy sweats that rode low on his hips. Some might think he was dressed for bed, but Katrina knew better. A lazy smile tugged at his lips. "You're early."

Her stomach rumbled and the food smelled appetizing, but she understood the steel in his bearing and the hint of danger in his bright green eyes. Cream rushed to her pussy. "Do you want me to leave and come back?"

He crossed his arms and leaned against the doorway. "The kids are with your parents. They're having all the grandkids overnight."

Katrina did not pity her parents, but at least they had Alex and Andrew. Her nephews were either good helpers or a walloping handful. There was no middle ground with them. Understanding Keith's message—he'd wanted to put her mind at ease with regard to the children so that she could focus on submitting to him—she lowered her gaze. "Can I have ten minutes to put my bag away and freshen up?"

"Yes. I set out what I want you to wear." His voice washed through her senses, overpowering her with peace and excitement.

"Thank you." Briefcase in hand, she turned to follow his instructions.

"Kitty Kat."

The unspoken order halted her. She turned back to him. "Yes?"

"I want a kiss."

Closing the distance she lifted her face. He caressed her cheek with one hand and wrapped the other around her waist to support her lower back, two points of contact only. His lips brushed hers, teasing at a third point. He massaged, a gentle pressure welcoming her home and to her role as his submissive.

Slave to his mastery, she sighed into it, dropping her briefcase and lifting her arms to twine them around his neck, and she pressed her chest to his. He deepened the kiss, plunging his tongue deep to taste and stab. The hand on her cheek slid into her hair, and the one on her back lowered to squeeze her ass. She forgot about everything. The stresses of her day fell away as she melted in the face of his demand.

He broke away to trail sucking kisses down her neck, stopping when the collar of her dress shirt got in his way. "Go," he said. "Take your ten minutes, and then you're mine."

Wasting no time, she ran up the stairs. She wanted to rinse off and put her hair up. The kids were gone, and it had been weeks since they'd played in the dungeon, so she hoped that's where they'd end up. Once she found the outfit he'd selected, she questioned the direction of the evening. Her old comfortable bathrobe did not conjure scenes of her kneeling at his feet, bondage, or sexual torture—not like lace lingerie might.

Ten minutes flew by. Upon her return to the dining room, she found it transformed. Gone were the electronics, stacks of papers, and evidence of children, and in their place was a white tablecloth. The curtains were drawn, and candles provided a romantic glow. Two places were set.

He hadn't told her to take a place at the table or where to kneel, so she waited in the doorway. Soon she felt his presence behind her, and his hands rested on her hips. "Hungry?"

"Starving."

"Good. Let's eat." He tapped her ass, indicating she should sit. "How was work? Did you get everything done?"

"Never." She sat across from him, all the way at the other end of the table where he'd set her a place. "But Elizabeth pitched a fit enough so that Judge Osman decided that one day helping out in Legal Aid was enough. Vina and I are back at the Justice Department on Monday."

"That's awesome. I wasn't looking forward to having you cross-examine me." He flashed half a grin. "I like for us to be on the same side."

Katrina did as well, but her mind was not on work matters. "Keith, why am I wearing a bathrobe? Aren't we going to scene tonight?"

He studied her as if looking for the flaw in his plan. "Yes. You're dressed how I want you dressed—in your birthday suit. The robe is just for dinner. As much as I like seeing your nipples pointy, I don't want you to be cold just yet."

They talked as they ate, barreling through a myriad topics like an old married couple. Keith told her about Angelina's bad day, how M.J. copied his plan for dinner, and what flavor ice cream her mother was making for the grandchildren tonight. She shared the feeling of helplessness that came from being thrown into an impossible situation. Despite her best effort, she hadn't been as effective as she could have been with more time and resources. Katrina felt sorry for people who couldn't afford private attorneys.

When they finished, Keith blew out the candles, took her by the hand, and led her down the stairs. His workout room was down here now, next to the dungeon and across from laundry and storage. He parked her outside the door. "Wait here."

Ever the obedient submissive, she waited. This was part of the game. Their sex life always followed the D/s dynamic, but that part of their relationship was subtle or missing in their daily life. Katrina missed this ludic side of Keith. He was an exacting Dom, but he was fun as well.

The door opened forever later, revealing her Dom. He'd put a lab coat on over his shirt and sweats. Only a man as inherently sexy as Keith Rossetti could pull off that look in a way that made her knees weak.

"Mrs. Rossetti?"

Katrina started. The wedding wasn't for a couple months, and she wasn't sure where she stood on the idea of changing her name. Remembering her place, she dropped her gaze. She would answer to any name he gave her. "Yes?"

"Time for your physical. I'll take your robe." He held out a hand. She untied the belt, let the satiny fabric slip down her arms, and handed the garment over. Then he stepped back and indicated for her to enter.

The dungeon hadn't changed since the last time she'd been down there. This room wasn't hers. It was utterly his domain. Unless he invited her inside, she did not enter. Following protocol, she kept her gaze downcast as she went directly to the thick cushion on the floor and knelt.

He circled her, slowly inspecting her body and her position. Shoulders back, spine straight, knees spread, palms up, gaze demurely lowered—she mentally checked the boxes as he looked at her. Seconds passed, each ticking by with excruciating lassitude as she wondered what he had in mind. Knowing it would just be in the way, she'd put her hair up. A thick leather strap encircled her throat, and Keith secured the buckle of the collar.

"Stand up, Mrs. Rossetti. Let's begin your exam on the bench."

"Yes, Doctor." She rose and went to the bench. He had a spanking bench, but since he was the masochist in their relationship, it had become a place where she administered painful bliss to him. In the meantime, he'd bought a punishing bench, a raised platform that put her on her hands and knees. A bar at her waist kept her ass high in the air, and there was nowhere to rest her head. The knee and elbow rests were thickly padded, as were the restraints that kept her from moving a single inch.

She climbed onto the bench, and he secured the restraints at her ankles, knees, elbows, and wrists. With her ass lifted too high, there was no way she could move.

"Comfortable, Mrs. Rossetti?"

Again, she wondered at his use of that name, but figured they were role playing, and that's the role to which he'd assigned her. "Yes, Doctor. Thank you."

He slipped a blindfold over her eyes. "We'll start with some sensory perception. I'll be administering a series of test, and you'll give verbal feedback as requested. Questions?"

"No, Doctor."

She felt his hands on her breasts, cupping and kneading. Her breasts were small, but he found them fascinating anyway. He played, pinching and pulling her nipples as she breathed into the pain that slowly morphed to pleasure. Her squeaks became moans, and his hands fell away.

She mewed in protest.

"Your breasts display a healthy response to phase one stimulation. Time for phase two." He pulled her nipple, and the sharp pain replacing his fingers let her know he'd used a clover clamp. "Breathe through it, Mrs. Rossetti."

She did, letting the worst of the sting flee with every exhaled breath. Once her breathing had calmed, he clamped the other nipple. Then he threaded a chain through them and through a metal loop on the collar.

"How are you holding up?"

"I'm fine, Doctor. Ready for anything."

He chuckled. "Good to know."

Next the falls of a flogger trailed over her shoulder, across her back and ass, and down her leg. It tickled her calf and the bottom of her foot. Then it made a return trip up the other side. Back and forth, it lulled her into an almost-trance. The snap of the falls hitting her ass pulled her from the edge, and a delicious sting radiated from the point of contact. As she assimilated the aftereffects of one hit, he swung again. He started slow, but the rhythm picked up before long, and all the sensations melted together. He peppered her thighs and calves, and then he moved on to her ass and the fleshy parts of her back.

If she'd been able, she would have writhed and bucked, fighting the onslaught even as she submitted to it. But strict restraint meant she couldn't move a single muscle, and so she utilized her only recourse—she cried out. Low moans alternated with grunts and cries, and then she was floating.

The flogging continued, keeping her in subspace for a while longer. When she came out of it, she found his fingers probing her mouth, an invasion that claimed her as his possession. Accepting his dominion, she moaned and sucked on the digits.

He laughed, a low sound that vibrated through her senses. "Welcome back, Kitty Kat."

Unable to respond, she moaned again.

"There's a string of anal beads in your luscious ass, and I've attached the leads for the TENS unit for the next test."

She flexed and felt every ball of the beads. The fingers in her mouth continued probing, simulating the sex act, and she sucked harder, begging without words for him to replace his fingers with his cock.

The air changed slightly, indicating that he'd leaned away from her, but the fingers in her mouth didn't stop their invasion. A switch clicked, and the TENS unit came to life. Electricity surged through sticky pads on her inner thighs and on her ass, stimulating the muscles so that they tightened and relaxed. The pattern made it feel like she was being fucked. Small noises, high-pitched mews, vibrated in her chest and throat.

His fingers withdrew, and the soft tip of his cock replaced it. He traced her lips with the sensitive head, and then he worked it into her mouth, wetting it by inches as he pushed deeper with each thrust. Katrina embraced her submission, and languor suffused her limbs. She was a vessel for his pleasure, and through surrendering, she was rewarded with complete bliss.

He leaned forward, thrusting into her mouth as deeply as he could go, and the anal beads slipped in and out of her ass. She admired his ability to multitask. Anal stimulation never failed to send her over the edge. The hot-cold feeling wrapped around her pleasure centers, and she detonated, crying out her first orgasm.

Keith, true to form, kept going. The TENS unit forced her pussy to keep pulsing. The steady in-and-out of the anal beads reminded her that she was not in control, and Keith's cock thrust lazily into her mouth. He had no intention of climaxing anytime soon. He forced her to remain as she was until his machinations bore additional fruit. Tension coiled, and she orgasmed a second time, moaning around his cock.

This time, he pulled out, and she whimpered at the loss. The TENS unit ceased, and the beads in her ass were slowly extracted.

"Beautiful, Mrs. Rossetti. Your submission, as always, is stunning to witness. Thank you for that."

Katrina wasn't sure how to respond. Keith frequently commented on how much he loved watching her submit. He routinely thanked her for the gift. But he'd never done it while they were role playing.

The blindfold came off, and he freed her from the restraints. Then he helped her up. Sore from being locked in one position so long, she moved slowly. He massaged her thighs and around her knees, and then he led her to a vinyl sofa where he'd spread a towel.

Other than the buttons on his lab coat being undone, he looked exactly the same. "Sit down. There's time for a break before your physical continues."

Aware of exactly how weak her legs were, she sank down, and when he returned with a glass of water, she drank it all.

He lounged next to her, his arm along the back of the sofa. "How are you, Kitty Kat? What's your color?" This was her Dom asking, the man who loved her beyond all reason and planned to exact more from her before the evening concluded.

"Green, Master. I'm fine."

He stroked an absent caress along her neck, sending shivers radiating in all directions. "You are so fucking beautiful, my Kat. You were meant to be mine."

She leaned back and snuggled her head against his shoulder. "I love you too, and I'm glad you finally accepted that I'm yours and you're mine."

With one finger on her jaw, he tilted her head up, and he captured her mouth in a kiss that branded her. It started slowly, a leisurely kiss to reaffirm his dominance and their connection. But a fire had already been kindled, and this sparked a raging inferno neither of them could resist. Forgetting that she was supposed to be resting, she straddled his lap and let that blaze consume her. Keith was a fever that ravaged her insides.

He responded in kind, his knowing hands roaming her body, grazing across sensitive areas and roughly caressing others. He urged her to rise up on her knees so he could free his cock from its confines. Then he guided her down. She ground against him, establishing the rhythm she liked best, but he took over. Clenching his fist in her hair, he pulled her head back, effectively robbing her of control. Then he laved his tongue over her breasts, and she realized the nipple clamps were gone. They were still sensitive, and she cried out when his teeth scraped her nipple.

His hand covered her stomach, a rough caress that squeezed her soft parts and raked over her ribs. Suddenly she was upright, and he was kissing her wildly. The rough fabric of his lab coat chafed against her chest. He pulled her hips down, sealing their bodies together as his hot semen bathed her insides.

His head fell back to rest along the top of the sofa, and she held him in her arms, comforting him as his orgasm subsided. After a while, he stirred, stroking the wisps of hair that had fallen from her ponytail away from her face.

"Your exam isn't over, Mrs. Rossetti."

She smiled against his neck. "I thought not, Doctor. What's next? Am I allowed to know?"

"Endurance test." He motioned to the gynecologist exam table in the far corner. "Get on the table. I'm going to have to strap you down for this."

Reluctantly leaving their comfortable embrace, she ambled to the table and climbed onto it. He was behind her, helping to lift her feet into the stirrups. Then he secured her ankles and hips with the adjustable straps.

"You're going to need your hands, my lovely patient." With infinite care, he wiped down her pussy and inner thighs with a cold, damp cloth.

Still weak from the first part of her "physical," Katrina's knees fell together.

Keith tsked. "Looks like we'll need to take care of that problem, Mrs. Rossetti."

The gyno table had drawers down one side and cabinets on the sides for convenient storage. Metal slid on metal, and Keith produced a pair of padded neoprene straps. He secured them above each knee. The bindings featured metal D-rings. He attached snaps with leads that connected to chains he'd strategically bolted to the ceiling. Now her legs were secured, wide open and out of the way.

He stepped back to look over his handiwork. In some ways, this was her favorite part. When she'd been on the punishing bench, the blindfold had prevented her from witnessing the way his green eyes glowed with satisfaction, pride, love, and possessiveness. His gaze roamed her exposed body, an emotional caress that swept from the top of her head to the tips of her toes. She had not climaxed during the break. That had been a purely submissive act—seeing to his needs after he'd so thoughtfully sated her during the scene. She had not sought completion because it had been about pleasing her Master.

Now, under his perusal, a longing sprang to life. Her pussy, open and welcoming, wept for his touch. Her breasts, sensitive from the clover clamps, pebbled to clamor for his attention. Her arms and legs relaxed, pliant and ready for whatever he planned, and her core tightened in anticipation.

"Mrs. Rossetti, you are one fucking hot woman."

"I'm glad you think so, Doctor."

"Are your nipples sore?"

The effects of the clover clamps sometimes lingered for a day or two. "Yes, Doctor."

He took one nipple between his thumb and forefinger. Though his touch was soft, she gasped, and she gasped louder when he increased the pressure. "Breathe through it."

Once she acclimated to the pain, he treated the other one to the same torture. He loved to play with her breasts. She couldn't count the number of times he'd come up behind her when she was alone—in the house or when they were at a friend's place—put one hand over her mouth while the other crept up her shirt. He'd treat her nipple roughly, pinching, pulling, and squeezing it until she squirmed against him, and then he'd release her to rejoin the others. For the rest of the day, his gaze would drop to her chest, and he'd wear his naughty smirk that made her panties damp.

Unsurprisingly he produced two metal clothespins. He pulled each nipple taut prior to clipping them on. Since she had been prepared, she breathed into the sensation, and her pussy responded as it always did. Moisture dripped, bowing to gravity and running in the direction of her anus.

He donned rubber gloves. Using his foot, he pushed the rolling stool to the other end of the table, and then he sat down, his face inches from her crotch. He had a powerful light that he aimed at her pussy, the warmth adding to her arousal. Wordlessly he pushed a

Re/Captured

lubed finger into her anus. She felt simultaneously invaded and owned, his to use however he wished. He added more fingers, but she wasn't sure how many, and they sawed in and out of her body, turning and stretching her rear opening.

Then his fingers left her, and she felt cold plastic slip into her. A minute later, it beeped. "Temperature within the normal range," he announced. Then he resumed his exploration. Katrina loved anal stimulation. Her body, already on edge, came alive. She moaned, and he slapped her ass. "Mrs. Rossetti, please refrain from making such inappropriate noises."

"I can't help it Doctor. What you're doing feels so good."

"One might begin to think you're a sex addict."

"Doctor, you're the sex addict. I don't mind if you use me to get your fix."

His fingers left her back entrance. He disposed of his gloves, and then he produced a bulbous plug, which he shoved into her ass, reaming her with the toy. As she forced her body to acclimate, he spanked her. The blows, centered on the plug, came fast and hard. Tears pricked behind her eyes, while pleasure bloomed in her nether region. "Bad patients are punished, Mrs. Rossetti."

"Yes, Doctor." Her inappropriate noises came faster and louder. The smacks echoed through the room as they landed on her ass and the backs of her thighs. "Sorry, Doctor."

The punishment ceased abruptly.

"Touch your pussy." He issued the command in a clinical tone, but devilry played behind his eyes.

She watched his face as she complied, turned on more by his reaction than by her actual touch. She circled her clit with two fingers, her touch heavy because he'd ignored that part of her so far. "Do you want me to climax?"

"You're the sex addict. We'll see how far you can get." As she masturbated, he clipped clothespins onto her labia. Then he handed her a dildo. "Put this in that hungry little hole, Mrs. Rossetti."

She inserted it slowly, Keith dribbling lube on it as it disappeared into her body. Then she fucked herself with it, her gaze never leaving his face. With the plug still filling her ass, it didn't take long to climax. With a soft cry, her body arched as much as it could under the restraint, and she came.

He took the dildo away, his attention never wavering from her quivering pussy. "Link your hands behind your neck, and don't move,

Mrs. Rossetti. This next part may prove unpleasant. Exhale." As she did so, he removed the butt plug.

The sound of a drawer opening made her anxious. When she was on this table, Keith was sometimes unpredictable. Though well aware of her limits and preferences, he liked to try new things, often without discussing them with her—as long as he felt the new item fell into approved toy categories. This time, he went with something old. He inserted the lubricated speculum into her vagina and cranked the thing open. Then he shined his bright light inside.

He poked and prodded, adjusting the speculum as he went. It didn't hurt, but neither was it pleasurable. After some time, he removed the speculum. "Mrs. Rossetti, your pussy is healthy and ready for a thorough fucking."

"It just had a good fucking. A couple, actually."

"Sex addicts overuse their equipment, so I'm going to run an endurance test. We're going to see how much you can take."

Orgasms were wonderful unless the pussy was overstimulated and needed a break. Then they were torture. Eager to please him and endure anything for his pleasure, Katrina nodded. "Yes, Doctor."

"You're going to cry." A tremor passed through him as he openly anticipated her discomfort. "You're going to beg me to stop."

She had no doubt both things would happen.

"But I won't." He indicated her arms. "And I won't bind your arms. You'll need to keep them where they are."

Things like this were always easier when she was tied up and all choices had been removed. She swallowed her objection. "Yes, Doctor."

He removed the lab coat and his shirt, revealing an appealing expanse of chiseled chest. Then he lowered his sweats, freeing his hard cock, which he fed into her waiting pussy. He leaned forward, resting his hands on either side of her waist, and he fucked her with quick, circular strokes, the kind that hit her sweet spot and drove her crazy. Keith knew her body better than she did, and he drove her to the edge. As she came, he removed the clothespins from her labia and nipples.

Unsated, he withdrew from her pussy. He leaned down to rummage in another drawer. This time he came up with a bullet vibrator. A little lube, and he inserted it into her vagina. He stood next to her, remote in hand, and watched her squirm as he varied the speed. Over the next hour, he drove her to orgasm repeatedly. Each time it took her longer to get there again, but he forced the issue. The lingering aftershocks of pleasure sapped her energy and turned to torture. She begged until tears leaked from her eyes. She'd submitted to him from the start, so this was just for his pleasure—and he enjoyed every moment. Taking himself in hand, he stroked his thick cock and shot his load on her stomach. She barely noticed as yet another climax liquefied her bones and all feeling left her body.

She had no control over her muscles. She couldn't move at all. Her whimpers and cries tapered off. He removed the vibrator and cleaned her up. She was vaguely aware of the bindings dropping away. He lifted her, wrapping her in a soft blanket, and carried her to the sofa.

He held her in his arms for a long time, the soft rumble of his voice soothing her with words of praise and love.

Later that night, as she lay enveloped in the warmth of his body, she pressed a tired kiss to his shoulder. "Keith? Why did you keep calling me Mrs. Rossetti?"

He shifted, tightening his hold, and growled his response. "Because you're mine."

Michele Zurlo

Chapter 5

Monday morning found Keith in ASAC Lexee Hardy's office. Two years ago, when Brandy Lockmeyer had been tapped to head an elite task force, Lexee had been promoted to Chief, and now she was in charge of units that investigated white collar crimes. Prior to that, Keith had worked with Lexee on a handful of operations. He respected her ethics and her authority.

She was a petite woman, perhaps five feet tall and a hundred pounds soaking wet, but Keith wasn't fooled by her diminutive appearance. Having sparred with her, he knew she was a formidable fighter. Outside of work, he'd socialized with her a handful of times because Lexee had become friends with Layla Hudson, who was Katrina's cousin and his buddy Dustin's fiancée.

"What's up, Chief?" He settled into the chair across from her desk and sipped hot coffee from a paper cup.

All business, she did not flash a smile. "I have some bad news. This morning, all charges against Mason Charles Norris were dismissed when the prosecution was unable to produce chain-of-custody logs for the evidence."

Feeling left his fingers, and his lips went numb as white-hot anger suffused his limbs. He wanted to punch something. He wanted a drink of hard liquor. He wanted to down a gallon of whiskey while punching things. Through sheer force of will, he combated those urges.

"I know how hard you worked on that case—the long hours, partnering with VC. This is a tough blow."

His fraud investigation had turned up a murder, and he'd partnered with a colleague at Violent Crimes to build an airtight case.

"You were in court Friday, so you know what happened there. Someone dropped the ball at the DOJ, and the defense attorney used the opening to get this guy off. This wasn't us."

His protective instincts rushed to the fore, superseding the urge to get drunk and beat things. "Katrina was his lawyer on Friday. She rightly pointed out the missing logs. Even if Norris had been convicted, that could have been grounds for mistrial. It's not her fault."

Lexee studied him, assessing with intelligent eyes. "I wasn't aware she was working that side of the courtroom."

"She doesn't normally. Judge Osman is gunning for elected office, and he assigned her to work Legal Aid for a day. She found the problem and asked for a recess, and then she was taken off the case." He rubbed a hand over his face. "Chief, this is unacceptable. We bust our balls to put these motherfuckers behind bars. We handed Yessina Cremin a win, and she fucked us all." They couldn't use any of the evidence because there was nothing to prove they'd found it where they said they found it.

Lexee folded her hands. "Murder is off the table, but fraud is not. What do we have that wasn't turned over to the DOJ?"

"Nothing, that's what we have." He leaped to his feet and paced away from her, fury radiating from the core of his being. "Fraud was part of the motive for murder. That's how we got him. They might not have charged him with fraud, but they had all the evidence to do so. It was a judgment call. Green thought the fraud case was circumstantial, so he went for murder." At the time Keith had been pissed that ADA Gideon Green hadn't pressed more charges. The evidence he'd uncovered had been substantial—not at all circumstantial, but the paper trail would be harder for the average jury to wrap their heads around.

"So we have nothing—no grounds to even monitor his activities." Though she had to be pissed, her tone was measured and even. "That's what I thought. I'm sorry, Keith. I didn't want you hearing this from anyone else."

He appreciated her professionalism and poise. He ran a hand through his hair. "I need to hit the gym."

"Not so fast."

Pausing in his exit, he faced his boss.

"That was the bad news. I have some other news. You might, perhaps, view it as good news." She motioned to the seat he'd vacated.

Though he needed to blow off some steam, he sat back down, but he didn't get his hopes up. At best he was about to be assigned a new case.

"Rafael Torres is going to offer you a job."

Torres was in charge of counterintelligence, which was not Keith's area of expertise. After the Marines, he'd landed at the WCCU by chance. It turned out he had a gift for finding fraud. Though, since Malcolm had left the FBI and Brandy had taken Jordan, Avery, Liam, and Jed for her task force, things at White-Collar Crime hadn't been the same. Even having Lexee for a boss was difficult, not because he had an issue with her personally, but because he knew he'd been in the running for the position.

Keith studied his hands. "Why?"

"He thinks your skills would be a valuable asset to CI." She cleared her throat. "And I agree. I love working with you, Keith, but I don't think we're utilizing your skills as well as we could. You're a gifted agent with an incredible intuitive sense. Furthermore, you thrive on challenge, and CI can challenge you in a way WCC no longer does."

Too much was happening on too many different fronts.

Lexee continued. "You're welcome to stay, of course. You're my best agent. Losing you would leave a huge gap. It would be a pain in the ass. But I'll understand if you choose to go."

Something occurred to him. "Why are you talking to me before Torres does? You don't know for sure that he's going to offer me anything."

"Of course I do. Rafael and I are friends." She folded her hands on her desk. "I've known you for a long time, Keith. You're a good man, loyal to a fault. I don't want that fault to get in the way of you advancing your career. You'll still be catching criminals, but your impact—and the stakes—will be bigger. I wish you nothing but the best."

"Thanks." He stood, and they shook hands.

On the way to the gym, he phoned Kat to tell her the news.

"Damn," she said. He pictured her eyes closing with regret. "I'm sorry. I really thought Cremin would submit the logs. That's not a difficult request. I'm so sorry, Keith. I didn't see this happening."

"It's not your fault. You were right to catch it. Down the road, it could have been grounds for a mistrial or for having the entire conviction thrown out. What you did gave the case a fighting chance." He soothed her with his voice, knowing she was beating herself up.

"How are you holding up?" Always a giver, she turned her concern to him.

"I'm going to the gym. I need to hit something."

"I can flog you after the kids go to bed." She'd lowered her volume so that he barely heard. From the background noise, he knew she was at her desk in the midst of a bustling office.

He chuckled, already feeling better. Kat was the salve for anything that ailed him. "Look at you, being naughty in public."

"Shush, you. I mean it, though. It's been a while for you."

Keith was a masochist, but he wasn't submissive. Back in the day, he'd hired sadists to dole out the punishment. Kat was the only submissive he'd allowed to even know he liked pain, and she was the only person he trusted to administer it. "Maybe. We'll see. If you wear those high-heeled boots and that black lacy teddy I got you last summer."

"It's a deal. Listen, on a completely unrelated note, Mrs. Glyss called. I have a meeting with her at three. I didn't know if you could get away today."

His schedule wasn't always flexible, but today he didn't have anything scheduled after eleven. He had work to do, but nothing that couldn't be put off until tomorrow. "I'll be there."

"Good. We'll present a united front. She's not moving to a different class." On the other end, Kat sighed. "She's come so far, Keith. I wish they could see that. She has a good heart."

When Angie had first come into their life, she hadn't acted out. Once she'd become comfortable, her behaviors had shocked them. She'd trotted out a large vocabulary for her age, full of colorful expressions and ethnic slurs. When angry, she lashed out, hitting, kicking, scratching, and spitting. Her fits and tantrums had lasted for hours. Now she controlled her language, though she still had a spectacular vocabulary for a six-year-old, the fits had stopped, and she was rarely violent. She was unfailingly gentle with her little brother and anyone else she considered as needing care. When someone was upset or hurt, she was the first one there to offer a hug or a shoulder.

"I know, Kitty Kat. I know."

Later that day, after Torres had stopped by to formally offer him a position with Counterintelligence, he met Kat in the parking lot at the school. They were a few minutes early, so he indulged in a lingering kiss.

"I thought about you all day," she said.

"Good thoughts, I hope." He kept his arms around her because he liked having her close.

"Naked thoughts. You always get horny after a flogging. I wonder how you handled that when you paid people to beat you?"

"They didn't elicit the same response." He maneuvered her between two cars where no one could see him squeeze her ass cheek and grind his pelvis against her abdomen. "This is all for you, Kitty Kat."

She giggled and grasped the arms of his jacket. "We're at an elementary school, Agent Rossetti. You could get arrested for this."

"For kissing my bride-to-be? Nah." For good measure, he kissed her again. "Oh, I almost forgot. Rafael Torres offered me a job at Counterintelligence. I'd be a Supervisory Special Agent. It means a raise, more travel, and I won't be working so closely with you anymore."

Kat blinked. "Oh. Well, that last part would kind of suck, but I want to be a judge, so that was just a matter of time, right? The rest—that's great, Keith. You deserve this. Did you take the job?"

He hadn't been sure. Part of him disliked change, though that didn't stop his life from evolving. Three years ago, he never would have predicted he'd be engaged to the woman of his dreams and have adopted two children that were now the focus of his world. "I said I'd think about it."

"For what it's worth, I think you should go for it. Then you can convince Malcolm to go back to the FBI."

They shared a laugh. Darcy wanted Malcolm out of her hair, but mostly they were concerned that he wasn't happy working as a tech consultant. Some of his work came from the FBI, but most of his jobs came from the private sector, including SAFE Security.

He took Kat's hand and led her toward the school. "He'll never go back. That's one bridge he won't rebuild." Since he'd quit, not one of his family members had been in danger. Prior to that, his wife, his sister, his cousin, and his sister-in-law had been targeted by criminals.

She sighed. "I hope he finds what he's looking for. He's good at catching bad guys. I can't remember a time when he wasn't fixated on standing up for truth, justice, and the American way."

As soon as they went inside, the office staff rushed them into the principal's office where Mrs. Glyss walked them through a new behavior plan for Angie.

"After meeting again with the Smiths, we've decided not to move Kyle to another classroom. Instead, we've instituted a stay-apart mandate for them. Kyle and Angelina are not allowed to play together. They can't be in groups or on teams together. They can't sit at the same table in the classroom or on the playground." Mrs. Glyss smiled at her creative solution.

Kat blanched. "That's horrible. Those poor kids. Kyle is her best friend, and from what I understand, the other kids pick on him when Angelina isn't around."

He set his hand over the one Kat had clenched on her lap. "This seems harsh."

"Too severe for a first offense." Kat's bearing morphed from parent to U.S. Attorney Mama Bear. "This is how you handle all classroom altercations where no bodily injuries were sustained?"

"There was a bruise," Mrs. Glyss offered. "She hits quite hard. She's hit me before, so I know."

Kat leaned forward. "A bruise? That's quite severe. Did it require medical treatment?"

Mrs. Glyss's face wrinkled in response to Kat's blatant sarcasm. "Well, no. But she has a history of violence, so these measures are warranted."

Keith intervened. "How long is the sentence for this crime?" Okay, maybe he didn't improve the situation. He knew they were probably being assholes, but he hated anything that hurt his little girl's feelings.

"For the foreseeable future. The Smiths insist."

Keith took that to mean that the Smiths were still threatening litigation. He turned to Kat. "We should have the Smiths over for dinner."

She stared, probably trying to figure out if he was serious. Wheels churned in her head as she weighed the pros and cons. Finally she nodded. "Sounds great. Mrs. Glyss, would you happen to have contact information?"

"I can't share that with you."

Kat made a face. "Don't worry. We'll find the information we need. It's kind of our jobs."

Angelina joined them for the next phase of the meeting where they explained the terms of her sentence to her. She took it like a trooper. "Actions have consequences," she said. "Me and Kyle will always be friends no matter what."

Afterward he took Angie home while Kat went to her parents' house to pick up Corey.

Corey limped into the kitchen where he and Angie were fixing dinner to show off his injured knee. Kat followed, setting her briefcase on the sideboard where they shoved all kinds of odds and ends.

Angie jumped down from her step stool where she'd been arranging ingredients for a salad, and she knelt down to inspect the bandage. "What happened, Cor? Are you okay?"

"Grandpa said I'll live." He wiped a hand across his forehead, indicating he'd dodged a bullet on that front. "I learned to ride a bike today. This was from when I still didn't know. I fell down on the cement. Scraped the skin right off."

Angie kissed the bandage. "That'll help it heal faster. I'm glad you learned. Now we can go for a ride together."

Kat ruffled Angie's hair. "Why don't the two of you go play? I'll help Daddy make dinner."

"Okay." The pair squealed and ran toward the garage.

"Stay in the driveway," Keith said. "Or the sidewalk in front of the house." He indicated Kat's power suit. "Go change first. I'm making chicken and potatoes. There's nothing immediate that needs your attention."

Plus he wanted her to rest up. Flogging him required some serious strength and stamina.

The dungeon was his domain. No matter what was scheduled to happen inside that room, he was the undisputed Master. Once they'd confirmed the kids were asleep, Kat shooed him out of their bedroom so that she could prepare.

"I was kidding about the lingerie and boots." He paused in the doorway. "As long as you're balanced and comfortable, whatever you're wearing is fine."

"And no underwear." She snagged his arm as he turned to leave. "I was thinking."

When most women said something like that, their partner cringed. They knew that trouble was on the horizon. But Kat was different. As a generous and thoughtful person, she approached everything with the best of intentions. Keith waited patiently for her to continue.

"The cross tilts. Maybe incline it or lay it flat. That way you can really relax tonight instead of worrying about holding yourself up."

He'd considered altering the angle before, but in the back of his mind, he suspected that if he did that, he'd lose control of the situation. Though she was the one doling out the pain, he was the one in charge. Anything she did, she did because he commanded it. If he let himself fall under the influence of the endorphins, then wouldn't that put her in charge, albeit temporarily?

Always in tune with the drift of his thoughts, Kat stroked her palm down his arm. "Of course I'll do whatever you want. My thought was only for your pleasure."

"I'll think about it." He kissed her cheek. "Don't be long."

Two flights of stairs later, he contemplated his St. Andrew's cross. Years ago, he'd bought it for himself, and then he'd perversely refused to let anyone even know that he was a masochist. Kat had found out because he'd let her get close to him, and she'd watched his reactions every bit as closely as he'd watched hers. Where he'd discovered that she endured pain for his sake, she'd discovered that pain heightened his pleasure. During sex, if she wasn't bound, she always scratched, bit, pinched, or squeezed to sweeten his orgasm.

Since Kat had found out, the secret was no longer closely guarded. His friends knew and accepted it. Malcolm found glee in

Re/Captured

showing Kat different techniques to elicit pain on a man. It was one small way to passive-aggressively punish Keith for breaking his promise to stay away from Kat.

After setting out the implements he wanted her to use, he tilted the cross, angling it at sixty degrees. It wasn't quite flat, but it would allow him to rest his weight against the thing. As he locked it into position, two raps on the door let him know that Kat waited outside. As this was his domain, she wasn't allowed inside unless she was invited or had specific permission.

He opened the door to find her wearing jogging shorts and a matching shirt. She'd wrangled her luxurious brown tresses into a French braid. Flogging him was a workout, and she almost always dressed accordingly. "Come in, Kitty Kat."

She proceeded to the pillow on the floor near the center of the room and knelt in the alert pose. This meant her bottom didn't rest on her heels, though her knees were spread and her hands were behind her neck.

Standing behind her, he let her feel his presence, soak in his domination. Gently, he stroked her hair, noting the silky pattern of the braid shifting under his fingers. "I've put out the elk, horsehair, and bull." The bull flogger had a flat braid, much like her hair. "Come, and put me on the cross, Kitty Kat."

She rose gracefully and followed him to the cross. He shed his shirt, pants, and briefs, handing each item to her for folding. "Master, will you wear the belt?"

"Yes." Though she had become an expert with various floggers, she felt better when he wore a back brace designed for orthopedic support. While he didn't need the support, it protected his kidneys and lower back, areas that should never be flogged. He secured the brace, and then he positioned himself on the cross.

Kat attached the ankle and wrists cuffs. "I'm glad you tilted it down, Master. I want you to relax and enjoy my service to you. Would you like a blindfold?"

"Not tonight." There was nothing for him to look at but the wall and floor.

"Elk, horsehair, bull." She repeated the order, confirming how she'd use the three floggers.

"Yes. You can begin."

She ran her hands over his back, ass, and thighs, preparing the areas she intended to abuse. Then she pressed a kiss between his shoulder blades. He exhaled, forcing his body to begin to relax. Ever since that morning, he'd been on edge. His case had been torn apart by an inept prosecutor, and then he'd been forced to witness his daughter facing the consequences of her actions. To top it all off, he had to decide whether to keep his career on a safe, predictable path with few chances of advancement or jump into the deep end of something new.

The soft falls of the elk brushed his skin as she applied a steady forehand/backhand pattern. It concentrated on his right shoulder before moving to the left. She went after his ass and thighs next. Predictability was important. He needed to anticipate each kiss of the leather to control his response. Soon the force behind the strokes increased, and endorphins trickled into his system. He closed his eyes and concentrated on the way the pain made him feel calm and alive. The thoughts nagging his brain stopped being coherent, and a light, floating feeling suffused his limbs.

He noted the change to horsehair and how she altered her technique to use a pinwheel motion. A million pinpricks stung his back, ass, and thighs. They melded together, and he lost control of the endorphins flooding through his blood. By the time she moved on to the braided bull, he barely registered the change. For the first time in his life, his mind took flight and he was powerless to stop it. Or maybe he trusted Kat so deeply that he knew it was safe to let completely go.

Time passed. His body thrummed, and his mind was uncharacteristically calm. He became aware of Kat massaging his ass.

"What are you doing?" His words were slurred, almost unintelligible.

She stroked his cheek. "Shhh. It's okay, Master. I'm putting arnica on you."

"Aftercare?" He'd never required aftercare before. Usually after a session, he turned on her, his inner beast hungry for a taste of her honey.

"Yes. I didn't realize you were in subspace at first, so I kept going. And then when I realized what had happened, I thought I'd keep you there for a while. You deserve that kind of bliss, Master. But I'm afraid you're going to have some decent bruises."

She hadn't known to stop? Of course she hadn't. He was the one who always said when it was enough. He lifted his arm, testing to see if she'd freed him from the restraints. She had.

She stilled his movement with a hand on his wrist. "Oh, don't move yet. I haven't done your thighs. I would have brought you to the aftercare room—the table in there is much more comfortable—but I can't lift you."

Re/Captured

He was still on the cross. Though he had pads for it, he'd never used them. Perhaps it was time to reconsider. He let her finish ministering to him, and then he leaned on her as he got to his feet.

"I'm glad you tilted the cross. I think you had a better experience."

"Yeah." He wasn't going to disagree. He'd never felt like this after a session. This was how he made her feel—helpless and out of control, but filled with bliss and all sorts of sappy emotions. He wasn't sure how he felt about this turn of events. On one hand, the sense of peace and calm were unparalleled. But he'd ceded total control. Doms didn't do that. Ever. Yet he couldn't summon anything except slightly mixed emotions. He kissed her forehead. "Where are my clothes?"

"I'll get them, Master."

She kept an arm around his waist as they navigated the stairs, and once they made it to the bedroom, he collapsed onto the bed. "I feel drunk."

"Well, no alcohol was involved, so your sobriety hasn't been compromised." She unbuttoned his pants. "Lift up."

He let her undress him because he liked to sleep in his underwear and he didn't have the coordination required to take off his own clothes. She helped him get under the covers, and then she changed into pajamas to join him.

He didn't remember falling asleep, but he slept deeply and woke up before the alarm, revitalized and refreshed. The house was quiet. He heard the distinct tick of the grandfather clock Papa L had given them, a family heirloom he had passed to them that now occupied a place in the hallway near the stairs.

There wasn't enough light for him to make out more than the general shape of the woman sleeping next to him. He wondered how long the session had lasted and if her arms were going to be sore. If he hadn't lost himself last night, he would have massaged her shoulders before they went to bed. Yet he didn't get the sense that he'd let her down. Though he hadn't fully followed what she'd said to him after the session, he had a clear recollection of her saying that he deserved that kind of bliss.

She wanted him to be happy. Was he happy at WCC? He wasn't unhappy. This issue wasn't simple, and it was going to take some time to sort out his feelings and his goals. This was a decision he refused to rush.

The sound of water woke Katrina. She cracked one eye open to find that she still had a half hour before the alarm went off. With a groan, she turned over and pulled the covers over her head. Closing her eyes produced an image of Keith naked and wet.

Last night had been incredible on so many levels. He'd relaxed, fully relaxed, for the first time in all the years she'd known him. She wouldn't go so far as to say he'd submitted to her, but he'd definitely let down his guard and allowed himself to experience bliss. When he flogged her, that feeling was her reward. She felt immense satisfaction that she had been able to give that same thing to him.

But he might not see it that way.

Last night he'd been too tired for sex, and this morning, he hadn't made a move. That wasn't like Keith. They joked that he was a sex addict, but the fact of the matter was that he rarely went a day without sex. She'd expected to awaken to him pushing into her body, finding a respite only she could give.

She threw back the covers and padded into the bathroom. "Keith, are you all right?"

"I'm excellent. I've decided to take my time thinking about the job with Counterintelligence." His perky response came through the shower door.

Caught off guard, she started. Though he was always thoughtful and thorough, she'd thought he would have made a decision. She rubbed the sleep from her eyes. "That's good. Did last night help?"

"Yes, thank you. I'm sorry I didn't get to massage your shoulders. Why don't you join me in here, and I'll take care of that for you?"

In seconds she was naked. She opened the door and slid into the shower with him. It was a large stall, easily big enough for them both, with a tiled shower seat at one end. She found him sitting there with the spray falling over the top of his head and cascading down his back.

"Can I see your back?" She expected the red marks to be gone, but she had no idea how many bruises he'd bear.

He stood and showed off his back. She found a series of small bruises on his upper back, another on the right side of his ass, and nothing on his thighs. Typically she went easier on his thighs because they were more sensitive. "I'm fine," he said.

"I'll put more arnica on you when you get out of the shower."

He turned around and pressed his naked, wet front to hers. "Last night was weird."

"I've never sent you to subspace before." She spoke softly, remembering with awe the moment she realized his mind had taken flight.

"Let's not call it subspace."

Her gaze snapped to his. She studied his clear green eyes as she thought about his order. "Because you're not a sub?"

"Submitting...It doesn't sit right with me." He stroked his fingertips along her spine. "I'm not a sub, Kitty Kat."

Regarding him with complete somberness, she nodded. "No, there's nothing submissive about you, Keith. You're alpha to the core."

"I'm glad you understand."

"Of course I understand. I know you better than anyone. I know what drives you, and I love you."

"I love you too, Kitty Kat." He pressed his forehead to hers.

"But you did submit. Maybe not to me, but to the lash. You surrendered, and that's not a bad thing. I think it's what you needed to clear your head." Perhaps he hadn't made a decision, but now the idea no longer seemed to weigh him down.

"I'm going to turn you over my knee," he said.

"For being honest?" She knew his threat was hollow. Keith never punished her outside of a scene. He knew how hard she took it when she upset or disappointed him. She also wasn't the kind of person who backed down when she knew she was right. "I'll take any reward you want to dish out, Master."

He sighed. "Arguing with a lawyer is impossible."

"It's insanity," she agreed. "But I hear what you're saying. Last night, though awesome, bothers you. You need time to process it and come to terms with the fact that you like that spacey feeling." She aimed to give him different terms to describe it because anything that hinted at submission was going to rub his machismo the wrong way.

"Turn around, Kitty Kat. I'll rub your shoulders, and then I'm going to have my way with you."

Michele Zurlo

Chapter 6

The week flew by. Katrina's dress came in, and she left work early on Friday for her first fitting. Layla, flanked by their mothers, met her at the bridal boutique. Being sisters, their mothers were also close friends, and so Layla and Katrina had forged a close bond as children. They'd drifted apart after high school when life had taken them in different directions, but over the past couple years, they'd reestablished their friendship.

Katrina's mom, Donna, reached her first and hugged her tight. "Dad took Corey and Colin to the grocery store. Those three will be gone for hours." Mario Legato loved to shop, and more than that, he loved a deal. He'd talk the boys through the math on every discount, sale, and coupon before selecting an item to purchase.

Aunt Cindy hugged her next. "I can't wait, Trina. You and Layla are going to make such beautiful brides."

Layla grinned. Her wedding was right around the corner as well. They hadn't wanted to schedule them too close together, but when Katrina had been forced to postpone hers, it had happened anyway. Now their weddings were two weeks apart.

Layla threaded her arm though Katrina's. "My dress came in today too, so it's a double fitting."

Katrina leaned down to whisper in her cousin's ear. "You brought our mothers? I thought this would be just me and you."

"Sorry. They're so excited. We'll go out after, just you and me, and get a drink." Layla squeezed her arm.

"I'll see if Keith can pick the kids up." She fired off a text to Keith as they were ushered back to the changing rooms.

Donna and Cindy settled on chairs provided for all the moms who wait. Katrina checked that thought when she saw a man there as well. His daughter was wearing what one might politely term a classic gown, and she was not happy about it.

"Dad, this dress is hideous."

"Erica, you need to make it work. Grandma made one request, and you have to honor it."

Erica, who looked to be about the same age as Katrina and Layla, checked her reflection in the mirror, her eyes wide with horror. "I'm going to elope. Then she won't be paying for a thing."

Her father stood behind her and placed his hands on her shoulders. "Sweetheart, you can't do that."

Erica's lips twisted bitterly. "Because it'll reflect badly on your career? It's my wedding, Dad. I don't care what a bunch of—" She broke off, noticing for the first time that four people had joined them. Her face turned to stone. She was still upset, but now it was tinged with bitterness.

Katrina felt sorry for the woman. Thankfully her mother had not offered her wedding dress. She'd long ago had it made into christening gowns for M.J., Malcolm, and Katrina.

"Hi," Layla said, her friendly greeting and brilliant smile shattering the awkward silence. "When's the big day?"

Erica frowned.

Her father answered. "August sixteenth."

"Four months." Katrina studied the dress. It had long sleeves, a full bodice that came up to the neck in a tight collar, and a train that went on forever. "The fabric is beautiful. I've never seen such exquisite lace."

The dad took a step back. "It was my mother's wedding dress. She has excellent taste." He held out a hand. "I'm Robert. This is my daughter, Erica. Normally she's delightful, but today has been difficult for her."

Katrina shook his hand. "Katrina. This is my cousin Layla, and those are our mothers, Cindy and Donna."

"Nice to meet you. Erica's mother passed away a few years ago, so she's stuck with me."

"Dad," Erica implored, her brown eyes growing larger. "Don't say it like that. I'm glad you're here."

Katrina reached toward Erica's dress. "May I?"

Erica looked down, judging where Katrina wanted to touch. "Knock yourself out."

Picking up the half-moon piece that fell from the collar, Katrina said, "The bib has to go. And these puffy sleeves...I'd take them off, go sleeveless. Oh, more lace. I love this lace."

"Actually," Layla came closer, lifting the bib. "The bodice has a killer sweetheart neckline. I'd go strapless. August is warm, so you might appreciate the airflow."

Katrina circled around Erica. "You have a rip back here next to the zipper."

Michele Zurlo

"Grandma tried it on," Erica said dryly, "but she's gained a few pounds since she first wore it. No matter what, the back is going to look horrible. There is no good way to repair satin."

Katrina snapped her fingers. "Put a cutout in the back. Use the lace you're taking from under the bib to fill it in. It'll look incredible. Nobody will have a dress like that."

Erica's frown turned thoughtful. She shook out the skirt. "What about the skirt? This is way too much beadwork."

"I don't think so." Layla ran her hand over the eight inches of beadwork looping and swirling on the hem. "It'll look less busy once you redo the top half. I'd leave the skirt alone."

Katrina agreed. "It's a lovely dress. It just needs updating."

Erica nodded absently, her mind focusing on the image Layla and Katrina had painted.

Robert turned away, but not before Katrina noticed him dabbing a tear from his eye.

The seamstress and her assistant came in. She smiled politely at Erica's dress. "Let's mark where it needs to be taken in or let out."

"Actually," Erica said, "I'm going to need a few more alterations."

Katrina turned to go into a dressing room, and Robert caught her arm. "I cannot thank you enough. You don't know what this means to me."

She patted his arm. "Weddings shouldn't be so stressful." As she entered the fitting room, she caught her mother's eye. Donna's face reflected the pride and love she felt for her daughter, and that made Katrina's eyes feel damp. Pushing back the gooey emotions, she resolved that this wasn't going to be a big deal. She and Keith lived together. They'd adopted two children. A marriage was just a piece of paper, a formality to legally label the life they already lived.

In the changing room, she stripped down to her panties and bra, and Keith's ringtone sounded on her phone.

"Hey, there."

"What are you doing?"

Her text had been brief, asking if he was working late or if he could pick the kids up. She had expected him to work late, as he frequently did, so she hadn't elaborated on her reasons. "I'm semi-naked, standing in front of a mirror, and talking to you."

He was quiet for a second. "This doesn't feel like you're coming on to me."

She laughed. "I'm at my fitting, silly. My mom, Layla, and Aunt Cindy are waiting for me to put on my dress."

"Oh." His interest piqued. "Is there a problem? Are you running late?"

"No, no problem. Layla asked if I wanted to get a drink with her after this. I don't know what your schedule is like today." She knew he had planned to meet with Rafael Torres, the ASAC for Counterintelligence at the Detroit field office.

"Torres canceled on me, so my schedule freed up. I'll get the kids. You spend some time with Layla, maybe get some dinner. It's been over a month since you two have gone out."

"You're so sweet. I'll see if she has plans."

"Text me. Let me know. And call me if you need me to pick you up. I don't want either of you driving under the influence."

"I will."

"Put your dress on. Tell me how you look."

Though he couldn't see it, she parked her hand on her hip. "Keith, this is highly inappropriate, and it's bad luck." Her pulse raced. Though she thought of the wedding as a formality, she couldn't help but get a little excited for the actual event.

His husky chuckle crackled through the phone. "I don't believe in bad luck, and I can't masturbate to mental images of you in that dress if I don't know what it looks like."

Her fake chagrin melted. She whispered her reply. "You want to masturbate to mental images of me in a wedding dress? That's weird. You have actual pictures of me wearing lingerie." He also had a picture of her pussy that he refused to delete. Good thing his phone was password and fingerprint protected.

"I like those pictures." His voice dropped as the Dom in him asserted itself. "But, Kitty Kat, the wedding dress says unequivocally that you belong to me. Nothing is sexier than that."

Her breath caught at his tone. "You're such a romantic."

"How about a picture?"

"Nope." She smiled as she refused him. "I'm not bending on this. You can't see my dress before the wedding."

"At least tell me what the neckline looks like. And how long is the skirt? What are you wearing under it?"

She laughed. "No clues. You'll have to wait."

"Tease."

"A tease would send you pictures of random dresses."

"True. I love you, Kitty Kat. Be good. Call if you need me, okay?"

"I will. I love you too."

Michele Zurlo

With that exchange in mind, she put the dress on. The dress was simple, a sleeveless satin gown with an elegant V-cut in the front and back. The bodice hugged her curves, while the full skirt billowed around her legs. In keeping with its simplicity, there were few beads, and the only lace was found in the short train.

She noted that it would have to be taken in around the chest. Her boobs were not large, and this bodice had enough leftover space to accommodate an extra pair. She went into the alteration area to find Layla already on the second platform. On the first one, Erica still described changes to the seamstress. Her father had disappeared.

Layla had chosen a strapless sheath that conformed to her petite figure. Hers came with a huge train that seemed to flow like a waterfall from the back of her dress.

Layla looked Katrina up and down. "Looks like you have the same problem I do." She let go of the top of her dress, and it slid down. "No boobs. I blame our mothers."

Donna and Cindy, sitting off to the side, snorted and laughed. Both were curvy women with ample bosoms. Cindy shook her head. "Blame your father for those genes, Layla. Grandma Hudson has a flat chest, and so do both of your father's sisters. With that blonde hair, slim build, and those blue eyes, you take after your father's side."

Donna chimed in. "Trina, your size is proportional to your figure. Be happy with what you have."

"I wasn't complaining." She'd never been self-conscious about her body. Keith loved it, and that's all that mattered. She watched as a seamstress pinned Layla's gown. "You look so lovely, Layla. Dustin is going to flip for you all over again when he sees you coming down the aisle."

Layla's smug grin was her only response.

"I can't believe our girls are both getting married." Cindy sniffed. "It seems like yesterday they were both running around barefoot and screaming about how gross boys are."

"Now I have grandchildren," Donna said, her voice soft. "Six wonderful grandchildren."

Cindy recovered. She cleared her throat. "I'm still waiting. Layla has informed me that she's in no hurry."

Katrina could relate. If fate hadn't brought Angelina and Corey to her, then she wouldn't have kids either. Before them, she hadn't really wanted kids. She'd wanted a career that led to a judgeship. She still wanted to become a judge, but right now that didn't seem to be in the cards.

Re/Captured

When it was her turn, Katrina stood still while the seamstress marked all the alterations. Besides the chest area, there were few to be made. In the background, Layla and their mothers chatted about wedding details. Katrina hadn't been as proactive as Layla. She'd let her mother and Keith take the lead on most of the planning, and Darcy's sister, Amy, had been helpful as well. As an event planner, she had samples and contacts that she'd eagerly shared with both of them. When Katrina had offered to pay for her services, Amy had refused.

The fitting didn't take very long. Cindy and Donna both cried. Katrina could understand Cindy getting teary-eyed—Layla was her only child—but Donna had seen both of Katrina's older brothers married. She hugged her mom. "Thanks for coming."

"You're so beautiful, Trina. I'm glad you finally convinced your prince that he wasn't a frog."

Keith hadn't thought of himself as a frog. He hadn't thought himself worthy of love, but she'd helped him to see the light. Katrina faced Layla. "Did you still want to get a drink? Maybe grab some dinner?"

"Sure." Layla's effervescent smile lit up her face. "Dustin won't be home until later."

Erica emerged from her changing room dressed in the exact same skirt and jacket Katrina was wearing. The two of them stared. With their dark hair and eyes, they looked remarkably alike. Laughter burst from Layla.

Katrina smoothed her skirt. "You have great taste."

Erica's mouth twitched into a smile. "So do you."

"There you are." Robert came into the alterations area. "We need to get going or we'll be late." He looked between Katrina and Erica, but he didn't comment on the similarity.

"In a minute, Dad. I have to give the dress to the seamstress." Erica smiled sweetly, and her father exited the area. Then she turned to Katrina and Layla. "I'm envious of you two. I'd much rather get a drink with you than go to dinner with my dad and his friends. It's a bunch of old people talking about health care, pensions, and the latest things they've bought."

Layla frowned sympathetically. "Well, then join us." She glanced at Katrina to belatedly make sure she didn't have a problem with adding to their number. "Trina and I are best friends, and you look like you'll fit right in."

Erica cocked her head thoughtfully. "Can you add someone to your reservation this late on a Friday night?"

Michele Zurlo

They didn't have reservations. Katrina handed her dress over to the assistant. Layla and Erica followed suit. "Sure. We were just going to go to Friday's or something like that. If there's a wait, we'll sit at the bar."

"If you'll allow me to do you one better?" Erica's eyebrows lifted. "Since you did one for me?"

The lawyer in Katrina didn't agree to deals until she knew the details. Layla wasn't a lawyer. "Sure," she said. "What did you have in mind?"

"My dad can add as many people as he wants to his party, and he'll pick up the tab. Join us. That way he'll be happy that I'm there to put on a show for his friends, and I'll be happy that I have friends of my own along."

This screamed awkward. Katrina opened her mouth to bow out, but Layla beat her to it, only she didn't bow out. "Why not? It sounds like an adventure."

Katrina, left with no choice—she wasn't going to let her cousin go off with virtual strangers—murmured polite agreement. "Perhaps you should check with your father first?"

Erica waved away Katrina's concern. She strode into the showroom filled with hundreds of gowns and tuxedoes. "Dad, I've invited Trina and Layla to dinner. You don't mind, right?"

Robert hid his surprise. "That's fine. I'll phone ahead so the club knows to add two place settings."

Katrina felt the need to give the man an out. He'd been caught off guard. "Really, Robert, we don't want to impose. If this isn't a good time, we can get together with Erica another time."

He smiled indulgently. "It's not an imposition. This way Erica will have some people her own age to talk with. Our conversations can get quite tedious. Will you be riding with us?"

Erica linked arms with Layla and Katrina. "I'll ride with them and show them where it is."

And so Katrina found herself driving Layla and Erica to an exclusive golf club thirty-five minutes from where she lived.

"Pull up to the front. My dad has valet service on his account." Erica leaped from the car as soon as she stopped.

Katrina glanced into the backseat, throwing Layla a dirty look. "You owe me, big time."

Layla threw up her hands. "I had no freaking clue she'd take us to a place like this. At least you're dressed nicely. I'm wearing jeans, and my shirt says that I'm addicted to chocolate."

As soon as she reached for her door, the valet opened it. He handed her a token in exchange for her key. She joined Layla and Erica at the door.

Erica turned to them. "I just realized I didn't think this through. I was so focused on the fact that I wouldn't have to be alone with all those stuffed shirts that I didn't stop to think about if this is the kind of place you'd like. I understand if you want to leave, but I'm begging you to stay."

Layla pointed to her shirt. "I feel a little underdressed. I have some great cocktail dresses at home, but I run a community center, so I tend to dress in kid-friendly clothes."

For the first time, Erica seemed to notice what Layla was wearing. "I have the perfect thing. Come on."

They followed Erica into the club. Erica led them down a wide, paneled hall and into a small boutique. She beelined for a rack featuring a wine red dress. "You're petite, so probably this size?" She held it up to Layla. "Go put it on."

Layla took it, intending to look at the price tag, but Erica ripped off the tag and took it to the register. Eyes wide, Layla stared at Katrina.

Katrina shrugged. "She's right. That will look great on you." While Layla changed, Katrina texted Keith and Dustin, giving them the name of the club and warning them that they'd be later than they originally thought.

Waiting patiently next to her, Erica smiled. "Is that your fiancé?"

"And Layla's. He'll want to know where she is."

She wrinkled her nose. "Is he one of those guys who has to know where you are every minute of the day?"

So many of the people in her life were connected. They knew each other, and so they didn't see things like this as controlling. They saw them for what they were—a status update to set minds at ease. Even her parents knew the score when it came to the Doms in their lives. But it wasn't one-sided. Keith also texted her when he wasn't where she expected him to be.

"He doesn't have to know, but he likes to know. Dustin does as well."

She tilted her head. "If he told you to come home right now, would you?"

Katrina didn't hesitate. "Yes."

Erica tapped her lips, thinking. "You asked him for permission before you came out tonight, didn't you?"

Michele Zurlo

The judgment in Erica's tone smacked Katrina upside the head. Pressing her lips together, she squared up to Erica. "Of course I did. It was my day to pick up the kids. I needed to know if he could get them and if he didn't mind me being gone this evening. I asked if he wouldn't mind me getting a drink with Layla, and he suggested dinner. And then he told me that if we had too much to drink to call him, and he'd come get us. I don't care for how you're judging me."

Layla had joined them during Katrina's speech. The wine-colored dress looked incredible on Layla, and the cut played up her slight curves. On her feet, she'd selected plain black heels. Layla put her hand on Katrina's arm. "Thank you so much for the dress. Really, you didn't have to." She flashed a smile before continuing. "Trina and I are subs in D/s relationships. Dustin and Keith are good men. Caring men. Generous and demanding. And they're kinky as fuck, which we both love. We wouldn't change either of them for the world."

Erica's gaze dropped. While Katrina was a natural people pleaser, she wasn't a pushover. Layla wasn't a people pleaser, and she only submitted to Dustin.

Finally Erica cleared her throat. "Sorry. It sounded—I dated a guy who was controlling for a while. He was a selfish jerk. I know it's wrong to paint all men with the same brush." She smiled, but it was thin. "You and your fiancé have kids?"

Thinking of Angelina and Corey, Katrina's face softened. "Yes."

"There you are." They looked over to see Robert motioning them over. "Everybody is ready to order."

Erica strolled out of the store. Layla hiked her bag, now stuffed with her clothes, higher on her shoulder. She slung an arm around Katrina. "Next time I do something like this, tell me to shut up, will you?"

"It wouldn't work," Katrina said. "Like Dustin says, a gag only muffles you. Nothing shuts you up."

At the table, Robert and two other men hopped up to pull out chairs. Far from the informal, no-holds-barred chat-fest she'd intended for this evening, it had turned into a rather formal affair. They'd joined six people dressed in suits or dresses.

"Sorry we're late," Erica said. "We were getting fitted for our wedding dresses."

A woman with a pinched face leaned forward. "All of you?"

"Yes," Erica said. "I'd like to introduce my friends, Layla and Katrina. We're all summer brides. We met at the bridal shop." She didn't add that they'd been acquainted for less than two hours. "This is State Senator John Benty and his wife, Shirley."

The pair nodded their greeting.

"Next to Shirley is District 12 Representative Doris Hoffman."

Doris smiled politely. She was the one who had inquired about all of them being fitted for wedding dresses.

"At the other end of the table next to Doris is her husband, Alan. Then we have State Senator Henry Otille, and you've already met my dad, Senator Robert Kenyon."

Katrina had thought Robert looked familiar, and now she knew why. She'd voted for him. He looked different in person, taller and more real than he had appeared on television or online.

Having met politicians before—sooner or later they all showed up at the Department of Justice—she put on the smile she gave to juries. "It's great to meet all of you. Thank you for allowing Layla and me to join you tonight on such short notice."

They tittered polite reassurances. Katrina found herself at the end of the table between Senator Kenyon and Erica, with Layla across from her. The senator attempted polite conversation. "What's your line of work, Katrina?"

"I'm a federal prosecutor, mostly white-collar crimes."

He lifted a brow. "Really? That's fantastic. I started out at the DOJ. What are your long-term aspirations?"

"The bench, ideally. I like being a lawyer, but I've always had my heart set on becoming a judge."

"District court?"

She grinned. "Sky's the limit, Robert."

Though he smiled, his eyes regarded her shrewdly. "What did you think of the Gorham vs. Prosperity decision?"

This recent case in the Third Judicial Circuit Court had redefined seizure of evidence rules in favor of the accused. She hadn't agreed with the interpretation of the law that led to the ruling. "It defined the statute too narrowly. It makes it harder for the FBI to effectively do their job. The last thing we need to do is cripple our first line of defense against—"

"Dad." Erica pulled their attention back to her. "Trina came here to hang out with me."

Robert flashed a guilty smile. "Sorry. I love the law. We'll pick this up later. I'm interested in hearing your reasoning on the matter." He turned his attention to the politicians he'd come to meet.

Erica drew her and Layla into conversation. All told, it was pleasant. They had a lot in common, and despite their rocky beginning, Katrina found herself liking Erica.

Michele Zurlo

When the dinner plates had been cleared away and her father had stepped out for a phone call, Erica leaned forward and lowered her volume. "I'm dying to ask you guys about the kinky stuff."

Layla didn't blink. "I knew you were one of us."

Thinking back to Layla's apologies, Katrina chuckled. She loved her effusive cousin with the short attention span. "What kinds of questions do you have?"

She looked from Katrina to Layla and back again. "Do you really have to do everything he says?"

Layla answered first. "If it's an order, yes."

Katrina weighed in to explain. "As long as it's something you've agreed on. You start with negotiation. You sit down, talk about what's allowed and what's not allowed—hard and soft limits." She hadn't done that with Keith even though he'd asked. Because she had been new to the details of the lifestyle, she hadn't developed a reference point for anything. He'd helped her with that.

Erica's eyes scrunched up again as she thought. "So, you're saying that you have to do whatever he says as long as you've already agreed to do those things?"

"Pretty much," Layla said. "You can negotiate as much or as little as you want. Most people don't live the dynamic 24/7. That's hard, especially when you both work or if you have kids."

Katrina chimed in. "When you're with someone who has an alpha personality, he's going to be that way all the time. That's another reason negotiation is good. It helps draw clear lines and keep communication open."

Eyes still scrunched, Erica sipped her cocktail. "Can you give me a for-instance?"

"Keith picks out my clothes when we scene," Katrina offered. "And sometimes outside of a scene he'll ask me to wear a certain outfit."

Layla tapped the table with one finger as she thought. "Dustin can start a scene whenever he wants, but I have a safe signal and a safeword I can use if it's not a good time."

Erica turned to Katrina. "Do you have the safe things?"

"A safeword? Absolutely. It's essential. I also have a safe signal for when I can't use my mouth."

As the reasons why Katrina might not be able to use her mouth occurred to Erica, her skin flushed red. "My fiancé, Burke, asked if he could tie me up. Have you ever done that?"

"All the time," Layla said.

"Yeah. I find myself restrained quite often," Katrina agreed.

Erica laughed, though her blush did not diminish. "From your expressions, it sounds not scary."

"Trust is necessary," Layla said. "You have to trust your partner to have your best interest at heart."

Katrina put her hand on Erica's wrist. "If you want, we can introduce your fiancé to Dustin and Keith. They'd be willing to sit down and talk him through the basics, especially if he's reticent. And if Burke is interested in rope bondage, my brother is an expert."

"Your brother?"

Layla nodded. "Last year at our play party, he led a session where he taught people how to do a corselet. He's an artist, for sure. Malcolm could point Burke in the right direction."

Erica's gaze dropped. "Burke is afraid of going too far, of hurting me."

"We should all get together." Layla raised her glass in a toast. "Let our freak flags fly."

Michele Zurlo

Chapter 7

"Daddy!" Angie ran across the gym to him, arms open, and launched herself into the air when she was still a few feet away, trusting him to catch her.

Bending his knees slightly, he braced himself for impact. With Angie, love was a contact sport. They worked to gentle her without breaking her spirit. He caught her easily and brought her close for a hug.

She wrapped her tiny arms around his neck and squeezed. "Is Mommy here too?"

"No. She had to try on her wedding dress to make sure it fits, and then she's going to have dinner with Layla. It's you, me, and Corey tonight. We'll rough it." When Kat was gone in the evening, he liked to pull out all the leftovers. He'd spread them on the table, and they'd pick at everything while Angie and Corey told him about their day. Eventually one of the kids would convince him to be a horse or dragon, and they both ended up on his back while he wreaked havoc on the countryside. He'd never played like that as a kid, and he found that he enjoyed this second chance at a childhood.

Angie's eyes lit up. "Did my dress come too? Mommy bought me a flower girl dress. It's white, and it matches her dress, but I can't tell you what it looks like because it's a secret." She cupped his face in her small hands. "If you ask me the secret, you have to bribe me with ice cream."

While he wanted to know what the dress looked like, he wasn't going to cheat to find out. Kat wanted her traditions, and he was going to make sure she had them. Of course, that wouldn't stop him from trying to tease it out of her.

The director of after school care came to speak with him. He set Angie down. "Go get your things, baby girl."

She glared at him out of the sides of her eyes. "I'm not a baby."

Ms. Janie smiled after Angie. "She had a great day today. I know we always tell you the problems, so I wanted to make sure to tell you the positives. One of the kids was upset about something, crying his eyes out, and she went over and soothed him. Where two adults failed, she comforted him, got him smiling and playing in, like, two minutes. She's amazingly compassionate."

Keith beamed with fatherly pride. "Yes, she is. Thank you. She needs the positives more than the negatives. She's had enough of that in her short life."

"Have a great day, Mr. Rossetti." Ms. Janie beamed at Angie as she returned to them. "Bye, Angelina. Have a great weekend. I'll see you Monday."

On the way out, his phone rang, the familiar strains of the X-Files theme song letting him know it was the FBI. He let it go to voice mail. The next call came while he was driving, and this ring tone was generic. He sighed and answered. "Rossetti."

"Keith, this is Lexee. You need to get back here."

Before he had kids, he would have turned the car around without question. Things were different now. Priorities had changed. "Can't. Kat is working late. I have Angie, and I'm on my way to pick up Corey."

"It's an emergency."

Not wanting Angie to hear anything she shouldn't, he took her off speakerphone. "What's going on?"

"This is something you need to hear in person."

"Are you firing me?"

"No."

"Demoting or transferring me?"

"No, but Keith, trust me when I say this isn't a phone conversation."

"Trust me when I say that I'm not driving back to Detroit tonight, not without a damn good reason. So far, you haven't given me one."

"Fine. Have it your way. Pull over, then."

He turned down the street to Trina's parents and stopped in front of a random house. "I'm stopped. What's so urgent?"

"Someone delivered a bouquet to the DOJ, addressed to Katrina Legato."

"So?" His tone was measured. Katrina sometimes got flowers from victims who she'd vindicated. Even if they were from an admirer, he knew she didn't return their interest. This was not a reason to return to work. It wasn't even a reason for a phone call.

"When it went through security in the mail room, they detected something odd, so they opened it. Keith, it's a bouquet of roses being held by a severed hand."

His blood ran cold. "What the fuck?"

"Daddy, you can't say the F-word in front of me."

Michele Zurlo

Angie's reminder barely registered, but her presence caused him to couch his questions. "Was there a note? Is the owner of the, ah, digits waiting to get them back?"

"It's with forensics right now. They're trying to find out if we're looking for a living or dead vic. They're also running DNA. There wasn't a note or postmark. The package was plain, but we're trying to trace point of purchase."

Keith breathed to control his upset. "Lex, thank you for telling me, but if I came back there, I couldn't be of any use. Legally I can't touch the case."

"I know. I just—I know how you are. Wait—did you say Trina is working late?" The background noises got louder.

"She's getting fitted for her dress." He had said she was at work, but he'd meant that she wasn't here to take care of the kids so he could go back to work. "I'll take care of her. You find the sick bastard who sent the package."

"We will, Keith. It's top priority."

"Who's working on this?"

"Rakeem Bahu is taking lead. Jordan Monaghan is back. He's in the midst of transferring from the task force to VC. He's working with Bahu."

Keith felt good that Jordan was working on this, though he had no idea that Jordan had planned to leave the task force. They were friends. This was the kind of thing friends should know. He filed that away as a conversation to have later. He didn't know Bahu except by reputation. Between the two of them, they'd find this fucked up bastard. "Good. Keep me informed."

"Absolutely." That meant she'd tell him as much as she could without compromising the case.

He ended the call and headed to the Legato residence. When Angie got out and ran to the door, he grabbed her backpack. While he wasn't going back to the McNamara building tonight, he was definitely going to make sure Kat was safe.

They had no indication that she was in immediate danger. The delivery had come at the end of the day on Friday, so the perp didn't expect her to get it until Monday morning. Jordan was a great agent. There was a good chance he'd find the bastard before the weekend was over. Until then, he'd keep Kat where he could see her.

Angie burst through the front door, announcing her arrival by loudly calling for Corey. "Corey, I have something for you!"

Keith followed closely. "Angie, use your inside voice. What if Zella is sleeping?"

Re/Captured

Mama L entered the front room with Corey on her hip. His little blond head rested on her shoulder, and he blinked the sleep from his tired green eyes. "This one is almost ready for bed. He shopped with Poppa all afternoon."

Corey had stopped napping regularly six months ago. Keith held out his arms. "Hey, buddy. Are you feeling okay?"

He leaned forward, confident Keith would make sure he got from point A to point B safely. He took his son from Mama L.

"Corey?"

"I'm hungry."

"Growing," Mama L, amended. "Tired and hungry means he's growing."

He kissed Corey's head and set him on the sofa, and then he turned back to Mama L.

Mama L regarded him warily. "Uh-oh. I know that look."

He motioned to the kitchen. "Can I talk to you and Papa L for a minute?" At her nod, he addressed Angie. "Ang, why don't you and Corey go upstairs and watch cartoons?"

She watched him warily. "Daddy said three bad words in the car." She didn't level an accusation as much as she tried to connect dots. At six years old, she was too mature and aware of what grownups were doing.

He ruffled her hair. "I'll put money in the swear jar when we get home. Go upstairs, Angie." He watched his kids until they got to the top of the stairs, and then he went into the kitchen to face the only people who'd ever been parents to him.

Papa L sat at the table while Mama L fluttered nervously at the counter.

"Mama L, please sit down."

She exchanged a look with Papa L, but she sat down.

"I need to leave Angie and Corey here while I go get Kat."

Mama L pressed her lips together. Papa L frowned. "Let's not do twenty questions. Just tell us what's wrong."

"Someone delivered a grotesque bouquet to her office this afternoon. I got a call about it on my way over here."

"Grotesque bouquet?" Papa L frowned. "Like body parts?"

"Yes. They don't have reason to believe she's in imminent danger or even a target. They have the very best agents on the case, but I don't want to take chances. I'm going to go get Kat and make sure she gets home safely. And stays that way."

Mama L looked at him strangely. "She said nothing about this at the fitting. She doesn't know, does she?"

"Not yet."

"Well don't tell her." Mama L sprang from her chair, spritely and agile though she was nearing seventy. "Maybe you and Dustin happen to show up at the same place they're eating? You can keep an eye on her from a distance. That way she won't get freaked out."

Papa L folded his arms and leaned forward and nailed Keith with his firm gaze. An older version of Malcolm, hair silver instead of black, Mario Senior was a force with which to be reckoned. "Son, you do what you need to do to keep our girl safe. We'll take care of Angelina and Corey."

"I will." Keith went upstairs to kiss his children.

Corey's attention stayed on the cartoon, but Angie's knowing eyes met his. "I love you, Daddy."

"I love you too."

"Tell Mommy that we love her, okay?"

"I will. Be good for Grandma and Poppa. I'll be back later. You might be asleep."

Angie watched him. "I might not."

In the car, he checked his messages. "Where the fuck is Forest Hills Country Club?" He plugged the address into his Federal-issued GPS and called Dustin to explain the situation.

Dustin swore liberally. "I think working at the DOJ is more dangerous that being in the field. Come get me. I'm at my sister's house." Dustin's sister lived in the next subdivision over. Five minutes later, the two of them were headed to Forest Hills. "Trina texted me an hour ago. I've never heard of the place."

"Me, neither."

Dustin put the flashing light on the dash, and Keith floored it. Due to the later hour and the direction they traveled, rush hour traffic was not a problem.

"Plan of attack?" Dustin said as they neared the exit. "Are we going to extract them or watch over them as they finish eating?"

"We'll need to check her car, make sure nobody has tampered with it."

"I say we leave it and bring bomb-sniffing dogs back tomorrow." Dustin thought out loud. "It'll take that long to requisition them."

"No threats were made, so I think we're okay checking it out ourselves." She'd been driving it all day with no problem.

"Let's go in there, check out the situation. If they're in no danger, we'll let them finish gossiping and drinking. If they are, we'll pull them out." Dustin ran a hand through his blond hair. Though he and Keith were very similar—around the same height and build—Dustin looked like the proverbial boy next door while Keith had a harder, more dangerous edge to him. Dustin's looks charmed the ladies and misled the criminals. The man had lethal skills, and he used them to fight for good.

They arrived at the club to find the parking valet-only. Keith emerged from his SUV and flashed his badge. "You parked a silver Ford Edge about an hour ago. I need to see it."

The valet, a slim boy who looked barely legal to drive, blinked. "I'll ask my manager."

Dustin whistled to get his attention. "Key rack is over there. Can you recognize the key?"

"She has a family photo on the keychain." Keith jogged after Dustin. The two of them searched the rows of hanging keys.

"Sir, can I help you?" A man wearing a slightly more mature version of the valet uniform approached.

Dustin flashed his badge. "Special Agent Brandt. And you are?"

"Tony. I'm the valet manager."

"Tony, we may have a situation. Please remain calm while Special Agent Rossetti and I check it out."

Tony motioned over his shoulder. "I should go get the owner of the car. They'll want to know."

Dustin and Keith both nailed Tony in place with one firm look. Dustin's affable nature disappeared. "You'll stay here and keep all your employees here while we check this out. In the meantime, don't say a word to anyone. The last thing we need is panic, and I'm sure this place doesn't want that kind of press."

Color drained from Tony's face. "Of course not, sir. Will it take long? Dinner service is almost over, and people will want their cars."

"Got it," Keith said. "J3—where is that?"

Tony pointed down the long driveway. "The rows are in order, and each spot is numbered." Keith took off before Tony finished, having understood the gist of the system.

"We'll be quick." Dustin jogged after Keith. Together they checked over the car and engine.

Dustin, already wearing grubby clothes because he'd been helping his sister install a new hot water heater, slid under the car. He used the flashlight on his phone to check for incendiary devices.

Keith finished his check of the interior and waited impatiently for Dustin to complete his inspection. "It's clear. Nothing has been tampered with." Dustin wiggled out. Keith held out a hand and helped his buddy to his feet.

"Let's go inside, get eyes on Kat and Layla." Keith hurried back to the main building to find that Tony had followed Dustin's orders to the letter. All five valets stood waiting, as did several guests.

Tony watched them anxiously.

"It's clear. Resume normal operations." Keith handed Tony his card. "If you see anything out of the ordinary, call me."

Mouth open, Tony read the card as if it was a winning lottery ticket. "I will, Agent Rossetti. We can never be too careful when we have a senator and some representatives inside."

Dustin's mouth twitched. He didn't place more value on the life of one person over another. "We're going to sweep the inside."

"Sure." Tony motioned to a valet to get to work. "I'll keep an eye on things here."

They went inside. Kat had said she was having dinner there, so they scanned the entryway. The restaurant was to the right. Huge glass French doors let them see inside. As they opened, they heard the sounds of conversation mingled with that of a string quartet. Outside the door was a podium sporting a man wearing a suit.

Dustin glanced at Keith. "I thought they'd go somewhere easy, like Friday's or Applebee's."

"Yeah." Keith's brow wrinkled as he pondered what might bring the ladies to a country club so far from home. "This isn't what I expected either."

"Can I help you gentlemen?" The maitre d' took in Dustin's jeans and grungy shirt, his nose wrinkled in distaste.

They flashed their badges. "FBI," Keith said. "We're looking for a couple of guests. I have pictures." He pulled up a photo of Kat and Layla sitting at the kitchen table of his house. Kat hadn't known he was there, and he'd been struck by her smile.

The head waiter looked at the photo. "Yes. These ladies are guests of Senator Kenyon. Shall I ask them to come out here?"

"We're going to need visual confirmation." Keith peered past the maitre d'. It didn't take long to find Kat or Layla. They were seated at the end of a table populated with politician-looking types. The two of them appeared deep in conversation with a brown-haired woman who was significantly younger than the rest. The tension in his shoulders fractionally eased.

"Who are they talking to?" Dustin asked.

"Ms. Erica Kenyon is the senator's daughter."

That explained how they got here, but not why. Keith knew all Kat's friends and co-workers, but he did not know this one. He shot a silent question to Dustin. The shake of Dustin's head was almost imperceptible.

"How long have they been here?" Keith asked.

"About an hour. They have finished with dinner. Dessert should be served any moment now." The head waiter glanced back at the dining room. "I cannot allow you inside unless you're wearing a jacket and tie." He eyeballed Dustin. "I can loan you the required clothing."

Dustin's expression turned inscrutable. "I'll sweep the kitchen and outer areas. You go inside." Without waiting to see if Keith agreed with the plan, he disappeared down the hall.

Keith nodded to the restaurant. "I'll just be a few minutes."

Resigned, the maitre d' opened the door. Keith went inside, trying to be inconspicuous. His confident gait said he belonged there, and his eyes missed nothing. In two minutes, he had counted guests and waitstaff, and he'd noted which couples were fighting and who was cheating on their spouse. Nothing set off his internal alarm, so he parked himself in a corner near the kitchen. He was out of the way, and he could see the whole room. From this position, he settled in for closer scrutiny.

The more he watched, the more he saw people having a fancy dinner out on a Friday night. Kat and Layla huddled around Erica, talking and laughing. The trio seemed quite separate from the rest of the table. Keith noted that in addition to Senator Kenyon, there were two state senators and a U.S. Representative at the table.

In order for Kat to get the judgeship she wanted, she'd need the recommendation of one or two of the people at that table. His thoughts shifted as he tried to guess her endgame. Where had she met the senator, and why had he invited her to dinner? Time passed. Dessert came, and they all dove into some kind of pie. The senator, seated next to Kat, turned to her, and from the expression on her face, Keith guessed they were discussing the law.

Though puzzled, he was proud of his bride-to-be for networking so effectively. His phone buzzed with a text message. Surreptitiously he checked it.

What's going on?

He glanced up to see her looking at him. He shot her a smile and texted back. Enjoy your dinner. We'll talk after.

Michele Zurlo

She frowned as she read his response. Are you undercover? Because your cover is blown. People have noticed you're watching them.

While he toyed with what kind of response would set her at ease, another one came through.

Where are the kids?

That one, he could answer. With your parents. They're safe.

And I'm not. She hadn't included a question mark, so he knew she'd pieced together the essence of why he was there.

He sought to reassure her. Dustin is here too. You're safe.

Layla? Is she in danger?

No. Finish your dinner, and then we'll take you home.

Senator Kenyon said something to Kat, and she answered. The two conversed more, and Keith waited until their party rose to leave. He met Dustin in the foyer.

Keith reported first. "Just your average Friday night watching your fiancée and mine have dinner with a gaggle of politicians."

"Nothing untoward happening in the kitchen. The food is excellent. I had chocolate cheesecake and tiramisu."

The group emerged. Katrina and Layla approached, bringing Erica with them.

Layla's brow wrinkled in confusion. Her back had been to him in the restaurant, and it was obvious Kat hadn't told her that Keith and Dustin had arrived. "Dustin?"

His eyes lit, and he held his arms open. "How was dinner?"

"Good." Not caring that he was grungy, she slid into his embrace, a myriad questions brimming in her blue eyes. "What are you doing here? Did you eat?"

Kat sidled up to Keith. He kissed her hello, a brief press of his lips against hers due to the serious nature of the business at hand, and parked his hand on the small of her back. She hid her discomfiture better than Layla, smiling through her unease. "Erica, I'd like to introduce you to Keith Rossetti, my fiancé. Keith, this is Erica Kenyon. We met at the bridal shop. Her wedding is in August."

Keith offered his hand. "It's a pleasure to meet you."

"Likewise." Erica openly checked him out, and he met her gaze coolly.

Layla jumped in next. "And this is Dustin Brandt, my very handsome fiancé."

Dustin shook hands with Erica as well, but his comment was aimed at Layla. "Thank goodness she didn't introduce me as ugly again. That would have been awkward."

Erica laughed. "It's a pleasure to meet you both. Trina and Layla have told me so much about you."

Senator Kenyon approached. "Erica, they're bringing the car now." He nodded to Layla and Kat. "Thank you both for joining us tonight. You made Erica's day."

Kat smiled, but it was her professional one. "Senator Robert Kenyon, I'd like to introduce you to my fiancé, Special Agent Keith Rossetti, and this is Special Agent Dustin Brandt, who has the distinct honor of being engaged to Layla."

Confusion washed over the senator's face as he shook hands. "It's a pleasure to meet you. I saw you in the restaurant, and I got the impression you were Feds, but I didn't know you were here for Trina and Layla. You should have joined us."

"Next time." Dustin flashed a smile. "We're here on business tonight."

Robert's brows lifted. "Nothing serious, I hope?"

Kat put her hand on the senator's arm. "Robert, thank you for dinner. It was lovely."

"We'll have to do it again. Erica has your information. I'll get it from her." He nodded at Keith. "You've landed yourself a very remarkable young woman. I like the way her mind works."

Keith liked the way her mind worked too, like how she'd changed the subject so that he wasn't in the position of having to refuse to share details with a senator. "I agree. She's very special."

Robert waved at the foursome as he took Erica's arm to steer her toward the door. Erica shook him off. "Give me a minute, Dad. I promise I won't be long."

Keith and Dustin both stepped back so the ladies could talk. Erica hugged both women. "You saved me tonight. Thank you so much for letting me crash your cousin bonding night."

They hugged her back and the trio had a quick, whispered exchange. Keith shot a look at Dustin. He didn't have a problem with the whispering or even Kat keeping her girlfriend's secrets, but he did wonder what they were saying. The idea that the bouquet could have come from one of these people occurred to him, but he dismissed the idea. None of them had been acquainted before this afternoon.

Dustin took Layla home in Keith's SUV, and so Keith rode with Kat in her car. He leaned back in the passenger seat, one eye on the surroundings and the other on Kat. "So, how did all that happen?"

Michele Zurlo

"Nuh-uh. You go first. Why did Special Agent Rossetti feel like he had to drive all the way down here to keep an eye on me? You gave up an evening with Angelina and Corey, so this is big. What's going on?"

He was going to have to tell her eventually. "Someone sent a bouquet of roses being held by a severed hand to you at the DOJ. Mailroom security found it when they x-rayed the packages. Lexee called me when I was on my way to pick up Corey, so I left the kids with your parents."

"So you could watch over me."

"Yes." In the flashes of headlights from oncoming traffic, he saw the corners of her mouth curl up. She liked his protective side.

"Was there a written threat with the hand? Who sent it?" Her voice came out strong and even, curiosity trumping any fear she might feel.

He kept his tone neutral as well. "There wasn't a note. Forensics is analyzing everything right now. Lexee is going to keep me informed, but she can't say too much. I'm not on the case, but that's not going to stop me from making sure you're safe."

Now her mouth turned down. "Who would send something like that?"

"Don't know. Jordan is back. He left the task force and is working VC now. Rakeem Bahu is partnering with him on this. I don't know Bahu, but I trust Jordan." He thought about how he'd worked to track down the person who'd blown up Amy's house in an effort to kill her and Jordan. He knew Jordan would work just as tirelessly on making sure this threat was eliminated.

"He quit? That was fast. Amy mentioned that he wasn't happy being gone so much, but that was only a few days ago." She shook her head fondly. "He's so in love with her. It's sweet."

Needing to touch her, Keith rested his hand on her thigh. "There's nothing to say that you're in immediate danger, but if some sick-o is sending you gruesome gifts, it's only a matter of time before it escalates."

"Well, at least we know it's not another lawyer this time." A couple years before, a colleague had targeted Kat, trying to advance his career by ruining hers. When that backfired, he'd turned violent. "This makes no sense."

He agreed. "The type of person who would cut off another person's hand isn't inclined to make sense. It's a completely bizarre mentality in the first place."

Kat sighed, accepting the news with a hint of annoyance and no fear. She opted to change the subject. "We met Erica at the bridal shop. She had on this hideous dress that she had no choice about wearing. Layla and I helped her figure out how to alter it so that it looked good. Afterward, she overheard us planning to grab a bite. Layla, with her big heart, invited her to join us. Robert insisted she had to accompany him, and so he invited us. I thought we'd end up at a nearby restaurant. I did not know he was a senator."

He couldn't help but smile at her summary. Layla was a handful. She was fun and vivacious, with a huge heart and impulsive nature. He liked her, and he knew Kat loved her, but he heard her unspoken wish that Layla hadn't been so generous. "A U.S. Senator. The kind who can recommend you for a judgeship. And he seemed to like you. Did you guys talk about politics?"

"The law. We discussed a few recent rulings, and he was interested in my thoughts on immigration law. It's not my area of specialty, but I know what's going on." She glanced over. "I was surprised to see you tonight, and when you didn't come over to see me, I got worried. Very worried."

He squeezed her knee. "I'll always take care of you." And he knew that she could take care of herself. Two years ago, when he and Malcolm had come to rescue her from her kidnappers, they found she'd already neutralized them.

She turned down the street that would take them to her parents' house. They both wanted their family safe at home.

Michele Zurlo

Chapter 8

The next morning, Katrina felt like someone had wrapped her head in cotton. She hadn't slept well, mostly because Keith hadn't slept at all. He kept getting up to check everything in the house. Toward dawn, he fell into an exhausted sleep, so she was careful not to wake him when she slid out of bed.

She kept the kids as quiet as possible, which was a feat considering that it was Saturday morning and she wouldn't let them leave the house. Angelina took the news better than Corey, who wanted to bury dinosaur toys in the backyard so that he could excavate them.

Malcolm called as she was cleaning up the remnants of a mid-morning snack. "Trina, I just heard. How are you?"

She strove to set his mind at ease. Her big brother had always looked out for her. "I'm fine. Keith didn't get to sleep until after four this morning, though."

"Is he asleep now?"

Responding to the censure in Mal's question, she defended Keith. "Yes, and I'm not waking him up. He's exhausted."

"I'm coming over."

"Mal, we're fine. I'm keeping everyone in the house even though I think it's overkill. We have no evidence that I'm in danger."

"Some sick fuck sent you a severed hand holding a dozen roses." Malcolm's volume rose. "You're in danger, Trina, and the person who is supposed to be protecting you is sound asleep on the job."

"Don't malign Keith, Mal. As freaking awesome as you and I both know he is, he's not Superman. He's human. He needs sleep." She ran a hand through her hair. "I know you're worried, but don't be. We're fine. Jordan is on the case, and some other guy I don't know—his name escapes me—so you know they'll catch the bad guy."

"I know Jordan is on the case. How do you think I found out about this whole thing, since you didn't bother to tell me?" His irritation came through, loud and clear.

"Mom and Dad know. I thought maybe they called you. Hey, you knew Jordan was back? Keith didn't. When did he transfer?"

"Yesterday. Amy came over, all but floating on air. I guess he did it suddenly and sprang it on her as a surprise yesterday morning. He caught this case first thing." Malcolm lowered his voice. "Trina, I can't help thinking that you should find another job. I mean, is being a prosecutor worth painting a huge target on your back like this? There's always private practice. You can make a shit ton of money, and I know you've had offers."

Two firms regularly extended invitations to her to join their practice, and other offers came sporadically. She was good at what she did. Could she make more money in private practice? Definitely. But it wouldn't further her goal of making it to the bench. She huffed. "I'm not going to give up my dreams because some twisted psychopath sent me some flowers." Yes, it had been more than just flowers, but she wasn't going to say that where little ears could overhear.

"Of course you're not." Keith's sleep-scratchy voice had her whirling around. Wearing only sleep pants, he was a tousled sight to behold. "Who are you talking to?"

"Malcolm." To her brother, she said, "Keith's awake. You can relax now."

"I'll relax when this guy is caught. Let me talk to Keith."

With an exaggerated roll of the eyes, she handed the phone to Keith. "He wants to talk to you because I'm a poor, defenseless woman."

Keith pulled her to his chest and planted a kiss on her forehead. "He doesn't think you're defenseless. He knows I'm here." He tucked her closer so that she couldn't smack him, and then he took the phone. "Hey, Mal. How are you?"

She tried to wrest out of his embrace, but he merely turned so that he could pin her between his body and the counter. Though the timing wasn't appropriate, her pussy woke up. It was his fault because he'd trained her to expect restraint to lead somewhere sexual. Since her hands were free, she traced a path from his bare shoulders to the waistband of his pants. Her caress teased up and down his chest, until she decided to see if she could widen her foray.

"Yeah, I figured." Keith responded to something Malcolm said, but he wrapped his hand around hers, halting her quest, and his eyebrow lifted in warning. "I'm considering that."

Katrina toyed with the idea of being naughty, but she reasoned that this wasn't a good time. Keith had enough on his plate without worrying about having to discipline her as well. She relaxed, and when he let go, she wrapped her arms around his waist and rested her cheek on his chest. He stroked her back as he listened to Malcolm.

"Jordan is supposed to call with an update today. I'll call you after. Okay, sounds good. Talk to you later." He ended the call.

Katrina leaned back to look at his face. "You're considering what?"

"Putting a GPS tracker on you."

She scoffed. "You thought about implanting me with a GPS tracker? My brother suggested putting a tracker on me? Like I'm a pet or something?"

"You were taken once," he said. "It took precious time to locate you. You could have been killed, Kat."

But she hadn't been. Despite a skull fracture, she'd kicked butt and taken names. Still she could understand their concern.

A line appeared between Keith's eyebrows as he continued. "I hadn't considered subdural, but now that you mention it, that's probably the best option. That way you can't lose or break it."

Katrina hadn't seriously been considering giving consent. While she understood their fear, she wasn't about to let them put a tracker in her. "No. Absolutely not."

She tried to pull away, but he set his hands on her shoulders and captured her with his steady, dominating gaze. "If it's what I want?"

Studying his face, she analyzed his level of seriousness. Finally she answered in a soft tone. "If it's what you really want, then I would do it. But it's not what I want."

"Kat, if anything happened to you—"

No way in hell she was letting him complete that thought. "Stop. Nothing is going to happen. Jordan and his new partner will get this guy. I'm not worried."

"Daddy's awake!" Corey announced Keith's status in an excited shriek. He barreled across the kitchen. Katrina stepped aside so that Keith could catch the brunt of the blast.

He scooped Corey up effortlessly, and he added Angelina to his arms a few seconds later. "Good morning, you two. Want to keep me company while I have breakfast?"

As they settled into a lazy Saturday, Katrina noticed that, though Keith relaxed, his vigilance never waned.

Later that afternoon, they watched a movie. Angelina and Corey spread a blanket on the floor and sprawled on it. Katrina set a pillow on the floor at Keith's feet. This ritual brought peace to both their souls. She knelt on it and rested her head on his thigh. Automatically all her stress and worry melted away. She hadn't lied when she'd said she had confidence in Jordan's ability to find the culprit, but the long hours of not knowing weren't easy.

Keith absently stroked her hair as they watched the movie. After a time, Corey scooted back and rested his head on her lap. She rubbed circles on his back until his eyes fluttered closed.

"He's growing," Keith noted.

"He ate more for breakfast than Angelina and me combined." She tilted her face to smile up at him. "I think he's going to be tall, like you."

The doorbell rang. Katrina sat up, silently questioning Keith.

Angelina leaped to her feet. "I'll get it."

"I'll get it, Angie." Keith went after her. "You don't know who it is."

Corey hadn't moved a muscle. Katrina picked him up and got to her feet. She heard the front door open, and Keith greeted Jordan. Relief flowed through her, and she chastised herself for having such frayed nerves. If it hadn't been Jordan, it would have been her parents or M.J. or Malcolm and Darcy. They'd each called at least once today to express their concern and offer support.

She carried Corey to the front of the house, intending to take him upstairs to finish his nap.

Jordan's massive frame filled the doorway. With his dark brown, shaggy hair, dark eyes, and unshaven face, Jordan was one of those guys who looked dark and menacing, but he was one of the sweetest men she'd ever met. He was also the tallest and most thickly muscled. He ducked his head to come inside. "I texted that I was coming, but you look surprised to see me, so I guess you didn't get it."

Angelina clapped and jumped up and down. "Uncle Jordan, I didn't know you were coming over."

"I had to come see my best girl." He picked her up and planted a kiss on her cheek, and she squeezed his neck in a tight hug.

"Ease up, Angie. Jordan needs to breathe."

Katrina approached, one arm under Corey's bottom and the other on the back of his head. "Hi," she whispered. "I'm going to take him upstairs. Don't start without me." As she brushed past the crowd, she noticed two more people in the doorway. One was Amy, and she assumed the other was Jordan's new partner.

When she came back down, only Amy remained in the hall. Technically she and Amy weren't blood relatives, but over the past few years, they'd become like sisters. It helped that Amy's sister was married to Katrina's brother. Amy tried to smile, but it turned watery, making her eyes look even larger. Like Darcy, Amy's pretty face was framed with brown hair, and her cornflower blue eyes were her most startling feature.

She threw her arms around Katrina. "Jordan told me a little about what's happened. I'm so sorry."

Katrina patted Amy's back. "It'll be fine. Everything that comes into that building is monitored and recorded. They'll have video of it arriving, and they have dozens of forensic tricks to trace the materials back to the purchaser."

Amy let her go. "You sound like Jordan." She motioned toward the back of the house where the men had disappeared. "I came to entertain Angelina and Corey while you guys talk. I figured you could focus better if you knew you didn't have to worry about the kids."

"You're so thoughtful. Thank you." Katrina liked Amy's thoughtful side. She was one of those generous friends who was always looking for ways to help out. Amy and Jordan had a Daddy/little dynamic, where Jordan indulged Amy's childlike tendencies as a non-sexual part of their D/s relationship. While Jordan worked as an FBI agent, Amy ran a successful event planning business.

They found the men in the kitchen, gathered around the island. The rectangular feature had stools along one side, but nobody was sitting.

"Ah, a kitchen full of hot guys," Katrina said. "This is every woman's wet dream."

"Eh," Amy said, unimpressed. "If they were cooking dinner and folding laundry, then they'd be every woman's wet dream."

Keith ignored her attempt at levity. "Kat, this is Rakeem Bahu."

Rakeem was tall, about six feet, which appeared short next to Jordan. His dark brown hair was longer than Keith's, though still short, and he regarded her with friendly brown eyes. He had a scar that ran along one cheekbone, and it lent him a rakish air. His brown skin was slightly darker than honey, and it had undertones of cinnamon. He shook her hand. "It's nice to meet you, Ms. Legato, though I wish the circumstances were better."

"Call me Trina. Everybody but Keith does." She loved his nickname for her, and she had an aversion to anyone else using it.

Angelina slid in front of Katrina, studying Rakeem with a furrowed brow. "Did you get that scar in a fight with a bad guy?"

"I did."

"Does the other guy look worse? That's what Daddy says when he gets a boo-boo from a criminal."

Rakeem grinned. "He did. Now he's all healed up and in prison."

Amy held her arms out to Angelina. "How about we go do something fun?"

Angelina mulled over the offer. "Okay, but this time I get to be the dragon." With that, the pair disappeared into the living room.

Katrina stood near Keith, more for his benefit than hers. She knew he liked having her close, especially today. She looked from Jordan to Rakeem. "So, how's it going?"

Jordan began. "We have video of the perp delivering the package. He drove a flower delivery van. But we didn't get a clear shot of his face because he wore a hat and sunglasses, and he kept his face turned away from the cameras."

Katrina knew better than to interrupt. She'd deposed Jordan enough times to know he would include all the details.

"He's about 5'10, Caucasian, brown hair, medium build." Rakeem rattled off the stats. "Probably about 180 pounds. In other words, he looks like an average white guy."

So they really had nothing on the perp.

Rakeem continued. "The vic was deceased before the removal of his limb. Fingerprints came back as Jason Harris, age nineteen. He was the original driver of the delivery van."

Katrina closed her eyes. That poor boy had lost his life because some psychopath wanted his van. "Oh my God." Keith put his arm around her and pulled her into him.

Jordan cleared his throat. "The van was abandoned in a vacant lot about a mile away. We found Harris's body in the back. He died from blunt force trauma to the head. CSU is still combing the van for evidence, but it had been wiped clean of prints."

"Any leads?" She wiped her eye, a response to stress. Most of her bravery had been based on a belief that Jordan would wrap this up quickly.

Rakeem's eyes softened apologetically. "We need to go through every active and recent case you've worked on, probably for the last month."

"Sure, of course. Do you want those now or Monday?"

"Now, if you can," Jordan said.

She could. She logged onto her laptop and spent the next two hours sending all her files to Jordan and Rakeem.

Michele Zurlo

The next two weeks flew. They were a whirlwind of work, kids, and wedding preparation punctuated by brief meetings where Jordan and Rakeem updated her on the fact that they'd hit a wall, but they were not giving up on the case. Judge Osman annoyed the hell out of her by assigning her and Vina to help out at Legal Aid twice more. The press had magically heard about this assignment, and they were singing Osman's praises. Katrina and Vina had been approached by a reporter asking for comment, but they'd declined. As they'd walked away, a reporter had overheard Vina saying that the assignments were a pain in the ass because they still carried their full load of work for the US Attorney's Office. That comment had made it into news reports.

Katrina relaxed, deciding the gruesome delivery was a one-time deal. Keith's vigilance did not wane. When her phone rang Tuesday evening while they were in the kitchen discussing dinner options, and it indicated an unfamiliar caller, he insisted on answering.

He stared at the number, and she knew he was memorizing it. "Hello?" He listened. "No, this is her fiancé. Who is calling? Oh. No, she's here. Hang on, I'll get her." He covered the speaker as he handed the phone to her. "It's Robert."

As she searched her brain for all the Roberts she knew, she pressed the phone to her ear. "Hello?"

"Katrina? This is Robert, Senator Kenyon. We met a few weeks ago."

She laughed. "Hi, Robert. How are you?"

"Good, good. I hope I'm not interrupting anything."

Keith went into the freezer and held up a frozen pizza. She shrugged. Their discussion had been more about what would take the least effort and still be nutritious and less about what they were in the mood to eat.

"You're not. We're trying to decide what to make for dinner that the kids will eat."

He chuckled. "I remember those days. Erica went through a macaroni and cheese phase. I used to sneak peas and carrots into it, otherwise she wouldn't eat vegetables."

"I like that idea. Hang on." She moved the phone away from her face. "What about mac and cheese? You could put cut up veggies in it."

Keith mirrored her shrug and returned the pizza to the freezer. They'd eaten pizza two days ago, and though the kids loved it, they both felt like losers if they had it too often.

"Thanks, Robert. I hope it's a parenting win for us. What can I do for you?" She doubted he'd called to chat or give parenting advice.

"I wanted to pick your brain on a bill I'm writing. Do you have about twenty minutes?"

She wasn't going to tell him that she didn't. "Sure. What's it about?" As she listened, she jotted a note to Keith to let him know what was going on.

With a proud grin, he kissed her cheek. Then he pointed up, indicating that she should go into their bedroom for privacy.

The moment she hung up from the call—a good hour later—her phone rang again with more familiar number. She answered. "Hello?"

"Trina? I'm so sorry about that." Erica's voice came through breathy and low, as if she didn't want to be overheard.

"It's okay. I'm kind of flattered that with all his resources, he called to ask for my opinion." Flabbergasted and confused as well. He'd grilled her on the intricacies of corporate fraud for a bill he was sponsoring that would close some of the existing loopholes. She wholeheartedly supported the legislation.

"He does that. It's his pattern. He flatters, uses you for advice, and then you never hear from him again."

Even if she didn't, she felt good knowing her voice had been heard by her senator. "That's okay. No big deal. How are you?"

"I'm great. Good. Okay. Sort of."

"Well, that doesn't sound promising. Is it the dress?"

"The—no. Actually the dress is the great part. I can't believe how much better it looks. I mean, it's my style now." She laughed. "Burke and I tried bondage last night. It didn't go so well."

Katrina had never been with a beginner. She didn't know what kinds of problems they'd encounter. "Was anyone hurt?"

"No. He used handcuffs on me. We thought we'd start small. Then we, you know, did it. It wasn't as good as I thought it would be. It was kind of like when he's horny, but I'm tired, so I'm like go for it, but I'm going to sleep."

Katrina couldn't imagine sleeping through sex. Even with her previous boyfriends, she'd always been mentally present for the big event.

"Hello? Are you still there?"

"Sorry." She hadn't realized she'd gone silent for so long. "I was processing what you said. So, he put handcuffs on you, and then you had pretty much vanilla sex?"

"Yep. Total dud."

Katrina couldn't help herself. "Is it always like that?"

"Yeah. Don't get me wrong—he's not bad in bed. He tries to make sure I orgasm, but sometimes I fake it because I'm bored. Okay, a lot of the time I fake it."

"Erica, why are you marrying a guy who doesn't excite you?" Katrina closed her eyes. "Never mind. That was rude. I shouldn't have gone there."

"No, it's fine." She exhaled a stream of defeat and acceptance. "He's really, really nice, and I do love him. He'll be a great life partner and father. He's loyal, really loyal, so I know he won't cheat. I can see myself being content with him for the rest of my life. The sex will fade, but romance, love, and friendship are what keeps a marriage afloat."

Katrina didn't disagree. Having kids definitely put a damper on her sex life. She couldn't walk around as a naked sex slave when she was being a mom. But she would miss the excitement and intimacy sex brought into their relationship. She tried to find the bright side. "He sounds like he's willing to try new things."

"Oh, he is. He's enthusiastic about anything I suggest. Like I said, he's a good man." Erica's volume dropped. "Maybe I could bring him over, like you said, to talk to your fiancé? I think we need help from people who've been there and done that."

"Sure," Katrina said. "Let me talk to Keith and some of the others, and I'll get back to you."

A few hours later, she texted Erica with an invitation to dinner that weekend.

Chapter 9

It wasn't often they had new people over because their circle of friends and family was rather constant. As Katrina stirred bits of tomatillo, onion, yellow chile, and Serrano chile in her sauce pan, she heard the front door open and close. Keith came into the kitchen as she reduced the heat and set it to simmering.

"What are you making? It smells delicious." He was probably talking about the food, but he planted his face in her neck and rested his hands on her hips.

She reached back to acknowledge him with a hand on the back of his head. "I thought I'd do enchiladas. Fresh—not frozen." Being working parents meant they cut a lot of corners. Though Katrina liked to cook, especially from scratch, she didn't get to do it very often. When they had only an hour or two in the evening with the kids, they liked to make that time count. Though, now that Angelina was six, she had started helping prepare dinner.

"I love your cooking. It's one of the reasons I'm marrying you." He kissed a path up her neck and bit her earlobe.

She laughed. "Wow. If that's the case, you're not getting a very good bargain. You cook dinner more nights than I do."

He turned her to face him and folded her in his arms. "With you, I'm getting more than I deserve. I hit the jackpot, Kitty Kat." He captured her lips in a searing kiss, tormenting her with the promise of his skilled tongue. She melted against him, submitting to his mastery.

When he released her, it took a moment to remember what she had been doing. She added sweet onions to a hot pan. "Darcy called about a half hour ago to say they were almost here."

Keith grunted. "No time for a quickie, is what you're saying."

She inclined her head doubtfully. "Sorry. I didn't think it would take you so long to drop the kids off at my parents' house."

"Your dad was fixing the bathroom sink." Keith was the kind of person who would offer a hand to Mario whether or not he needed one.

Katrina smiled at the image of her father, future husband, and son all working together. "Did Corey help too?" Corey had recently taken a shine to helping her father with home improvement projects. He liked to be the one who assisted with the tools.

"He did. I can't believe he's four and knows the difference between a flathead and a Phillips." He tucked a strand of hair behind her ear. "So these people who are coming over—how late do you think they'll stay?"

She laughed at his hopeful tone. She'd set up this night so that Erica and her fiancé, Burke, could come over and ask questions about the D/s lifestyle. She'd explained to Keith that they were feeling a bit disheartened. "I don't think it's them you have to worry about. Malcolm and Darcy are dropping the kids with my parents, and they're staying the night."

"That's why you put new sheets on the bed in the guest room." He looked away, thinking. "Did I know they were staying the night?"

"You keep forgetting." This development amused Katrina. Before they were a couple, Keith never minded having Malcolm around. Sometimes the pair would spend days together. Even after Mal had moved an hour away to live with Darcy, he'd kept a change of clothes in the guest room. Now that Katrina and Keith were together, Keith maintained that Malcolm gave him menacing looks whenever he touched Katrina.

"I keep hoping they decide to go home."

"They'll be down the hall, not in the same room as us. We can still have sex." She cradled his face in her hands. "Mal isn't going to stop messing with you until it no longer bothers you. You should give as good as you get."

He studied her. "What are you suggesting?"

"Tonight we're using protocols, right?" Not only did they enjoy that part of the dynamic, they wanted to model it for Erica and Burke. "Let's not scale it back for my brother's sake. Let me kneel at your feet. Let me call you by title. Let me serve you."

Keith had put restrictions on what she could do in the presence of her family, especially Malcolm. She could defer to him, but she wasn't allowed to serve him. Instead of kneeling on the floor, she was to sit beside him. Rather than call him 'Master,' she called him by his name. She understood his reasons—he still felt guilty for pursuing her after Malcolm had expressly forbade it—but she didn't agree with them. Being his submissive completed her. It fed vital life to her soul. It made them both happy. She had come to resent scaling it back in front of her brother. As Keith's best friend, he was at almost all play parties, and he was there most times they entertained others in the lifestyle.

If Layla had been able to come tonight, this wouldn't have been an issue. Layla and Dustin had even more protocols in place than Katrina and Keith did. Because Layla and Dustin had plans with other friends tonight, Katrina had asked Malcolm and Darcy to attend. She felt that Darcy would be a great resource for Erica because she'd also started in the lifestyle with a partner who was a beginner.

He opened his mouth, and she could tell by the regret in his eyes that he was going to deny her. He didn't want to, and that gave her cause for hope.

Her lower lip quivered with emotion she couldn't release. She grasped his shirt and peered deep into his troubled green eyes. "Please? At least try it. If you get uncomfortable, then you can give me a signal, and we'll go back to the other rules."

The doorbell rang, but neither of them moved. Seconds ticked by, marked by the grandfather clock in the main hall. At last, Keith exhaled a long stream of air. "We'll try it. But if I tell you to revert back, you do it. No questions, pouting, begging, or trying to talk me out of it."

She hopped to her tiptoes and planted a kiss on his lips. "Thank you, Master."

He went to answer the door, and she poured the contents of her sauce pan into the blender. She added cilantro and garlic, and then she set it to liquefy the ingredients.

Malcolm and Darcy entered the kitchen after Keith. She turned, a welcoming smile on her face, but she said nothing.

A beat passed before Keith remembered his role. "Kat, say hello to our guests."

She came forward, arms open, and hugged her brother. "I'm so glad you could make it."

Malcolm hugged her tightly, communicating his unease about the fact that the person who'd sent the gruesome bouquet hadn't been caught. He called and texted daily to check in on her. He kissed her temple. "I didn't know you were doing Mexican. I brought ingredients for Caprese."

Thanks to their parents, all three of them were good cooks. She hadn't known that Mal was planning to bring part of the meal, but she should have asked. He was that kind of guy. "We can set out Caprese as an appetizer."

Malcolm glanced over his shoulder, giving silent permission for his submissive to speak. Darcy, her sister-in-law, was one of those people who was shy at first, but once they opened up, they were fun and interesting. It had taken some time, but she and Darcy had become friends.

Darcy hugged Katrina as well, though she didn't squeeze like Malcolm had. "It's great to see you. Thanks for having us. I feel like I haven't seen you since the last time we were all at your parents' house for dinner."

Their parents liked to have everyone over the last Sunday of the month, and that had been a few weeks ago, before the hand incident. "I think you're right," Katrina said. "It's been a busy few weeks. But bridesmaids are due for their fittings on Wednesday. Don't forget."

For her wedding, Katrina was having Layla as her maid-of-honor. Her sisters-in-law, Jen and Darcy, would be bridesmaids, as would Vina, her friend from work. She's asked Amy, who was her friend and Darcy's sister, but Amy had politely declined, citing her busy schedule. Katrina wasn't upset or offended. As an event planner, this was Amy's busiest season.

"I won't." Darcy looked around the kitchen.

Malcolm put a hand on Darcy's shoulder. "Sweetheart, go sit down."

Darcy took a seat at the island, and Keith slid onto the stool next to her. The grinned at each other, and Darcy said, "Those Legatos are great cooks."

Keith chuckled. "We don't exactly suck."

"But we're nowhere near their caliber. It's okay. I've come to accept my limitations." Darcy winked at Malcolm, an overt, flirty gesture that had a light blush spreading over Mal's cheeks.

Rather than respond, Malcolm turned to Katrina. "How can I help?"

"I have chicken slow-roasting in the oven. It should be ready. It needs to be shredded."

Malcolm moved to do that, and Darcy asked, "So, this friend of yours that we're meeting tonight—how well do you know her?"

"Not well. Layla and I met her at the bridal shop when we were getting fitted for our dresses. We went out to dinner afterward." Katrina browned the tortillas in a pan while Mal handled the chicken. "She told me that her sex life was not fulfilling. Her and her fiancé are interested in trying out kink."

Darcy frowned. "It's a lifestyle, not a solution to bedroom issues."

"I know, and I've tried explaining that, but it didn't seem to penetrate. I was hoping that by seeing how we are and being able to ask questions, they could make informed decisions."

With Malcolm's help, it didn't take long to get the enchiladas put together and in the oven. She returned the favor by helping him make toasted Caprese. The doorbell rang, and Keith went to answer it.

Katrina rinsed dishes for the dishwasher while Malcolm checked the bread in the broiler. "Mal, can Darcy set the table?"

"She'd be happy to."

"Kat, say hello to our guests." Keith's order was delivered softly, like an invitation, but his tone was firm enough to clarify that it was an order.

Katrina dried her hands and came to stand by his side.

"This is Burke Cornwall."

Perhaps not expecting to be introduced first, Burke's eyes widened. He was a good-looking man with red hair, a strong jaw, sculpted cheekbones, and a smattering of freckles across his nose and cheeks. His polo shirt stretched across his strong shoulders and tucked neatly into his khaki pants.

Katrina shook his hand. "It's great to meet you. Erica has told me so much about you."

The woman in question studied Katrina as if trying to figure out what was different. "Hi, Trina. Thanks for having us over." Her eyes went to the two strangers in the room.

"My pleasure. I hope you like Mexican. I made enchiladas."

Burke's head bobbed in approval. "Love Mexican."

Keith indicated Malcolm. "This is Malcolm Legato. He's Kat's brother and an experienced Dom. He and I learned the ropes together."

Malcolm's lips curved in a polite smile. He shook Burke's hand. "For the record, I learned the ropes a lot better than Keith."

Katrina and Darcy both giggled. While Keith concentrated on bondage for restraint, Malcolm loved ropework for the sake of ropework. Katrina would bet that somewhere on Darcy's body, she was wearing one of Malcolm's designs.

"I take it that means something different from what it sounds like," Erica said. "Is it an inside joke?"

"Nah," Keith said. "Mal stopped checking out my ropework when I started tying up his sister." He shot her a secret grin to make sure she was proud of the fact that he'd fired back. She was.

Malcolm grunted. "So, this is Darcy, my sub. Say hello, sweetheart."

Michele Zurlo

Darcy paused in gathering plates and cutlery to take to the dining room. "Hello Burke, Erica. It's a pleasure to meet you. Please feel free to ask any questions. We know you're curious and possibly puzzled."

"Okay," Erica began. "Not to sound like a jerk, but Trina, why did you ask your brother if Darcy could set the table instead of just asking her? She was standing right next to you."

Darcy smiled softly. "Because if she'd asked me, I would seek his approval first."

"What if he's not around?" Erica continued. "What if it's just the two of you?"

"Then she'd ask me, and I'd do it. Or I would probably offer to do it. We don't use protocols all the time, and we don't use them when we're apart." Darcy hefted the plates. "And we make allowances for people who don't practice D/s. Would you like to help? You can grab the forks and napkins."

The two went into the next room, and Burke turned to Keith. "Okay, so the introduction thing? Am I not supposed to talk to the women directly or without a Dom present? Is that some kind of fifty shades of bro code? Like—welcome to the 1600's and hands off my woman?"

Neither Keith nor Malcolm spent time teaching others about the D/s lifestyle, and she could tell by their expressions that they felt judged. That was another reason Katrina wished Dustin was present. He was used to those who were new and curious. She set a hand on Keith's arm, asking for permission to respond.

He lifted an eyebrow. "You're sure?"

"Yes."

"Go for it." He crossed his arms and waited.

"There are many reasons for this protocol, but basically it boils down to trust, respect, and relationships. A sub trusts his or her Dominant to make sure he or she is safe. Part of that deal is waiting until he makes that judgment and gives or withholds permission. If Keith decided you weren't the kind of person who would treat me with respect, he wouldn't allow me to associate with you, and he'd put himself between us—physically, if need be—to keep me safe. Another reason for this protocol is to establish roles of dominance and submission for all present."

Burke listened, but his reservations weren't allayed. Erica and Darcy returned to the kitchen in time to hear his concerns. "But part of respecting a woman is not trampling on her autonomy. You should be able to trust your life partner to respect you as an equal and treat you accordingly. Can't you make your own decisions?"

"Sure," she said. "I do it all the time. That's another reason this appeals to me—at the end of a long day at work, I get to come home to a man who is going to take care of me. He's going to see to my emotional and physical needs. I'm not seeking autonomy. This is a partnership. We bring different things to the table, and we make it work for us."

Burke shook his head. "It's weird. It goes against everything I've been raised to believe about the way I should treat women."

Malcolm removed the pan of toasted Caprese from the broiler, and those delicious smells mingled with the enchilada spices. It was an interesting mixture of flavor palates. He put the hot pan on the stove top. "It's different, yes, but so is the whole concept of marriage. When you combine your life with another person's, neither of you are autonomous anymore. You're a team, a pair, partners, lovers, co-parents. If there's autonomy to be found, it's to be found together."

Darcy slid her hand from Malcolm's elbow to his shoulder, stopping short of resting her hand on top of his shoulder. A soft smile lit her face. He put an arm around her waist, and she turned to Burke. "Our way may not be your way. You need to begin with things that are in your comfort level. You can grow from there. Let's eat, and I think, over the course of the evening, you'll see that Trina and I are very happy. We are respected, cherished, loved—"

"Spoiled," Malcolm added. "Worshipped."

"That too," Darcy continued. "When meeting a new person, or even greeting an old friend, having Malcolm take control frees me. Some people find comfort and peace in the ritual and the certainty of knowing what's going to happen, knowing they can relax and not be on guard. Please understand that all these protocols are negotiated. Different couples will have different protocols. Some may not observe the 'meet the Dom, then greet the sub' rule. You'll find as many variations as you'll find couples. There is no one true way. You have to do what works for you. Keith and Malcolm, though, have similar rules. They're best friends, so it stands to reason they have this in common too."

While Darcy spoke, Malcolm transferred the toasted slices to two serving platters. "Let's go into the dining room and continue this. I'm starving."

They followed Mal to the next room. Keith seated Katrina next to him. Burke pulled out a chair for Erica, and Malcolm patted the chair where he wanted Darcy to sit.

Michele Zurlo

Katrina took one plate and passed it to Erica on her right, and the other she sent to Keith on her left. Keith put two slices on her plate before putting one on his own. Then he passed the platter to Darcy. At the other end of the table, Burke frowned yet again.

Keith took a bite. "Mal, you've done it again. This is amazing."

"Thanks," Malcolm said. "I hope it pairs well with enchiladas."

"You made this?" Erica said. "I thought the subs would do all the cooking?"

Katrina washed down her first bite with sparkling water. "Not with us. Keith makes dinner more nights than I do because he's often the first one home."

"Mal and Trina are excellent cooks," Darcy said. "Keith and I make passable food, but there's something in the Legato gene pool that makes them better. Their older brother, mom, and dad all possess amazing culinary skills. If I'm very good and ask nicely, Malcolm will make barbequed brisket for me."

"Does he also determine what and when you'll eat?" Burke lobbed that one at Darcy, but his questioning gaze went to Keith.

"No," Darcy said. Then she sat back, her eyes pointing toward the ceiling as she thought. "Well, sometimes. It depends on what else is going on. Sometimes when the kids are asleep, he has me sit on his lap and he feeds me. Or he combines bondage with a meal. It's always very sensual."

Keith finished off his Caprese, and then he folded his arms on the table. "What's your damage, Burke? I accepted you into my home because Kat said you were seeking guidance, and you keep challenging me. If you don't want to have this dynamic with Erica, then don't. The worst thing you can do in a relationship is be someone you aren't."

Katrina had taught him that. When they first got together, he'd morphed from the man she knew and loved to a cold, distant man that she didn't recognize. He'd said it was his Dom side, but she'd known better, and she'd given him the freedom to be the best version of himself.

Burke pointed to Katrina. "She didn't want Caprese. She handed the plate to you, and you put it on her plate. A woman should be able to choose what she does and doesn't want to eat."

"I agree," Keith said. "She wanted it, so I gave her some."

"She didn't take any. She didn't say she wanted it. And I looked for some kind of signal—I picked up on the one Darcy gave to Malcolm in the kitchen—but there was nothing."

Frost glazed Keith's green eyes, and the Special Agent that struck fear in the hearts of hardened criminals everywhere appeared. Katrina tensed. Under the table, she set her hand on his thigh, but his demeanor didn't soften.

When he spoke, his voice was eerily calm. "Do you know all the foods Erica likes and dislikes? Are you aware of the last time she had something to eat? Do you know when she's hungry? Do you know her eating habits better than your own?"

Burke didn't back down. His Irish skin tinged with ire, he set his napkin on the table. "She had an antipasto salad for lunch and a latte on the way here—all items she chose to eat, all consumed at a time and location she chose. I don't know what she had for breakfast because I left early to work out, and she slept in."

"A good Dom—a good life partner—takes the time to notice every detail about his sub. I've known Kat for close to fifteen years. In that time, I've memorized everything about her. She's been drooling over the Caprese since Malcolm mentioned that he'd brought the ingredients. She wanted to eat it, but she's one of those generous types who will give it all away and take nothing for herself, all in the name of being a good hostess. I wasn't going to let that happen." Keith's volume dropped to a menacing low. "I've tied her naked to a chair and fed her. I've had her sit on my lap and fed us both. I've had her kneel at my feet, and I've fed her that way. I've had her pick up a pizza on the way home from work. I've surprised her on her lunch break with a sandwich from her favorite deli. No matter the circumstances, I take care of my sub, and I do not care for the way you're sitting at my table, in my house, judging me and my relationship with Kat."

A stunned and awkward silence settled over the room. Katrina was mortified, as was Erica. Malcolm's silence was the supportive kind, though he kept an eye on Keith to make sure the situation didn't turn violent. Darcy didn't seem bothered by the tension in the room.

Katrina tore her gaze from Keith and implored Burke. "Please don't—"

"Stop." Keith issued the order in the same tone with which he'd spoken to Burke. Katrina obeyed, though the sense of dread weighed heavily in her gut.

Keith continued. "You were supposed to come here with an open mind. But you came here with a chip on your shoulder, which I don't think even Erica knows about. What is your problem with me?"

Burke's lip curled. "You fucked my cousin, got her pregnant, and then dumped her, leaving her to raise the kid alone."

Michele Zurlo

Katrina pasted on the questioning expression she used when a witness said something that impacted the jury, but she knew she was going to tear that testimony apart.

"Wasn't me."

Hatred blazed in Burke's eyes. "Keith Rossetti, FBI field agent. Same face, same address. I bet you have the same dungeon setup in your basement."

Bristling under the gag order, Katrina snapped at Burke. "Actually, the setup has changed quite a bit."

Keith shot her a full warning in a half-second glance.

"He looks like you," Burke continued. "Blond hair, green eyes. Did you know that only one percent of the world's population has green eyes? He's seven now. My cousin struggles to provide for her son. She works two jobs and still can't quite make ends meet. She has to take public assistance and ask for handouts from the family, and you're here, wanting for nothing. I hate men like you."

"Her situation is difficult, but the child isn't mine," Keith repeated.

Burke's lips twisted. "Would you be willing to submit to a paternity test?"

"You'll need a court order." Katrina ignored Keith's quelling look. She might be his sub, but she was also a lawyer. "Maybe you want to ask yourself why, if she was so certain Keith was the child's father, she hasn't already filed for paternity? Surely, if she's in the situation you say she's in, she could have used help, financial or otherwise."

"She said that he would have insisted on being part of Tony's life." The fire of Burke's hatred grew. "She said you hated women. That you're cruel and insensitive. That women serve one purpose for you. She didn't want to raise her child near such a tyrant." His gaze flickered to Katrina. "I see the way he treats you. From what Erica and Robert have told me, you're a good person. You deserve better."

Malcolm sighed at hearing the reasoning he'd employed to convince Keith to stay away from his sister being used by an outsider. "Fuck me. I guess I can never use that line again." He lifted an impatient brow at Keith. "Just tell him." When Keith didn't so much as twitch, Malcolm growled. "Damn it, Keith. Get you head out of your ass. There's too much at stake for you to stand on pride."

The muscles in Keith's jaw flexed as he waged an internal battle. He looked at Katrina and lost the war. Giving in gracelessly, he faced Burke. "I can't have kids."

Burke didn't miss a beat. "You have two."

Re/Captured

"We adopted them when my sister lost custody." Again his gaze landed on Katrina. "It's entirely possible that the woman in question was one of my former subs."

Her heart thudded painfully, aching for him, for Burke's cousin, and a little for herself. Keith and Malcolm had shielded her from the worst of Keith's past, and though she had a small taste of it, his past misdeeds were something she largely pretended didn't exist.

Keith sought her hand, holding it on top of the table. "Before Kat showed me the error of my ways, I was a shitty Dom. Your cousin's description is an accurate representation of the man I used to be. I regret my past, and I'm sorry for the way I treated my previous subs, but I can't change that. I can only control who I am now and in the future."

Burke wasn't easily swayed. "I'd like a paternity test."

"I had a vasectomy thirteen years ago, and I always used a condom." Keith didn't go against the position she'd laid out. "I'm sure if you ask your cousin, her story will change. Otherwise, she's going to have to go the legal route. Have her contact my lawyer." Keith stood. "This evening is over. Malcolm will see you out."

Malcolm herded Erica and Burke to the door. Darcy placed a hand on Keith's arm. "Would you like us to go or stay?"

"Stay," he said. "The food should be ready soon. I don't see a reason to cut our night short."

Darcy looked to Katrina. "I'll check on the food." She left, giving them some privacy.

Keith sat down. "Maybe I should do the paternity test."

Sinking into her chair, Katrina frowned. "If you could get anyone pregnant, I would be pregnant by now."

"I know." He met her eyes, with steady, green steel. "I know you only wanted to defend me, Kat, but when I give you an order, I expect you to follow it."

Her intentions had been good, but he was right. He'd told her to stay out of it. Perhaps the outcome would have been different if she'd kept her mouth shut. Burke and Keith might have been able to come to an understanding. She liked Erica, but now it was doubtful they would become friends. Though Keith wouldn't prohibit her from associating with Erica or Burke, she couldn't honestly become close to someone who openly disdained the man she loved.

She lowered her gaze. Her stomach clenched, and sorrow pricked at her eyes. She hated that she'd disappointed him. She tried a few times to speak, to explain her actions, but she had nothing of substance to add. Finally she managed a response. "I'm sorry, Master."

"Well, you're going to get at least one of your wishes fulfilled tonight." He pressed his lips together. "You've earned a punishment, and I'm not going to let it slide because Malcolm is here. Go down to the dungeon. Undress from the waist down and wait on the spanking bench."

Katrina rarely misbehaved, and so she was rarely punished. Tears tracked down her cheeks, not because she was afraid, but because she was devastated. He'd done her a favor by hosting a couple who were looking to try out the lifestyle. Not only had she disappointed him by not following his order, she'd brought a man to their home who was hostile and disrespectful to Keith. These recriminations pummeled her as she took her position on the spanking bench.

Chapter 10

Keith leaned against the frame of the doorway between the kitchen and dining rooms, his mind a million miles away.

Malcolm came into the kitchen as Darcy peered into the oven. "Sweetheart, if the cheese is melted, it's done." He looked over her shoulder. "Yep. It's done."

"I'll get it." She turned off the range and donned two oven mitts.

Keith noted all of this, but too many thoughts raced through his brain.

Malcolm parked his hands on his hips, a casual stance as he faced Keith. "That went sideways. We're going to have to figure out damage control."

"Damage control?" Darcy snorted. "Fucker is lucky he left with his limbs intact."

"That's why I told you not to move or say a word." Malcolm chuckled. "Post pregnancy hormones have turned her into an American Ninja Mom, willing to protect her family at all costs."

Keith, to Darcy, was family. Their bond hadn't been immediate. It had taken time to grow, but now it had deep roots.

Mal leaned against the counter. "I know that maybe I'm crossing a line, but you need to get Trina under control. She's not bratty. I can't believe she disobeyed you like that, but then again, you're usually very lenient with her. Sometimes overly so."

Though he indulged her quite often, Keith didn't consider himself a pushover. Kat craved his dominance. She blossomed under his hand. She'd begged him not to act differently in front of Malcolm, and she'd been right to do so. Every time he did that, he let her down. No more.

"When you're around, yes, I'm different with her than I am when we're alone, and that can't continue, which is why she's downstairs right now waiting for her punishment."

Malcolm started. "How long are you going to make her wait?"

"Until I get myself under control."

Darcy looked him up and down. Then she turned to Malcolm. "What am I missing? I get that she's earned a punishment for disobeying a direct order, but I don't understand why you're both so upset. That guy was a jerk, and none of us want or need people like that in our lives. He's not Dom material at all."

"No, he's not," Keith said. "He rubbed me the wrong way from the minute I introduced myself. At first I thought he was just nervous, the way he kept coming at me. Then I figured he was a sub who was subconsciously rebelling against being thrust into a dominant role."

"I agree," Malcolm said. "He will never be a Dom, though I'm not convinced that he's a sub."

"Erica has a dominant streak a mile wide," Darcy said. "And she could do so much better than that asshole. Or maybe she just needs to tie him down and teach him who's the boss. And then kick him to the curb with the rest of the trash."

Keith faced the woman vehemently defending his character. Not only did he not deserve such generosity, but more was at stake than his pride. "Darcy, Erica's father is a US Senator."

Darcy pressed her lips together, ready to unleash a tirade.

"Sweetheart, just listen," Malcolm ordered.

Keith continued. "Kat wants to become a District Judge. She's dreamed about it for as long as I can remember. The President appoints district judges. When there's a vacancy, the President usually defers to the Senator from that state to suggest a name. There are two vacancies right now, and if Kat can get in good with Senator Kenyon—his daughter is one path—then she stands a good chance of getting that appointment. He's already called her a few times to feel out her positions on different legal matters. All signs indicate that he's open to considering her for judge."

Darcy's eyes widened. "Oh, fuck. You would have taken the paternity test even though you know it's not your kid—just to keep up friendly appearances. But she took a stand by saying that they have to go through lawyers, and you couldn't find another way around it." She turned her big blue eyes on Malcolm. "We can think of something, right? We're four intelligent people who spend our lives solving problems. We can do this."

"We'll spend the rest of the evening thinking of ideas." Malcolm enfolded her in his arms.

"But that doesn't explain why Keith needs to get himself under control." She lifted her head to peer at Keith without breaking Malcolm's embrace. "You're not mad at her."

"I'm dreading telling her that she probably blew her chance to be a judge because she was trying to defend a person who doesn't deserve it." Leaving that piece of misery hanging there, Keith descended the basement stairs. Darcy would argue, and Keith didn't want to hear her try to make excuses for the man he'd been. Nobody had forced him to use women. Nobody had forced him to be a dick. He couldn't even blame alcohol because he'd been sober. Darcy didn't know the extent of his sins. Neither did Kat, but she was stuck having to deal with the consequences.

He found her waiting, positioned exactly as he'd directed. Her hushed sobs drifted across the room and slammed into him like a determined fist. She started when he closed the door, and her sobs grew quieter. He grabbed a box of tissue, stopped next to the bench, and touched her shoulder.

"Sit up, Kitty Kat."

She eased herself up and turned over. He slid onto the bench next to her and handed over the box of tissues. "Let's talk about why you're being punished."

Taking two tissues, she balled them up and blew her nose. "I invited a man to our house who was nasty and disrespectful to you, unreasonably so. And I disobeyed your order."

"You couldn't have known he'd be like that. And neither of us could have foreseen that the cousin of one of my ex-subs was Erica's fiancé." He rubbed circles on her back, seeking to soothe her. She was more upset about the way he'd been treated than the fact that she had disregarded a command. "I would never punish you for someone else's behavior."

She met his gaze. "I should have known from the way Erica talked about him that he would be hostile to our way of life. His attempts with her have been a joke."

"That's irrelevant." Keith put his arm around her shoulder and pulled her into his chest. "This punishment is for disobeying my direct order. In doing so, you showed disrespect for me, and you also damaged your chance to become a judge."

She stiffened and sat up. "What are you talking about?"

His jaw fell open. "You can't be unaware that Senator Kenyon is considering you for the recent vacancy in District Court? And if Judge Osman wins his bid for State Appellate, that's another vacancy—another chance for you to realize your dream of becoming a judge."

Her dark, miserable eyes searched his face. "That's the only reason you suggested having them over, isn't it? Dustin and Jordan are temperamentally more suited for mentorships. You're really only patient with people you love." Fat tears rolled down her cheeks. "You did this for me. You did everything for me, and I ruined it."

Michele Zurlo

He tucked her into his chest and rocked her until her sobs subsided. "You didn't ruin it. None of what happened was your fault. But in disobeying me, you made the situation worse."

"Unless the woman in question is asking or you suspect that you might be the father, there's no reason you should take a paternity test." She sniffled and sneezed.

He gave her a minute to make use of the tissue. "That's beside the point, and it's ultimately my decision. I would have discussed it with you later, in private where such matters belong."

She nodded against his chest. "I'm ready to accept my punishment, Master."

He kissed her temple. "Get into position. Ten whacks with the paddle. You'll count them out and thank me."

Later he followed Kat up the stairs. She walked stiffly, though the worst of it would wear off within an hour. Her tears had dried during the punishment, and she seemed to accept that she wasn't at fault for Burke's behavior. He didn't care for the act of punishing Kat, but he liked the way it helped her accept and move past her mistakes.

Mouthwatering aromas greeted them in the kitchen. Malcolm and Darcy heard the door to the basement opening, and they came in from the living room. They held hands, and Darcy's hair had been hastily smoothed down.

"I kept dinner warm," Malcolm said. "Who's hungry?"

"I'm starving," Kat said. "Why don't you guys go sit down, and I'll get the enchiladas?"

It didn't take but a moment. Kat brought the pan, still warm from the oven, and she dished it up on everyone's plates.

Malcolm watched her, a sparkle in his eye. Keith fully expected Malcolm to behave in a passive-aggressive manner toward him, like he had the first and only time Keith had tried to correct Kat in his presence. So far, he didn't seem at all upset. Darcy must have distracted him well.

"Trina, aren't you going to sit down to eat?" He put a dramatic hand over his mouth. "Or has shooting your mouth off made you too sore?"

"Fuck off, Malcolm." Kat sat down gingerly on her tender bottom.

Malcolm gasped. "Are you going to let your sub talk to me that way?"

Keith used his fork to cut a bite-sized piece from an enchilada, and then he put it in his mouth. Spicy and sweet, it melted in his mouth. "Damn, this is really good. Darcy, what do you think?"

Laughing, Darcy swallowed her mouthful. "I think you're wise to stay out of it."

Malcolm put his hand over his heart and faked a heart attack. "Sweetheart, I can't believe you didn't take my side."

Darcy didn't look impressed. She continued eating. "Master, I am always on your side, but when you bait your sister, the rules of D/s shouldn't apply. You are clearly trying to get her in trouble." She flashed a sweet smile at Mal. "Now, I think we should figure out how to fix this, and then we can do something fun."

"Fun? Hmmm." Keith entertained wicked thoughts as he stared at Kat. "I have some ideas."

Even as her cheeks heated, a slow smile spread across her face. "I'm game for whatever you want to do, Master."

"Hell, no. Discipline, behavior modification—fine. I can deal with that. But not sex stuff. There will be no nakedness or sex stuff with my little sister in my presence. As far as I'm concerned, she's an innocent young virgin, and she will remain that way until the day she dies." With that pronouncement, Malcolm crammed food into his mouth.

Her good mood restored—Keith was increasingly glad that he'd taken the time to administer punishment right away—an impish grin curved Kat's lips. "Oh, come on, Mal. I'm thirty years old. I have two kids, and I'm living in sin with your best friend, the sex addict. We have sex pretty much every day. And five weeks from tomorrow, I'm going to marry him. On our honeymoon, we're going to stay for part of the time at that resort Liam Adair's wife's friend runs, Zangari's Fetish Inn."

Darcy clapped. "I've been wanting to go there ever since I heard about it. Once the baby is a little older, I want to take Mal there. When you get back, I want to hear every detail. Take a lot of pictures."

"No," Malcolm said. "No pictures. Sweetheart, you're heading for the loss of your spanking."

As a Painslut, Darcy's idea of bliss was some rigorous impact play. She shrugged. "You just said no sex stuff, so I figured that was already off the table."

"I said with her, not with you." Malcolm finished eating and pushed his plate away.

Keith watched Kat, looking for her comeback, but her mind was far away. He closed his hand over hers. "Kitty Kat? What's wrong?"

"I think I should call Erica tomorrow, see if she'll meet me for lunch. I might be able to mend fences with her more easily if Burke isn't there." She had eaten about half of her food, and she picked at the remains.

Michele Zurlo

Darcy said, "I can go with you if you want."

"Thanks, but I think she'll do better one-on-one. With two of us, she might feel cornered. I don't want her to be on the defensive."

"Keith needs to do a paternity test," Malcolm said. "Use your own doctor. Set it up so that it's at your expense, and all she needs to do is go down there with the kid and give a sample."

Keith agreed, and he was glad Malcolm had brought it up. For some reason Kat was adamantly opposed to the idea of him even taking the test. Was she afraid it would come back positive? Then he connected some dots. If the test came back positive—and there was always a chance of a false positive—it would crush her. It would destroy her if another woman had his child when she could not. As much as she professed that having Angie and Corey was all she ever wanted, he knew she wanted more. He'd seen her watch Darcy through her pregnancy and with the newborn Zella, and he knew she yearned to have that with him.

And he desperately wanted to be able to give that to her. He wanted to watch her belly grow with his child, be there when she gave birth, and bring evidence of their everlasting love into the world.

He became aware of her hand on his wrist. He met her questioning gaze with his decision. "Malcolm is right. It's the best way to prove to Burke that I'm not completely who he thinks I am. It's a good bet that if we can't win him over, we'll lose Erica, and she has a great deal of influence over her father."

"If that's what you want." She nodded stiffly. "I'll set that up."

Darcy whispered to Malcolm, and he stood up. "We're going upstairs for a little while. You guys go ahead and talk."

Keith didn't understand why they'd leave. Most everything had already been said. "You don't have to go."

"I do," Darcy said. "I need to pump before my breasts explode. Malcolm has to come with me because he's tied me into a modified corselet, and I need him to adjust the ropes."

Once they were alone in the dining room, the table as messy as always but this time with plates and food instead of papers and laptops, he pushed his chair back. "Come sit on my lap, Kitty Kat."

He held her, soaking up the exquisite perfection of the way she felt in his arms. He needed to tell her that he understood, that he was sorry he couldn't give her the babies she wanted, and that he would understand if she didn't want to go through with the wedding. She'd put if off for so long already. He would have married her two years ago, a quick ceremony at the courthouse, if she would have agreed. But she'd put him off, telling him that they weren't in a hurry, for so long.

There was a very real possibility that she was only going through with it because she felt trapped. Malcolm's assurance aside, he knew Kat was a people pleaser. Not only did she want to please him, but she wanted to please her parents and family. She wanted to keep Angie and Corey happy, and if that meant sacrificing her future, she'd do it.

He opened his mouth to tell her these things, but his phone rang with the ringtone he couldn't ignore—Jordan's. If he was calling this late on a Saturday evening, there was a good chance he had movement on the bouquet case.

"I have to take that, Kitty Kat."

Ever the good sub, she hopped up without a sound of protest. He went to the kitchen where he'd left his phone. "Rossetti."

"It's Jordan. Is Trina with you?"

"Yeah. Mal's here too." He swallowed down his growing trepidation. "What's going on?"

"There was another murder. Judge Thomas Osman was found at home this afternoon by his wife who had been away for the week visiting their daughter in Iowa."

Keith understood the DOJ connection, but he didn't see how it was related to Kat. "That's horrible. My condolences to the family."

"His right hand was removed with a hacksaw. Then it was placed in a white box with a dozen long-stemmed roses. The fingers were posed a little differently. There's no note, but at this point, this whole fucking setup is a calling card."

The whole time, Keith kept his eyes on Kat, watching as she cleared the table and put away the leftovers. This couldn't happen to her. She'd been subjected to surveillance and house arrest already. And there was more at stake than just her now. They had Angie and Corey to think about. "Fuck."

Kat froze at his comment, probably tipped off by his tone. She turned slowly and watched him with the same intensity he watched her.

On the phone, Jordan continued. "Jocelyn approved surveillance for your house, and Trina's office is already on security cam. You should see one of our vehicles down the street at all times, and we're looking to rent the house behind yours. It's currently for sale."

Jocelyn Alard was the director in charge of Violent Crimes and Jordan's immediate boss. She was someone Keith knew only by reputation. He focused on the places he could add intel. "My neighbor is motivated to sell. His wife had a job transfer to the other side of the state, and he found a job that starts next week. Most of their stuff is already gone."

"Great. Rakeem is going to get right on that." Jordan hissed. "That's all I have for now. I need to get going, but I wanted you to know about the detail we put on Trina."

He ended the call and set his cell down.

"That was Jordan." Kat didn't dance around the topic. "They found another body, didn't they?"

"Judge Osman." He watched shock manifest in every part of her body.

She breathed through it, swallowing a few times to keep emotions under control. "There's more."

If he held back information, she would be livid when she found out. "They found another bouquet. It wasn't addressed to anyone, but with the similarities, ASAC Alard put you under protective surveillance." He knew that if she hadn't lived with an agent, they would have taken her into protective custody, effectively jettisoning all her career aspirations.

She blinked rapidly, and he was at her side before her legs gave out.

Chapter 11

"I'm fine." Emotions overwhelmed Katrina. Having convinced herself that either Jordan and Rakeem would find the culprit or that it was a one-time deal, she hadn't really thought about the bouquet incident for nearly a month. Keith had helped nurture the fantasy by changing the topic anytime she brought up anything related to the FBI.

"You need to sit down." Keith scooped her up and carried her to the living room, though she probably could have made it on her own.

The world existed in a dreamlike state as different thoughts clashed in her mind. One thing was clear—this killer wanted her attention. But was she a means to an end, or was she the end?

"Kat, we'll find this guy."

Her surroundings snapped into crystal clear focus. She realized that she was sitting on the sofa, and that Keith was next to her. She had a death grip on one of his hands, and he was stroking her hair back from her temple in a soothing caress. She faced him, alarmed at his assurance. "You're not on this case. Jordan and Rakeem will find this guy."

A storm clouded his green eyes. "Do you honestly think I'm not going to do everything I can to keep you safe?"

His vehement reaction helped her get her emotions under control. "I think you know better than to engage this guy. I think you know better than to get his attention. He's fixated on me, either because he thinks I am a conduit for his perceived sense of greatness or for a personal reason." She let go of his hands and clutched at his shirt. "Keith, you're my whole world. If he sees you as a threat, then he'll target you. I can deal with this as long as I don't have to worry about you as well."

His lips pressed together as his expression turned grim. "I'm not going to lie to make you feel better, and you'd see through it anyway if I tried. I love you, Kat. I don't love many people, and there's no one I love more deeply than I love you. You're part of me. You're the beat of my heart and the brightest light in my dark soul. I won't rest while this bastard is out there."

Michele Zurlo

Deep down, Katrina knew he'd refuse her request. Though her logic was sound, he was operating on emotion. Keith wasn't a person who made emotional decisions very often. When he did, nothing could dissuade him. Her Master was going to protect her at all costs, even the kind she wasn't willing to pay.

To will away the shaking and combat the overwhelming feeling of helplessness, she had to do something. "I'm going to go through every case I've prosecuted for the past six months, and I'm going to find the connection." The last time, she'd turned her files over to Jordan and Rakeem, trusting them to find the connection.

This time she needed an active role, and though she understood Keith's need to do the same, she dreaded that he'd do something to end his career in the FBI. When Malcolm had left the service, Keith had been upset by the decision, but he'd never questioned his dedication to his chosen field. Mal was still floundering, flitting between consulting and freelancing, but losing his badge would deal too harsh a blow to Keith.

"I need my phone." She got up. Keith did so as well, hovering over her as if she was going to collapse again. She set a hand on his chest. "I'm fine. I'm going to call Vina. We worked together on a lot of these cases, and I trust her to question everything."

"Okay. That's fine. But it's Saturday night. She's probably not sitting at home with nothing to do."

Katrina considered this. Vina was dedicated to her job, and Judge Osman had also been assigning her to Legal Aid, so like Katrina, she had a lot of extra work on her plate. However that didn't mean she wouldn't take a break. "You're right. She's intelligent and attractive, and she just broke up with her boyfriend. I think she told me that she had plans to go clubbing tonight. I'll get started by myself tonight, and I'll call her tomorrow."

"How about I help you tonight?" Keith rubbed the back of his neck. "Some of those cases were mine, and with the others, I know what I'm looking at."

"Uh-oh." Malcolm came into the living room, a frown furrowing his brow as he regarded them. "The mood in here is a little too somber. I thought I'd have to announce myself, and then come in shielding my eyes, but for some reason, you're talking about work."

Darcy came in behind him. She looked from Katrina to Keith. "Who died?"

"Judge Osman." Katrina bit her lip. "He was murdered in his home. His hand was severed, and the murderer arranged it to hold a bouquet of roses."

Clapping a hand over her mouth, Darcy squeaked. Color drained from her face. "Oh, my God. I was kidding. Holy shit, that was bad timing. I'm so sorry."

Malcolm guided her into the nearest chair.

"It's all right," Keith said. "You didn't know."

"I can help you look through cases too." Malcolm spoke with quiet authority. "I know what to look for."

There were ethical concerns. Malcolm was no longer with the FBI. He had limited clearance, and some of her files were still confidential. But he was her brother, and she trusted him to use discretion. She nodded. "I'd like that."

"I'll handle the after-dinner cleanup." Darcy got to her feet. "And I'll keep you in coffee and snacks."

The next morning, Katrina woke up to find Darcy in the kitchen and a fresh pot of coffee brewing. They'd stayed up late, looking over files until their eyelids staged a rebellion. Darcy hummed as she rooted around the refrigerator.

Katrina was glad that someone else was awake. She didn't exactly want to be alone with her thoughts. "Good morning. I would have thought you'd still be asleep."

"I'm a slave to my mammary glands." Darcy closed the fridge door. "But now that Zella is starting on cereal, I'm hoping my boobs will get the hint and slow down production."

"Maybe." Katrina poured a cup of coffee and sat on a stool.

"Of course, they won't if Malcolm decides they're fair game again."

The coffee went down wrong, and Katrina choked.

Darcy waited through the coughing. "I didn't mean to imply that he's open to nursing, just that he is a fan of suction."

"Oh, my brain didn't go there." Katrina squeezed her eyes shut to stop the image from forming. "And it never will. I forbid it."

Darcy rummaged through a cabinet. "Do you have pancake mix? I thought I'd give you and Malcolm a break this morning."

Most mornings, Keith made breakfast, but Katrina wasn't going to turn down an offer like that. She pointed to the cupboard next to where Darcy was foraging. "There."

Darcy got out the ingredients and put them on the island opposite Katrina. "So, Trina, what are you planning to say to Erica when you call her today?"

That fiasco was the farthest thing from Katrina's mind. It seemed like it had happened so long ago. "I don't have time to call her. I'm going to spend most of the day going over my case files, and all the other time goes to Keith and the kids."

"Trina, you can't put this off. I was going to urge you to call her last night, but after what happened, I put it on a shelf."

Katrina sipped her coffee. "That's exactly where I've put it—on a shelf."

"You put what on a shelf?" Keith, shirtless and barefoot, yawned mid-sentence and slid onto the stool next to Katrina. His eyes were bleary from not enough sleep.

She rubbed his arm. "You're not quite awake. It's okay to go back to sleep."

"Coffee," he murmured as he ran a hand through his tousled hair. "Black."

Katrina poured a cup and set it in front of him. "One cup. You can take a nap later." Corey would probably sleep as well, so that meant she and Angelina would have some girl time.

He picked up the cup and took a sip. "You didn't answer my question."

"What question?"

"Shelf." He imbibed more java, perking up with the second shot. "You put what on a shelf?"

Though she didn't want to bring up the subject with Keith, especially not first thing in the morning, she didn't feign ignorance. "Calling Erica."

"Why?" He rubbed his eyes. "You need to smooth things over with her."

Katrina wrinkled her nose. "Given recent developments, I don't really care about that anymore. It's not a priority."

"Jordan and Rakeem are working this case." Darcy interjected her two cents. "I get that you want to help, but it's not your job to catch this guy. There's no reason you can't call Erica."

"Exactly." The discussion woke Keith up more than the coffee. "We can't let this psychopath derail your dreams. After breakfast, you'll call Erica. Arrange a meeting for as soon as possible. It's best not to let this fester."

This was the last thing Katrina wanted to talk about or act upon. Keith was usually reasonable. It was best to appeal to that side of him. "Keith, I don't care if I ever become a judge. I'd much rather concentrate on catching this guy. And who's to say that I won't be nominated for the next vacancy or by another senator?"

He downed the rest of his coffee. "This isn't open for discussion. You will call her. You will arrange a meeting where you will smooth this over by assuring them that I will take a blood test. I'll have the results expedited as well. Liam, Jed, and Tru are giving a demonstration next weekend as part of a BDSM conference at a private club. We'll invite Erica and Burke as our guests."

"That's a great idea," Darcy added as Malcolm joined them. "Mal is going to do a bondage demo on me. He's also considering doing one about flogging, but I get to subspace so quickly that he's worried it'll give the newbies unrealistic expectations."

Keith took Katrina's hand in his, and he captured her with his firm gaze. "Bottom line, Kat, is that I gave you an order, and you will follow it."

Held prisoner by nothing more than a dominant look, Katrina's breath caught. Keith rarely gave orders. He could have ruled her that way, but most of the time he made suggestions or issued requests. He was thoughtful and kind, but waiting just beneath the surface was an endless pool of determination and ruthlessness.

Simply by lowering her gaze, she indicated submission and compliance. "I will." This wasn't what she wanted, and she had to force the words out.

Awake now, Keith refilled his coffee.

Darcy set a plate of pancakes in front of Katrina.

"Thanks."

Keith took the long way back to his stool, stopping at the pantry to get syrup on his way. He set it down next to the plate. "Eat, Kitty Kat. You have a long day ahead of you."

"You know, I bet Trina could help with the flogging demo." Malcolm availed himself of the coffee. "We could put Keith up there. He never gets to subspace, but he enjoys a good flogging."

If he hadn't shared with his best friend that he'd achieved subspace or any other synonym that didn't include a reference to being submissive, then she wasn't going to say a word. Keith was still learning to own his identity as a masochist and Dom. "I'd rather not." She bathed her pancakes in syrup. "That's too private."

"Right," Darcy said. "It makes Keith really horny, and he can't hide it like I can."

Malcolm frowned into his cup. "Good point. Never mind."

When they left, Katrina started on the dishes. She opened the dishwasher to unload it, but Keith caged her between his body and the counter before she could put anything away.

"I would," he said. "If you wanted to."

Michele Zurlo

His presence—the sight and familiar smell of him—filled her senses. She tilted her face to make her lips available. "When you come at me like this, I always want to."

He chuckled as he nibbled her lower lip. "I meant the flogging demonstration. I didn't know if you turned Mal down because you don't want to do it or because you thought I wouldn't do it. I'm willing."

Katrina closed her eyes, and her body swayed closer to his. "I have too many things on my plate right now. I can't even entertain that idea."

"Kitty Kat? Are you entertaining other ideas right now?" The timbre of his voice dropped a notch. Barely making contact, he traced his lips over her cheeks and eyelids, along her temples and the line of her jaw.

"Most definitely." She pressed her palms to his bare chest, feathering light caresses on the hard, muscled surface.

He nipped her earlobe. "What kinds of ideas?"

"The X-rated kind." Curving her fingers, she raked her nails down his chest.

One of his hands eased into her pajama bottoms, and his palm pressed against her mons. "Like this?"

She tilted her hips, rubbing against the heel of his hand. "There's too much clothing involved for this to be X-rated."

"Tell me what you want. Beg for it." His command, husky and harsh, vibrated from deep in his chest.

That tone, coupled with that demand, always made her pussy wet. She stroked his chest and shoulders, extending coverage to the corded muscles on his arms. "Fuck me, Master. Please show me how much I belong to you."

His hand dipped under her panties. He stroked her wetness. "This pussy belongs to me."

She gripped his shoulders. "Yes. Oh, yes."

He captured the tip of her clit between this thumb and forefinger, and he increased the pressure until she gasped. "This clit is mine."

"Yes, Master. It's most definitely yours."

He released her, and his fingers traveled down, stroking and rubbing along her sensitive places. Then he plunged two fingers inside. "Mine."

"Yes," she breathed. "Yours."

"I'm going to finger this pretty pussy. I want to feel your orgasm, but you can't make a single sound." He wrapped an arm around her waist, but he put inches between their faces.

Re/Captured

She blinked, forcing herself away from the bliss so that she could process his command. "I'll try, Master."

He withdrew most of the way and plunged his fingers back in. "If you make a sound—a moan, a squeak, even a gasp—I'll stop."

She clamped her lips together in a silent promise, and he set to work. His fingers curved to stab at her sweet spot while his palm stimulated her clit. That, combined with his dominance, brought her very close. She pumped her hips, moving in rhythm with his hand. As the intensity increased, she dug her nails into his flesh to avoid making a sound.

"That's it, Kitty Kat. I love watching your face. Let me see your frustration and your bliss while the silky feel of your throbbing cunt squeezes my fingers. You're so fucking beautiful. Come for me."

The climax thundered through her body, shaking her to the core, but she didn't make a sound. His hand pumped into her, prolonging those precious waves. Once most of her orgasm had waned, he withdrew his fingers. She gasped, suddenly realizing she'd been holding her breath.

"Thank you, Master. Please let me return the favor."

"Oh, you will, Kitty Kat." Grasping her waist, he lifted her up and turned her around. Then he shoved her bottoms and panties out of the way. They fell down her legs to pool at her feet. "Widen your stance."

She did the best she could with the fabric binding her ankles. He bent her over the sink, and then he fed his cock into her still-pulsing vagina, stretching those tender tissues. She braced herself on the ledge. "Oh, God, you feel so good."

"You're going to come again, but this time I want to hear you."

"Yes, Master."

One hand gripped her hip, and the other slid up her side to cup a breast. He plucked and kneaded, his rough play opening the conduit from her breasts to her pussy that had her eyes watering and her clit tingling.

"Whoops." Darcy's voice cut through the haze of impending orgasm. "I thought you'd be upstairs doing that. Or downstairs. Ignore me. I left my breast milk in the fridge."

Keith froze at the first word. The refrigerator opened and closed, as did the front door. They heard the lock engage. "They have a key," Katrina said. This was not news, just a reminder.

"I guess I didn't think they'd use it when we were home." Keith rubbed his palm over her hardened nipple. "Okay, well, that changes nothing. You're still going to come."

Michele Zurlo

He renewed the onslaught, rapidly making up for lost time. Before long, another orgasm washed through Katrina, she cried out, and he pulled her up so that her back was to his chest. He wrapped his arms around her, his hips still moving with slow thrusts.

"I love you, Kitty Kat, and I treasure the gift of your submission." He tugged the sleeve of her shirt to reveal her neck. He kissed the sensitive place just above her collarbone, and then he bit her.

"Oh, God." She cried out as he marked her with a sucking bite. Her body jerked, but he held her in place with the iron bands he'd wrapped around her torso. Tears and shock blinded her. In all their time together, he'd never given her a hickey.

She found herself lifted and turned. He set her on the edge of the counter, removed her pajama bottoms, and buried his cock in her pussy. Still reeling from the lingering pain, she could only cling to him.

He kissed her, his luscious lips and skilled tongue drugging her senses and dulling the pain. Then he sealed his forehead to hers. He moved in her, slow circles that fed her climax so subtly that she wasn't prepared for it to hit again. Her body lengthened and arched. Too shocked to cry out, she surrendered everything to the man who possessed her body and soul.

Chapter 12

"Thanks for helping me go through this stuff." Katrina set a plate of crackers and cheese in Vina's reach.

The pair had been hard at work for two days. Vina had come over Sunday to help Katrina and Keith look through files, and then she'd come over after work on Monday as well.

Vina looked up from the computer screen, smiling though she now had dark circles under her eyes. On her they looked like smudges instead of bags. "You're welcome. I'd like to think that if I were in your shoes, you'd do the same for me."

"Absolutely I would." Katrina resumed her seat across the table. "Okay, so what do we have so far?"

"In the past six months, you've prosecuted thirty-two criminals with charges of violence in addition to fraud. Of those, twenty were assault, eight were manslaughter, two were accidental death, and two were murder. If we concentrate only on the first-degree murder cases, then we have nobody. They're both still in prison."

Keith came into the dining room. "The kids are bathed and watching a movie." He sat down next to Katrina. "How about the manslaughter cases? Were any of those plea deals?" Sometimes they cut deals with criminals to plea to a lesser offense. It saved a ton of time, money, and resources.

"Yes. But they're all still in prison." Vina ran a hand through her hair, ruffling her perfect coif. "What if we're looking in the wrong place? Where are the records of the ones who were recently released?"

"Jordan and Rakeem are following up on those." Keith drummed his fingers on the table as he thought. Despite his dismissal, Katrina ran a database search for recent parolees. "What about the time you've spent at Legal Aid? Any murderers there?"

"Just the one," Katrina said, "but I didn't close that case. I had it one day, and nothing happened."

"You got a continuance to give time for the prosecution to turn over the evidence logs." Keith scowled. "Mason Charles Norris. The judge dismissed the case when the prosecutor didn't follow through.

Michele Zurlo

What was her name? Yessenia Cremin. I heard she got her ass chewed out for that."

"That was your case," Katrina recalled. "I asked Elizabeth about trying him for fraud, but she said the chain of evidence for that was missing as well."

"He doesn't have a job right now, but he's on our radar. It's just a matter of time before he starts another scheme again. I always thought that if we had time, we could have nailed him for money laundering as well." He shook his head.

"Really?" Vina leaned her elbow on the table and rested her chin. "He can't do that alone. Are you investigating his known associates?"

"A-ha!" Katrina pumped her fist in the air. "Eddie Maddox was released six weeks ago. He was sentenced to eight years for manslaughter and twelve for identity theft. He said he'd get even with me when he got out."

Maddox had been one of the first people she'd put away. He worked at a company specializing in identity-theft prevention where he'd stolen not only from the company, but he'd stolen fourteen identities. He'd opened credit cards, and in two cases, he'd cleaned out bank and retirement accounts.

She peered closer at her screen. "Fucker served only six years. That is not justice. Osman was the presiding and sentencing judge."

"That's a possibility. I'll call Jordan." Keith went to the kitchen to grab his phone.

Vina stretched and yawned, and then she reached for a cracker. "I love cheese. Gouda is my Achilles heel." She munched while Katrina studied her laptop screen.

The problem with this approach was that it ruled out families and friends. The severed hands holding bouquets were gruesome, but they were, in a psychopath's mind, tokens of affection. Was there someone peripherally related to a case who had fixated on her? Maybe she'd put away their competition or the person who'd prevented them from killing?

She closed her eyes and massaged her temples. This part of the investigation was not her favorite part. She liked being a prosecutor because the FBI had already done all the heavy lifting. All she needed to do was give it the final push.

"I'm tired too," Vina announced. "I'm going to call it a night. Same time tomorrow?"

"No." Keith rejoined them. "You both need a night off. Rest. Recharge. We'll see where we are Wednesday."

Re/Captured

"Sounds like a plan." Vina gathered her things and stuffed them into her bag. "Oh, we have a fitting on Wednesday. I almost forgot. Thursday I have plans. Sorry. Friday is the earliest day I can get back here."

"Don't worry about it," Keith said. "We have a lot of agents on this. Killing a judge is serious business, not that killing a delivery driver isn't."

When she was gone, Katrina turned to Keith. "Tomorrow is a night off?"

"Yes. No investigating allowed."

She would rather investigate than follow through with the plans she'd made. "Does that mean I can cancel on Erica?" She hadn't been able to reach Erica until late Sunday, and Erica had agreed to meet her for coffee on Tuesday at one.

"Nope. And take the envelope on the counter. It has directions for where and how for them to get the test done on the kid." Keith had gone for his part of the test bright and early that morning. He'd texted her afterward, letting her know that the deed was done.

"It's stupid that you had to take half a personal day for this idiotic thing."

He pulled her in for a hug. "I'm sure if you had been fed lies about a person, you'd want more than their word that they were innocent. Don't waste your vitriol on them, Kitty Kat. They're a means to an end."

"The fact that we're using them doesn't make me feel better." Katrina snuggled into his chest.

"Well, you aren't. Not really. You are actually interested in being Erica's friend. Otherwise you wouldn't care so much." He kissed her forehead. "Let's put the kids to bed, and we'll cuddle on the sofa."

They were both exhausted, but Katrina was still surprised that he didn't suggest going straight to bed and making her even more tired. She vowed to make a move, but she fell asleep ten minutes after they finished putting the kids to bed.

Jordan stopped by to see her mid-morning. She was at her desk, churning out paperwork like a madwoman when he scooted a chair next to her desk and sat down.

Genuinely happy to see him, she smiled. "Hey, there."

Jordan was one of those agents who didn't follow the dress code. His dark, wavy hair fell past his shoulders in a shaggy cut that accented the sharp cheekbones and strong jaw. Genetics had endowed him with a naturally dangerous look. He favored worn jeans and cotton shirts that advertised motorcycles, and he usually wore leather boots. Today was no exception.

He returned her smile. "Hi Trina. How are you holding up?"

She shrugged. "I'm so busy right now that I wasn't thinking about it."

"Good. I want you to stop investigating the case."

Her mouth fell open. "Did Keith put you up to this?"

"He did not. I've asked him to stop looking into it as well. We can't have you accessing files and records, not when you have the ability to electronically alter them. We're going to catch this guy, and in order to put him away for life, I need to have an airtight case. I can't have you poking holes for the defense."

As he made his case, Katrina knew he was right. In her effort to help, she could jeopardize the whole endeavor. She felt horrible about what she'd already done, and her brain immediately identified a half dozen other ways the defense could twist her involvement to create reasonable doubt for a jury.

Jordan jumped out of his chair with amazing agility for such a big guy. He braced one hand on the back of her chair and leaned over her. "Breathe."

His order jerked her from the barrage of recriminations in her head. She inhaled, and much-needed oxygen flooded her lungs.

"Good girl. Again. That's it." Crisis averted, he sat back down, but his air of authority remained intact. "Don't beat yourself up. No blame, no regrets. You haven't done any damage yet. I wanted to stop you before it came to that."

She had a hard time doing that. Even when she messed up a little, she spent a lot of time torturing herself by replaying the mistake in her mind.

"Trina, don't disobey me in this." Jordan wasn't her Dom, but he was a good friend, and this was the first time he'd ever topped her. She respected and cared about him.

"I won't. I'm finished pouring over my old cases."

He leaned forward, inches closer, but the effect was amplified by his steady and authoritative gaze. "I know you won't. I'm talking about beating yourself up. You're a lot like Amy in that regard. I'll let Keith know he might need to follow up tonight."

She nodded. There really wasn't anything she could say to assure him. She would try, but she might fail.

"Next, I need to warn you that this has been leaked to the press."

"What?" Katrina knew there was no way those involved with this would leak details. Killers of this variety thrived on media attention, and this might encourage more murders.

"Cable news show. When they contacted us for comment, they showed us the photographs they have. They're not our crime scene photos, so it's likely the killer is the source."

What he didn't say, and she knew to be true, was that the FBI didn't comment on active investigations. And if the killer had released the photos, it meant he wanted notoriety. Jordan and Rakeem were going to need to change their approach to the investigation now that the media was a factor.

"Okay, now that that's out of the way, I have some questions about Maddox." He opened an app on his phone and slid a stylus from its holder.

"Jordan, I was thinking. What if it isn't someone who is connected to me through a case, not directly anyway? What if it's a friend or relative of a victim or even of a defendant? The flowers thing, that's like they're thanking me."

He tapped the stylus on her desk. "It could be any number of things. People send flowers for romantic purposes, and they also do it for funerals."

"Weddings?" She covered her mouth. "Oh, my God, what if this is a wedding present?"

"Trina, we have other leads. Right now, Rakeem is following up on two of them. After I leave here, I'm going to meet him. Rest assured that approaching this through your old cases is only one prong of our investigation. And we're not sure how much you're linked to the killer. He may have chosen you randomly as a way to get our attention." This time, his smile reassured. "Back to Maddox. Do you have a record of his threat to get back at you? Or were there witnesses?"

His questions didn't offend Katrina. She knew what ingredients went into a thorough investigation.

Keith called ten minutes after Jordan left. "I'm fine. I swear."

"Just making sure." Wind created static, and a car honked in the background. "I'm sorry, Kat. I should have known better. I wasn't thinking clearly."

"Neither of us were." She sighed. "But now we are, and Jordan said we haven't done any damage yet, so we can rest easy on that front."

"We can. Hey, your parents invited us to dinner, and I said we'd be there. Six-thirty. You know the address."

Michele Zurlo

Her parents were worried, and that meant her mom was probably cooking at this moment, even though it was only a few minutes past noon. "That sounds great. Was it your idea or my mom's?" Keith called her parents more than she did, and he often suggested they get together.

"Hers. I suggested the lemon meringue pie for dessert." He laughed. "Your mother is amazing."

"She is." Katrina glanced at the clock on her computer screen. "I have to go, Keith. I have a few things I need to finish if I'm going to meet Erica for lunch."

"Then go. No excuses. Don't forget to give her the envelope. I love you."

Katrina wanted to state for the record that her attendance at this meeting was completely involuntary. She'd been compelled by a higher authority. Yes, that higher authority had her career in mind, but right now worrying about her career seemed meaningless and frivolous.

The coffee shop down the street boasted all manner of gourmet and exotic blends. Bright and cheery, it catered to the energetic professionals in the area. As Katrina crossed the street, she spied Erica seated at a table next to the front window, sipping foamy java.

Katrina came inside, and Erica waved, half-standing with an uncertain smile on her face. "I got you a triple bean blend from Colombia. You said you loved classic coffee, and this is the closest they have." She wore her hair tied back in a messy bun, and a wayward strand tumbled down her temple.

Taking the seat opposite Erica, Katrina said, "Thanks, but you didn't have to buy me a coffee."

Erica grimaced. "I'm hoping it'll help you to accept my apology. I'm so sorry for the way Burke behaved. I was too mortified to speak up, and then I was too ashamed afterward to call you."

This was a surprising turn of events. Even if Keith had flown off the handle at someone, Katrina never would have apologized for his behavior—unless he instructed her to do so. "I'd like to apologize as well. Keith has no experience with beginners. I should have waited for Dustin, Layla's fiancé. He runs a group that meets once a month, and he mentors beginners."

The only time Keith had broken with his "no beginners" policy was when he'd agreed to teach her. And this second time, he'd done that for her as well. The first time had turned out much better.

Erica waved her hand in the air. "Burke was out of line. I'm surprised Keith wasn't more acerbic in his response."

"Well, I think he felt a little responsible. While he doesn't remember Burke's cousin, it doesn't mean they weren't involved. Before I helped him to see the error of his ways, he was a prolific slut." Katrina placed the envelope on the table. "He's had a DNA test. This has instructions for Burke's cousin to get the test done. Everything is prepaid, so she doesn't have to worry about that. If she needs transportation, she should call me, and I'll arrange for it."

Frowning, Erica stared at the envelope. "I thought he said he couldn't father children?"

"He can't. This is for Burke's peace of mind."

"Why would he do that? I mean, wouldn't he be well within his rights to forbid you from seeing me?"

Katrina sipped her coffee and thought about that. While he could have done exactly that, it wasn't just the idea that this might advance her career that had stopped him from doing so. "Keith would never restrict who I could see. Some Doms do things like that, I'm sure, but none that I know."

Erica picked at the cardboard ring around her cup. "He can't like you associating with me, not after last weekend."

"Actually it was his idea that I call you. He insisted on it." Katrina watched Erica shred little flakes from the cardboard. "He liked you, not just from Saturday, but from what I've told him about our other interactions. He encourages and supports my friendships."

She scoffed. "He makes you wait for permission to speak."

Katrina reminded herself that she needed to end this on a positive note. "When we're using protocol, yes, he does."

"Explain that to me." Erica leaned closer, her brown eyes intense and earnest. "Why would you—a successful, intelligent, self-assured woman—let a man treat you like that?"

She'd known this question was coming. She met Erica's inquiry with a steady gaze. "I spend my days in charge. I meet with law enforcement, review cases, decide what kinds of charges to bring. From the time my kids wake up until they go to sleep, I am in charge of making decisions, and it is exhausting. It drains me. I'm a people pleaser, always have been. In my heart, I'm a submissive. Ceding control to someone I trust strengthens me and gives me the energy to do all the other things I need to do."

In an effort to organize her thoughts, Katrina sipped coffee, and Erica waited.

"It's not for everyone. Nothing is. What replenishes me may not replenish you, and that's okay. Keith understands what I need, and he makes sure I get it. Yes, he's in charge, but there's no one I trust more to make sure my needs are met—not even myself. I'll sacrifice my happiness, my time, and my well-being to please others. Keith makes sure that I prioritize myself. He does that through dominance because that's who he is."

Erica waited in the silence that followed. Then she shifted. "But the speaking thing—how does that empower you?"

"It's a reminder that I belong to him, and it's a demonstration of our dynamic to others. We don't do it all the time, but when we do—" Katrina closed her eyes and inhaled, the memory of Keith's power washing over her, taming her unrest. "When we do, I feel free. All stress and worry melt away. At the end of a stressful day, there's nothing I want to do more than go home and kneel at his feet. When I do that, I know he'll take care of me. Sometimes he'll sit down, and I'll lay my head on his leg. Other times it begins a scene, and I love to scene."

She opened her eyes to see Erica staring at her, mouth agape. "The expression on your face says more than words ever could. I saw it in the way you looked at Keith at the club. Layla too, when she looked at Dustin. It's like you have a deeper connection than I've ever felt with another person. I love Burke, but I don't feel connected to him like that."

Katrina had noticed the lack. "I can't say that our dynamic creates the connection, but it has a role in maintaining and deepening it."

"I thought dominants were greedy types, all about power and control."

"Some are," Katrina admitted. "Those are the ones you want to avoid. Doms are people. Some are great and some aren't."

Lost in thought, Erica picked at the cardboard some more. She'd torn away most of it, leaving a thin ring that barely defied gravity.

"There's a demonstration this weekend at a private club," Katrina said. "Why don't you come with us? You wouldn't be able to play or anything, but you could watch. You could see how other couples interact."

She considered this. "Can I bring Burke? He is still interested in the lifestyle."

"Yes, but he will need to keep his comments and questions respectful. There is no one true way. There is only what works for a particular couple. Look for things you like, don't bother with the parts you don't like. But leave your judgments at home."

"Kat, we need to talk." Keith's voice came through the speaker in her car. She was on her way to pick up Angelina from school and Corey from day care. This was an order, a notice that serious topics were going to be discussed after the kids went to bed. He might want to discuss their last scene, what could happen at the play party tomorrow night, the division of parenting responsibilities, or a host of other matters.

"Okay. Will you tell me what about?"

"No. I just wanted you to be prepared. If you have issues to bring up, you can do so tonight."

"All right." She couldn't think of anything right now, but that didn't mean she'd arrive empty-handed. They hadn't engaged in sexual activity in five days. In the whole time she'd been with him, they had never gone that long. If he didn't bring up what was wrong tonight, then she would.

"Drive safely. I'll see you at home."

This kind of notice did not dampen her spirits or ruin her evening. Their talks were neutral territory, a forum for open discussion. While they could do this anytime, having a ritual pointed to the importance of communication in their relationship.

Before they left to go to her parents' house for dinner and lemon meringue pie—because her mother hadn't been able to make one Tuesday, she had invited them back for another meal—Keith presented Angelina with a small rectangular box. "You have officially gone a whole month without an incident. You got no yellows, no blues, and no reds."

At Angelina's school, they color-coded behavior. Students who behaved, treated others well, followed directions, and did their work stayed on green. An infraction moved them down to yellow. A second misdeed dropped them to blue, and red meant there was a consequence like a time out, loss of recess, or conversation with the principal. This past month, all reports had been glowing, and all phone calls had relayed good deeds on Angelina's part.

A proud smile brightened his handsome face. "We're very proud of you."

Angelina beamed. "I've been trying really hard to be good."

"It paid off, Angelina." Katrina kissed her daughter's cheek.

Keith set another box in front of Corey. "And you, buddy, are doing a spectacular job."

They didn't have behavior issues with Corey. Everyone loved his affable personality, and he was a great student as well. He suffered no aftereffect from having an alcoholic as a birth mother. But if they were going to reward Angelina's behavior—a plan hatched with her therapist—then they needed to do something for Corey.

The kids opened their gifts.

"This is so cool!" Corey dropped to his knees and played air guitar. He held up an eraser shaped like a toilet, and another that looked like a turd.

Katrina wrinkled her nose and mouthed to Keith, "That's what you got him?"

Keith grinned. "It's a boy thing."

She and Angelina exchanged a look that said they were both grateful not to be boys. Angelina climbed onto the bar stool and set the box on the counter. She took her time with the ribbon, and then she lifted the lid. Her eyes grew saucer-sized. "Oh, this is just beautiful." She held up a charm bracelet small enough to fit over her tiny wrist. "Mommy, Daddy—this is exactly what I wanted, and you even got the charm with the girl kicking booty."

Twice each week, Katrina had been attending Tae Kwon Do with Angelina. As Keith had predicted, the sport left her calm and focused. It not only helped her harness that boundless energy, it channeled it into an activity that improved her self-esteem. As of right now, Angelina wanted to learn to master all the martial arts, and then she wanted to open her own studio.

Keith held out a hand. "Do you want me to put it on you?"

In a blink, she was standing next to him, vibrating with glee. "Thank you, Daddy. I love it."

As he secured the clasp, he said, "Don't forget to thank Mommy."

Angelina threw herself at Katrina's legs. "Thank you."

Katrina hugged Angelina. "You'll get a charm for every good month."

Corey made a jealous noise. "Will I get a new eraser?"

"Yes," Keith said. "Absolutely."

"Okay." Corey raced to the front of the house. "I'm getting my shoes on. Let's go to Grandma and Poppa's house. I'm hungry, and I want to show Grandma my prize."

Angelina ran off to join him, and Keith handed Katrina an unopened envelope with a return address from a hospital. She looked inside to find the results of the DNA test. As he'd maintained all along, the child was not his. "Why didn't you open it?"

"I already knew what it said. I wanted you to see it first."

Her brows drew together in confusion. "I knew it would come back negative, Keith. I wasn't worried."

That night, after the kids were asleep, she made tea and met Keith at the kitchen table. She set a cup of lemon tea with honey in front of him. "I am so glad Corey is an easy-to-please kid."

Keith chuckled. "Somehow he ended up with your temperament."

"So, what's on the agenda for tonight?" Katrina was hoping that they could have a relatively quick discussion and perhaps a session in the dungeon. "Do you want to try something new on me?"

"No, but if you're thinking we need to spice up our sex life, I'm willing to entertain requests." He tried for a rakish grin, but the humor didn't quite reach his eyes.

She sipped her tea to combat the sinking feeling in her stomach. It was rare that Keith couldn't manage to flirt. "Okay, then. I'm listening."

"Senator Kenyon called me today. He invited us to a luncheon Sunday in Grand Rapids."

"That's clear on the other side of the state." The invitation didn't confuse her, but the fact that Keith would call a negotiation meeting for news like that did.

"Layla and Dustin are coming over Sunday morning to watch the kids. They'll be here by nine-thirty to give us plenty of time to get there. I booked a hotel room so that we could freshen up after the drive."

Katrina tilted her head, trying to find his angle. "Why did you agree to this? Does my surveillance detail know they're going to Grand Rapids?"

His brows drew together. "Since you live with me, and they're not convinced you're in danger, not in light of new evidence—and no, I don't know what that is—they've pulled your protection. I'm here, so it's not like you're unprotected."

She felt safer having Keith around than any other agent, and she understood how these things went, and so she wasn't upset about having the detail pulled. "Keith, why wouldn't you ask me about this first? Angelina has a fitting on Sunday for her flower girl dress."

"Layla can take her."

"I know, but we were supposed to have a girl day. We were going to get mani-pedis and ice cream."

"Layla can do those things with her. I know it's not ideal. Sorry." Keith managed to sound both regretful and not sorry at the same time. "Kenyon likes you, Kat. He's called you several times for your legal opinion, and he's asked you to look over the bill he's co-sponsoring. He likes the way you think, and he likes your politics. I know politics shouldn't enter into this, but it does. This is the game we have to play."

Michele Zurlo

She knew this was required, but that didn't mean she liked it. The law shouldn't be a victim of political whim or partisan maneuvering. "Okay, so that's what we're doing Sunday. Your good suit is clean, so I just have to pick out a dress."

Restless and discontent, he sipped his tea. Katrina didn't understand the cause of his brooding demeanor.

"Is there more?"

He set the cup down, but he didn't meet her gaze. "You're an amazing mother. I mean, I always knew you would be. Not only did you learn from the best, but you're a natural caregiver and a fierce mama bear. When they tried to keep Angie out of regular school, you fought for her. You went to meetings, researched laws—you really advocated for her. And then with Corey, you guys bonded instantly. You're the first face he wants to see in the morning, and the last image he wants in his head before he closes his eyes at night—which I totally understand."

Keith was an amazing father as well, having been equally involved in the raising of their children, but she didn't think he was fishing for admiration. He needed her to listen to what he had to say.

"I want you to be happy, Kat. More than that, I want you to be fulfilled. I want you to have everything your heart desires." He broke off and shook his head. He still hadn't looked at her. "But I can't give you that, can I? Not when I took something huge off the table years ago. I thought I was doing the world a favor, but now I see my actions for what they are. It was an incredibly selfish act, one I know you resent—at least subconsciously—just as surely as I know you'll deny it. That's just how big your heart is. I took the possibility of something away from you, and you just accepted my decision."

The fact that he refused to look her in the eye or get to the point worried her. He wasn't the kind of man who beat around the bush, not even with difficult topics. He was the kind who forced a necessary discussion no matter how painful it might be. She guessed that was what he was trying to do right now. She set her hand on his wrist. "Keith, whatever is wrong—you can tell me. You can tell me anything."

Finally he lifted his gaze to hers. "Monday when I went in to get the DNA test, I also had a procedure done, a vasovasectomy."

She blinked. While she'd known it was possible to reverse a vasectomy, it would never have occurred to her to ask him to undergo the procedure. Having it wasn't a decision he'd made lightly, and she understood his reasons for never wanting to father a child. "You had surgery without telling me?"

"I'm telling you now."

Re/Captured

Having a vasectomy reversed was a much bigger deal than getting a vasectomy. "But you planned it a while ago. You can't just walk into a doctor's office and say, 'Hey, while I'm here, can you perform surgery on me?' That's not how it works. You have to get blood work done. You have to—oh, my God. That's how you got in to see a doctor so quickly to get a DNA test. You had the surgery scheduled, and while you were there, you asked if they could swab your cheek."

His lips parted during her tirade. "Kat, you're overreacting to the wrong thing."

Telling someone they were overreacting was an effective way to take them from upset to livid. "I'm overreacting to the fact that you made a major decision—to go under anesthesia and have someone cut open your body—without discussing it with me or even telling me that you were thinking about having surgery? Fuck you, Keith."

He wisely chose not to mention her expletive. "It wasn't surgery. It was an in-office procedure. I was in and out in three hours."

"I should have been there." Her volume rose with her temper. "I should have been there in case something happened. I should have been there to drive you home. You had surgery, for God's sake, and then you went back to work. It's not like you have a desk job."

"I arranged for me to be at my desk all week."

"Great. So you told your boss, but not your fucking fiancée. I feel so special, Keith. I love that you made a major decision without me, had surgery without my knowledge, and told Lexee but not me." She shot to her feet. When she was this furious, it was impossible to sit down and have a cup of tea, not unless she threw it at his face. "I can't remember the last time you pissed me off this much."

He watched her warily. "Kat, I just—You're a wonderful mother. You have so much to give. I watch you holding Zella, and all I can think about is how I can't give that to you. I can't get you pregnant. I can't give you a baby of your own. And then I think about how you keep putting off the wedding, and I can't help wondering why you refused to even let me propose for the first year we were together. Part of me wonders if you're marrying me because it's expected, and another part of me wonders if you're reluctant to marry me because I couldn't give you the one thing you want most."

So much shit dropped on Katrina that she didn't know how to react or where to start. Stunned, she held up a hand when he tried to continue explaining. "Wait. You just said and did about fifty stupid things. I need a minute to process."

Michele Zurlo

She took her tea to the sink and poured it out. As the amber liquid disappeared down the drain, she realized that tears streamed down her cheeks. This was the result of anger, not sorrow. In her whole life, she could count the number of times that fury had moved her to tears—once when M.J. had decapitated her favorite teddy bear, and another time when she'd found out about Layla's abusive ex-boyfriend.

Wiping her eyes, she struggled to get her temper under control. Times like this, she wished she didn't live with an alcoholic because it would be nice to have a shot of whiskey right about now.

She resumed her seat, and held his deep green gaze. "Okay, so I'm most pissed about the fact that you did this without telling me, without asking for my opinion. I get that it's your body, and you have the final say on what happens with it. But my opinion should matter to you. The fact that it doesn't hurts. The fact that you didn't want me to be there hurts. The fact that you hid this from me for five days hurts. And I feel incredibly guilty at the fact that I was too wrapped up in my own worries to seriously question why you'd go so long without sex. I should have known something wasn't right."

"Stop." Anguish darkened his eyes and twisted his features. "No beating yourself up. You have some serious shit going on, clear and present danger to worry about." He took her hands in his. "I didn't mean to hurt you, Kat. Fuck, I knew you'd be pissed and surprised at first, but I hoped this would make you happy."

"Happy? You doing the dishes makes me happy. When you fold the laundry, it makes me happy. When you send me a text in the middle of the day that lets me know you were thinking of me, that makes me happy. When you hold me in your arms, that makes me happy. You do a million things every day that make me happy. Knowing that you don't value or respect my opinion—that doesn't make me happy." Sitting wasn't working. She wanted to punch something, maybe even Keith's balls. She leaped back to her feet and paced to the door that had a window overlooking the back yard. She heard him approach and saw his reflection in the darkened glass.

"I'm sorry." He touched her lightly, resting his hands on her shoulders. "Kat, I love you more than I thought it was possible to love another person."

She inhaled, fighting the red clouds tingeing her vision, and she responded to the raw emotion of his confession. He'd begun by telling her that he wanted her to have everything her heart desired. "I know you do."

His grip tightened, and he whirled her to face him. "I didn't do this to hurt you."

She focused on the midpoint of his tie, noting that he'd chosen a blue one today. "I know that too."

"I want to get you pregnant."

Once she'd fantasized about having his babies, but after she'd found out it wasn't possible, she'd stopped. And then Angelina and Corey had come into their lives, and she'd stopped thinking about it altogether. "We have two children already, Keith. I don't know that I want more."

"But now you might have a choice."

"Might?"

His shoulder lifted and fell. "I won't know if the surgery was successful for four-to-six months. Even then, it could be difficult to conceive. It's likely I'll have a low sperm count, so we might have to try insemination. I could also have sperm harvested, which increases the likelihood of pregnancy."

A host of feelings pummeled her. She closed her eyes to beat them into submission. "Keith, can we agree that, unless it's a life-or-death emergency, neither of us will ever have surgery without the full knowledge and consent of the other?"

"Yes." With one finger under her chin, he tilted her face to his.

She wasn't going to let him play the Dom card, not during this discussion. "How long until we can have sex again?"

"Another week. I have a follow-up exam scheduled for the Monday after next."

That was more than a week away, but she wasn't going to point that out. "You'd better put condoms on the shopping list. We're going to be using a lot more of them." Currently they only used them for anal sex.

"Yeah. Sure." He seemed disappointed that she wasn't over the moon about the idea of giving birth.

She decided to address that head-on. "Do you really think I was dragging my feet about the wedding because you couldn't get me pregnant?"

"Can you honestly say that's not a factor?" He lifted both eyebrows.

"We have two kids, Keith. I love them with every fiber of my being. I love being there for them. I love watching them learn and grow. I love that I can give them the time and attention they need." She set her fingertips on his cheek. "They're more than I ever wanted. When you told me that you couldn't father children, I was surprised but not upset.

Michele Zurlo

I wasn't sure I wanted kids at all. I don't regret that Angelina and Corey came into our lives, but that doesn't mean I want more."

He sucked on his lower lip as he studied her. His hands slid from her shoulders to her hips. "Maybe not right now, but that doesn't mean a few years from now you'll feel the same way."

It didn't mean she wouldn't. Then something that should have been obvious hit her over the head. "Keith, do you want more children?" Becoming a parent had healed many of Keith's emotional scars.

He glanced away. "Not if you don't."

She wasn't going to let him be evasive. "Keith, do you want more children?"

He let go of her waist, and she grabbed his wrists so he wouldn't put distance between them.

"Keith, be honest."

"Yeah. I do." His hand hovered over her abdomen, but shades of doubt flashed through his eyes. "But I understand if you don't."

His confession rocked her to the core. When Angelina and Corey had first appeared on her radar, she'd gone through great lengths to get him to agree to see the kids, both of whom had been in foster care at the time. Though he'd embraced his role as a father, that attitude change had not happened overnight.

This new desire of his hadn't happened quickly. Keith was thoughtful and deliberate with most things, and part of her was surprised that she hadn't known about this shift in his thinking.

"It's not that I don't," she said after a long silence. "I don't know, Keith. I don't have an answer for you either way."

The thing that scared her most was the idea she'd lose him if she ultimately decided that two kids were enough. Or, if she didn't lose him, would this cause a rift? Would that rift tear them apart, or would it form a crack that would always be between them, a subtle resentment that would stain their relationship? She didn't know, and no amount of discussion could allay her fear because even though he'd said he was okay with whatever she decided, the fact remained that he'd gone ahead with the procedure and that he purposely hadn't told her about it.

Usually a talk with Keith left her feeling closer to him. This time, it seemed like a gulf stretched between them.

He didn't like it either. Enveloping her in his arms, he murmured reassurances into her hair.

Chapter 13

Keith backed into the tiny parking spot while Kat stuck the stub indicating that he'd paid the lot fee in the front window. He cut the engine and stared straight ahead. The late afternoon sun set the city of Detroit ablaze, highlighting the mingling of old and new architecture. The newer buildings were huge behemoths of glass and steel, bright lights breaking the monotony of reflective black glass. Flashy and young, they screamed for attention, but nothing they did could compete with the stately majesty of the buildings that harkened back to a time when craftsmanship and elegance defined style.

Throngs of people were out enjoying the sunny Saturday afternoon. They meandered down the street, shopping, laughing, eating, and enjoying the fountains, chessboard tables, and outdoor seating. Off Woodward, on the outskirts of this revitalized area, The Leland, a hotel and bistro, had a club in the back that catered to BDSM. They had agreed to host an educational seminar series run by area experts. Malcolm and Darcy were scheduled to demonstrate basic rope bondage techniques. Liam, Jed, and Tru were set to talk about negotiating safe, sane, and consensual guidelines for kinky play. The Domme who owned the club planned to demonstrate flogging techniques, and a sub they didn't know was giving a talk billed as, "things all persons who play with a female partner need to know."

Keith had worked that morning, and Kat had roped Vina into going to a water park with her and the kids. They hadn't really talked since the night before. Though they'd settled everything, it felt unfinished to Keith, perhaps because there hadn't been time to dominate her since then.

"You're quiet today. Are you tired?" Half of him wanted that to be the reason it felt like something was dividing them.

"A little. I'll be fine." She unlatched her seat belt. She wore the outfit he'd selected, a black, silky half camisole that hung loose over her breasts but hugged her ribs. Her black pants tapered at the ankle, and she'd paired them with strappy black heels. It wasn't necessarily a kinky style, but it was classy and elegant, like Kat.

He'd chosen jeans and a plain black shirt. Around his waist, he wore a thick black leather belt that Kat had bought for him. He unlatched his seat belt as well, but when Kat went to open her door, he set a restraining hand on her thigh.

She looked at him, a simple question in her eyes.

"Are we okay?"

She didn't pretend to not know what he was talking about. "We're okay."

He loved that she didn't play games, but he didn't quite buy her line. "Are you sure? Last night was—" He broke off, not sure how to describe it. They'd agreed on a hard limit, but the issue didn't feel resolved.

"It was a lot." Her voice was soft, submissive, and her dark eyes delved into his depths. "It's going to take me some time to come to terms with it all."

He'd known it wasn't quite water under the bridge, but hearing her confirm it hit him in the gut. "Do you want to talk about it?"

She shook her head, managing to appear both strong and fragile. "We talked. We came to an understanding. I know you want to do something to make it right, but there's nothing you can do. I just need time."

As a man of action, sitting back and waiting didn't suit him. But forcing the issue would cause more harm than good. She needed time, and it was his responsibility to give it to her. He held her gaze, and he ceded to her request. "I'll give you whatever you need."

"Thank you." She twisted to face him. "I love you, Keith. That hasn't changed."

He leaned over and brushed his lips over hers. Sparks kindled something he couldn't finish. She yielded to him, softening and opening her mouth to invite him deeper. He took solace in the sweetness of her submission. When it ended, he traced her lips with the pad of his thumb. "I brought a collar for you to wear tonight."

"No." She didn't hesitate.

"No?" He arched a brow, and his caress stuttered. "I don't recall giving you a choice."

"A collar is always a choice."

"At an event like this, it's for your safety. It tells the others that you're taken." Ire and frustration battled with residual pain and guilt. Why would she refuse such a simple protection?

A sad smile jerked at the corner of her mouth before dissipating. "I'm sure you'll tell the others that I'm taken." She lifted her left hand. "I also have an engagement ring, in case anyone should get ideas while you're in the restroom."

He wanted to argue, but after last night, he wasn't certain of his position. Then he noticed Erica and Burke coming toward them, and he tabled his objection for another time. "They're here."

They'd met the pair at the venue instead of driving together in case it turned out this kind of event wasn't palatable to either of them. Kat had shared Erica's misgivings with him, and he already had a negative opinion of Burke.

She exhaled. "Here goes nothing."

Keith steeled himself for this encounter. Normally attending a seminar like this would be relaxing and fun. However, for Kat's career, he could get through socializing with a dressed-up piece of trash. "I'm not going to punch him."

She laughed, a lighthearted sound that was balm to his soul, and at that moment, he relaxed.

They emerged from his SUV as Erica and Burke made it to them. They'd dressed casually, following Kat's suggestion for them to stick to dark colors. Erica wore a tasteful black mini-dress, and Burke's version of dressing down meant he wore black slacks with a black-and-red polo shirt. Keith wanted to find something negative about it, but the man actually looked good.

Erica hugged Trina. "Thanks for inviting us. You look fabulous. I love that shirt."

"Thanks," Kat said, "Keith picked it out."

Erica turned her polished smile on him. "You have great taste. It's good to see you again." She stepped forward to hug him, but Kat stopped her.

"You can't hug a Dom who isn't yours without permission."

"Oh?" Erica frowned. "I thought we weren't doing protocol. You talked to me without permission."

"I had permission," Kat said. "When we're inside, hang back with me and let Keith introduce us all."

Burke's expression soured, not that it had been pleasant before. "We're not his subs."

"No," Keith agreed. "But you're my guests. You're there because I vouched for you. Everything you do reflects on me." He held up a finger, indicating Burke should wait. "I have something for you."

He extracted an envelope from his pocket and handed it to Burke. From the man's demeanor, he guessed that his cousin had not shared the test results. Burke took the envelope, opened it, and read the contents. His frown turned to a scowl.

"She swore to me that you were the father." His lips thinned. "Her son has blond hair and green eyes."

Keith had no recollection of Burke's cousin, so he had no idea what she looked like. Genetically it was probable that green eyes were on her side as well. He knew a family of brown-eyed brunettes who had one daughter with blonde hair and green eyes. It turned out the trait was recessive on both sides. "Maybe she has a type."

"It bothers me that you don't remember her name." Burke handed the papers back, and Keith threw them in his car before locking it up.

Erica whirled, finger poised. "Stop. I told you to be nice. I explained that Keith had changed from back then, and you know your cousin is an opportunistic little whore. So, stop. This is not an issue."

Based on that exchange, Keith put another tick mark in the "Erica is a Domme" column. A submissive, even an untrained one, wouldn't confront anyone like that. Back when they'd been just friends, if Kat had needed to say something like that to him, she would have moved them out of hearing distance from anyone else, and she would have phrased it nicer, a request instead of an order.

Kat slid her hand around his biceps, assuming the position he desired for them to enter and move around an establishment.

Burke dipped his head, acknowledging Keith. "I'm sorry. It's just that I was so sure she was telling the truth."

"Well you have proof that she was mistaken. Now perhaps she can track down the actual father, who might want to know he has a son in the world." Keith summoned a neutral smile to let the man know that he wasn't holding a grudge. He indicated the door to the establishment, an unassuming industrial door on the side of the hotel. "Shall we?"

Erica assumed a spot on the other side of Kat. "Do we have to do protocol stuff?"

"No, but you do have to respect that others will. Let Keith handle introductions. That'll make things easier. Most of the people there know we're bringing newbie guests, so you shouldn't get nasty looks if you forget to wait for a Dom's permission before speaking to their sub."

Keith held the door for them. Kat waited inside.

The club didn't look like much at first, just a wide marble staircase that probably used to be the employee entrance.

"This whole place has a naughty feel," Burke murmured. "The walls are painted black."

Re/Captured

Erica giggled. "Your idea of naughty is painting the walls black?"

"Seems like." For the first time since they'd met, Burke let down his guard. The grin he gave Erica denoted affection and playfulness.

At the top of the stairs, a spacious lobby greeted them. Decorated like a waiting room for a tech company, it had chairs arranged in two square patterns. In the center of each was a table with magazines spread over them, and televisions were mounted in two spots on the walls.

They hadn't been there before together, but Keith had frequented this place regularly prior to it closing down for a few years. It had reopened under new management, but he hadn't made the time to return.

A curvy brunette greeted them. She was about the same height as Kat, but her dominant presence made her seem bigger, almost larger than life. She wore a bustier top that barely contained her ample bosom, a leather skirt that was slit up both sides, and thigh-high leather boots. Excitement burst from her in tangible waves, and when she smiled, it revealed the depth of her beauty. In contrast to her energy, a lanky redhead who radiated calm waited at her side. He was dressed in tight leather shorts and tennis shoes. A complicated Shibari rope pattern crisscrossed his chest, and he sported a thick leather slave collar on his neck.

"Welcome to our first seminar evening in over a decade. I'm Mistress L, the owner of this fine establishment, and this is my subbie and husband, Ryan."

Keith liked her immediately, and he knew Kat would as well. He offered his hand. "Keith Rossetti." They shook, the firm kind that dominant types used with each other. "This is my sub and fiancé, Trina Legato, and these are our guests, Erica and Burke."

"Thank you for coming. Please have a seat. Ryan will go over house rules, and then he has some forms for you to sign." She motioned to the first grouping of chairs, and then she peered around them. "Welcome. I'm so glad you could make it."

Keith turned to see Dustin and Layla. He wore leathers with a white shirt, and she wore a simple jeans and cotton shirt combination. Keith guessed that Layla's outfit was either under that, or she planned to change inside.

More greetings happened, and it was clear that Dustin and Layla had met Mistress L and Ryan before. It made sense. A good seminar meant planning had to happen and people had to meet, and Dustin was going to demonstrate electro-play.

Dustin and Layla joined them, as did two other couples. They chatted amiably until Ryan came over with a stack of clipboards.

"So, I have a short spiel and some paperwork. Normally we're a members-only club, but we've opened it up today to host this seminar. This first form is a liability waiver. This establishment isn't responsible for any injuries that might occur as a result of play, and any equipment you use is at your own risk." He handed around clipboards. Each had the liability waiver and a pen attached.

Keith scanned the document, and then he looked at Kat. "I'm officially consulting my lawyer."

She laughed. "It's a standard liability waiver. No surprises. Basically if you swing from the rafters and fall, you can't sue them."

He lifted a brow. "You say that like people here wouldn't swing from the rafters."

"If you'll pardon my interruption?" Ryan waited for Keith's permission to address him. "We have a reinforced area for suspension bondage. An inexperienced rigger would present the most danger. We have mats on the floor, but a fall is a fall."

Kat's eyes sparkled with excitement. "I'm looking forward to that—the demonstration, not possible injury. If you don't mind me saying, your corselet is quite stunning."

He stroked the knotted designs on his chest. "Thank you. Mistress was practicing earlier, and we both liked it too much to take it off just yet."

She signed the release, and Keith followed suit.

Once everyone had signed, Ryan went over the rules. Since they weren't applying for membership, most of the equipment was off limits. For members, use of some equipment could be scheduled.

"Please remember that this evening is about education. If you're new to BDSM, ask questions. Each demonstration will include a question-and-answer portion. Please don't feel self-conscious. Everyone started out as new, and we want to encourage practices that follow SSC and RACK guidelines. Always play responsibly. And if you're not new to BDSM, still ask questions. It's impossible to be an expert in everything, but it is possible to keep learning."

Keith looked to Erica and Burke. "SSC stands for 'Safe, Sane, and Consensual,' and RACK means 'Risk-Aware Consensual Kink.' Everything that happens is by mutual consent, and all parties involved are charged with educating themselves on the dangers."

He indicated their clipboards. "The remaining form is a contract that states you will abide by the rules of the club, including following all directions and heeding the monitors. Failure to do so will result in your immediate removal."

Erica raised her hand.

Ryan lifted his chin. "Yes?"

"If we're not in the lifestyle, do we still call people by title?"

"The monitors will all go by 'Master' or 'Mistress.' Think of it like addressing your teacher as 'mister' or 'miss.' For other Dommes and Doms, our protocol is to use their first name. Unless they're your dominant, then it's whatever you've agreed upon."

Burke raised a finger, indicating he had a question.

"Yes?" Ryan accepted signed papers from those who'd done so as he called on Burke.

"What about the subs?"

"Never speak to a sub unless you have permission from his or her dominant, and do not approach unattached subs." He nodded to Keith. "If you have questions, direct them to Keith or a monitor. They'll help you with protocols."

Keith liked that this place had rules to protect subs. Whether male or female, subs could find themselves the target of unwelcome advances. He checked with Kat before signing.

Burke snorted. "It's like you're the sub and she's the Dom."

Determined not to let Burke get under his skin, Keith gritted his teeth. "Or it's like she's a brilliant lawyer and I trust her counsel."

Erica subtly kicked Burke. "As you have no doubt noticed, gender doesn't determine whether one is a dominant or a submissive."

"Statistically men are more likely to identify as submissive," Ryan offered. "And many people switch."

Keith filled in the blanks and signed his name. Ten minutes later, he found himself inside the great chamber. A man wearing a shirt that proclaimed him as a monitor greeted them. Like Ryan, he was built like a runner. He had short blond curls and stylish, rectangular glasses.

He flashed a brief smile. "Hey, you made it this far. Locker rooms are here." He pointed to the right and left. "Doms to the right, subs to the left. If you require a private changing room, there are three along that wall." He pointed behind them. "Lockers and cubbies are not monitored. What else? Oh, there's no dress code for the seminar, except that you have to wear clothes."

The instructions made sense to Keith. BDSM clubs often had dress codes for Doms and subs that relied heavily on fetish wear. While that wasn't required tonight, they didn't want people walking around naked. Layla went into the changing room for subs, and Dustin waited with them.

Keith glanced at Burke and Erica. "I assume you're not planning to change?"

Erica shook her head. "Unless we're peeling things off, this is what we're wearing."

A few minutes later, Layla emerged wearing a blue lace shirt that only had solid fabric where a bra might have been located. The red collar on her neck stood out in stark contrast to the midnight blue. On the bottom, she had changed into a matching skirt, thigh-high stockings, and ankle boots. Keith would have loved to see Kat in something like that, but he couldn't risk it. Even thinking about it caused his dick to jerk, and since he hadn't quite healed, a spike of pain traveled up his core.

Kat squeezed his arm. "Keith, are you hurting?"

"Little bit. Nothing I can't handle."

"Poor baby," she purred. "Serves you right for getting all hot and bothered because my cousin looks so tasty."

He leaned down and bit her earlobe. "Watch out, Kitty Kat. I might not be able to fuck you, but I can punish you. I was imagining you in that outfit, and now I'm planning all the ways I'm going to make you pay for that remark once I'm cleared."

She shivered. "I'm looking forward to it."

It did not escape his notice that she wasn't calling him by title. Unfortunately he had never required her to use his title. According to their terms, she could use it if she wanted. When they were first together, he'd used it to put distance between them, but since that time, it had come to represent their close bond. He hated that he couldn't require her to use it, but he was definitely going to bring it up at their next negotiation. That, and the collar. It rankled that she'd refused the collar.

They wandered around, checking out the vendor displays. Kat stopped in front of a violet wand display. Though Dustin was a fan of electricity-based sex toys, Keith had not tried them.

He watched her face as she read the materials and listened to the spiel. "They're super easy to use, and we have detailed instructions on our website. We'll be back here in October to do a full demo."

Nothing in her expression denoted anything but polite interest. Just in case, Keith asked, "Are you interested in this kind of play?"

"I'm not sure." She considered a starter kit. "Have you ever used one?"

"No, but I can learn."

Kat smiled politely at the vendor. "Maybe another time."

"Excuse us," he said to Erica and Burke who had agreed to watch a small demo of the violet wand. He led Kat a few feet away, and he loomed over her, invading her personal space. "Kat, stop pouting."

Her gaze jerked to meet his. "I'm not pouting."

"I said I can learn to use one. I've seen demos, and I know Jordan likes to use a violet wand, and Dustin does as well. My lack of experience with it shouldn't be a consideration."

Electricity crackled between them and gathered in her eyes. "I know. Both Amy and Layla have told me stories. I'm just not interested."

"Oh. Then what's wrong?"

"Nothing's wrong."

"You're quiet and withdrawn."

She sighed, an exasperated noise. "Fine. I don't like Burke. I didn't like his question about talking to subs, and I didn't like the way he looked at Layla when she changed. And he keeps eyeballing the people here. A minute ago, he was staring at Mistress L's cleavage. There's something in his tone that rubs me wrong. He gives me the creeps. But I'm trying to ignore it for you and because I like Erica, but I don't like him, Keith. I don't like having him here. I don't want him to see Darcy get tied up because I love Darcy, and he's a creep."

Keith blinked. Her response was completely unexpected. Perhaps his instincts about Burke had been accurate and not a response to the misunderstanding. "You think he'll do something to Darcy?"

"He's more likely to say something to her or stare at her chest."

"If he does, Mal and I will take him behind the woodshed and teach him some manners." Though his tone was light, he wasn't kidding.

"You can't," she said. "He's Erica's fiancé."

"Maybe we can introduce her to someone else?"

Kat laughed, a quiet exhalation that felt like a reprieve. "Come on. Let's get back to them. The mystery talk is about to begin."

Keith called to Burke and Erica. "Are you ready to find out what every person who has sex with a vagina needs to know?"

"Sure," Burke grinned. "I'm all about the vagina."

Past the vendor tables, the large room was divided by tall partitions. Each cubicle was the size of a regular room, and they were equipped with basic dungeon equipment. There was variety based on the fetish, but most were places where masochists met the business end of a flogger. Past the cubicles was a long, rectangular area. Folding chairs were set up in rows, and at the far end, a white projection screen hung on a frame. The title slide simply read, "Pussy."

The area was fairly full, and they couldn't find four seats together, so Keith and Kat sat one row back from their guests. He rested his arm on the back of her chair and played with her hair.

The lights dimmed, and from the front, they heard someone say, "Is this thing on? There it is. Thank you, Mistress." The submissive that had conducted their brief orientation stood in front of the screen, the shadow of his slim body blocking a slice of the title screen. "Hi, everybody. Some of you know me, some of you met me earlier, and some of you have no clue who I am. My name is Ryan. I belong to Mistress L. This educational seminar is for anyone who has a vagina, anyone who owns a vagina, and anyone who is lucky enough to serve one who owns a vagina."

Nervous laughter tittered through the crowd.

"If you're a guy who is only into guys, you're welcome to stay, but you probably won't find anything too relevant in this talk. We're doing the penis at our October seminar, so at least you have something to look forward to." He glared at someone in the front row. "Yeah, I ended a sentence with a preposition. Get over it."

Ryan knew his place. He was Mistress L's sub and no one else's.

A single tall stool was set up front. Ryan slid onto it. "It has always struck me as ironic that most straight men, when confronted with nonsexual pussy issues, cover their ears and run for the exit. The pussy is a many splendored thing. I'll get to the sex stuff eventually, but I'd like to start with something that's actually more important."

He stopped to look around.

"Health. A healthy pussy can do great things. It has orgasms and births babies."

Keith had been steadily stroking Kat's arm with his thumb, and so he noticed that she stiffened at the mention of babies. His caress stuttered, and he forced himself to regain the rhythm as Ryan went over the basics of the female reproductive system, pointing them out on the next few slides.

"Like a woman herself, the pussy is complicated, which is one of the reasons we love it. But when things are complicated, problems can arise. Endometriosis, for example, can make for painful periods. It can make it harder to conceive, and it can also make orgasm painful. If the vagina in your care experiences pain during orgasm, that's a warning sign. Always heed the warning signs. Don't listen to her when she says it's not that bad. Most women have an incredible capacity for tolerating all kinds of pain and discomfort, and they often will ignore their own pain even when they're extra sensitive to the pain of others."

Keith studied Kat as she watched the presenter and listened to what he said. In the dimness and reflected light, her olive skin seemed to glow. As if his stare had physical presence, she turned her head to meet his eyes. She searched his face for something, but after a few seconds, disappointment flashed across her face. She resumed watching the presentation.

Keith did as well. He learned things about menstruation he'd never known, like the fact that Kat was most likely to conceive twelve to fifteen days after the first day of her last period.

"There's no reason to avoid sex during her period. Some women experience larger and more prolonged orgasms during this time." Ryan smiled blissfully and sighed. "Just have some old towels handy."

Laughter rippled through the audience.

"And if she says she isn't in the mood, I recommend making sure her favorite chocolate is on hand. I like to make tea for Mistress and kneel at her feet while she drinks it. Sometimes ice cream and cuddling works better. Know she's more likely to be tired, so make sure she gets enough sleep. Whether she's your sub or your Domme, she's your world, and it's your job to give her what she needs."

Keith glanced at Kat. She was his world, and right now, his world seemed lost on the other side of the galaxy.

"So now let's talk about the female orgasm. I have to admit that I'm jealous of all the ways women can experience pleasure. Did you know that one percent of women can climax from having their breasts stimulated? It's rare, for sure. Whether your woman can or not, breast stimulation plays an important role in preparing for sex. Guys, women need foreplay. Biologically, they need it."

Burke turned to look back at them, a salacious smile marring his face. "This whole night is foreplay."

Not wanting to encourage him, Keith lifted his chin in acknowledgment. Kat's gaze didn't flicker from the presentation, but he noted the mulish slant to her lips. He couldn't remember the last time Kat had disliked anyone this much, not even the colleague who had turned out to be a stalker.

When the talk concluded, Darcy and Amy came over to them. Or, more specifically, to talk to Kat. Darcy's huge smile almost split her face in half. The two subs stood in front of him, eyes lowered, asking for permission to speak.

"Hi, Darcy. Hi, Amy. How are you both?"

Michele Zurlo

"Great," Amy said. "Can we borrow Trina for a few minutes?"

"Yeah, sure. Stay in sight." While he liked having a visual on Kat because she was so spectacularly beautiful, he was reluctant to let her get too far away physically. The emotional distance was almost more than he could bear.

Erica stood and stretched. "This place is really interesting. I'd love to look around."

A man wearing a Monitor shirt was passing by. Upon overhearing Erica, he stopped. "A tour is starting in five minutes. It's the best way to see everything." He pointed to a group of people standing near the screen. "Meet up there."

Burke spread his hands wide. "What do you think? Want to go on a tour?"

Keith did not want to leave Kat, and he knew she wouldn't want to go with them. While these were their guests, they'd be with a monitor and unlikely to get in trouble. "Not this time. I'll meet you back here."

They left, and he was alone for all of ten seconds. Malcolm took the chair Kat had vacated. He slid down and settled back, and his knee slowly wagged back and forth.

"Hey. What's Darcy so excited about?"

"Bachelorette party. Amy got a deal on cupcakes and sex toys."

Because their weddings were scheduled so close together, Kat and Layla were sharing a bachelorette party. He and Dustin and their friends had tickets to see the Tigers play. Being an alcoholic made social events a little difficult. A server came by, her tray full of colorful shots in test tubes. He'd been sober for ten years, four months, and six days, yet he could feel the sweet burn of a vodka shot sliding down his throat and settling in his stomach.

"Keith? Buddy? Are you okay?"

"Fine." His reply came automatically.

"Really? Because I can't remember the last time I saw you look at a drink like that."

He wasn't going to pretend he hadn't been lusting after a taste. "Addiction doesn't go away."

Mal was silent for a second. His best friend had been there for the worst of it. He'd staged an intervention, and he'd been the one who'd tapped into Keith's desire for a better life. He'd been there, a staunch cheerleader, from the beginning of his sobriety. "Do you need to talk to your sponsor? Or me? I'm willing to listen."

He met Malcolm's concerned gaze. "I'm not going to drink."

"Okay. Then do you want to tell me why you look like someone has kicked your puppy?" At Keith's look of confusion, Malcolm continued. "Most people wouldn't see it, I think. You're adept at hiding your emotions, but I'm your best friend. I know you, man. I know something's wrong."

Keith shook his head. "It'll be fine." Now he sounded like Kat, refusing to admit there was a problem that neither of them knew how to fix.

Malcolm scanned the room with the casual watchfulness of a trained agent even though he was no longer with the FBI. "You and Trina are having problems."

"Not problems. Just a—" Could he call it a disagreement? They hadn't really fought. He shook his head. "I can't talk to you about this."

Tracing the side seam of his leathers with his thumb, Malcolm didn't meet his gaze. "Yes, you can."

Keith distinctly remembered Malcolm telling him that if he hurt his sister, nobody would find the body. "She's upset enough. I don't need that from you too."

"For fuck's sake, Keith. I'm your friend. Maybe at first I struggled with the two of you together, but I don't anymore. I've had time to come to terms with it." He clapped Keith on the back. "What did you guys fight about?"

Before Kat, Keith didn't hesitate to tell Malcolm everything. Of course, before Kat, Keith hadn't cared enough to let a woman's emotions affect him. Taking a chance his friend wouldn't kill him for hurting his sister's feelings, Keith exhaled hard. "I had my vasectomy reversed."

A wide grin broke out on Malcolm's face. "Good for you."

"Yeah. Kat wasn't pleased. She says she doesn't want more kids. Also she was upset that I didn't tell her about the surgery until five days later." He bit his lip. "I think she was more upset about me not telling her about the surgery beforehand."

Malcolm frowned as he thought. After a few moments had passed, he scratched his arm. "Yeah, okay. I can see where she'd be pissed about that. It's surgery. Any time you go under anesthesia, you take a risk. Especially if you're an addict. Trina is a worrier. She would have wanted to sit in the waiting room and worry about you."

Knowing that's exactly what she would have done was one of the reasons Keith hadn't told her. "She's not pouting about that, though. She lit into me about that, and then she negotiated an agreement to tell each other about all surgeries and medical stuff."

"Seems like people who are in a serious relationship automatically share that kind of information." Malcolm rubbed his jaw. "Unless it's an emergency."

"You're not really helping." Keith watched Kat throw back her head as she laughed, and then she grabbed Darcy's arm as she responded.

"She's hurt."

"I'm aware. I apologized—several times."

"There's a bigger issue here." Malcolm shifted to face him. "You're the center of her world."

"And she's the center of mine. I did this for her, Mal. Every fucking day I watch her be the best mother in the world to two kids she never expected to have. Her love for them is selfless and unconditional. Then I saw her with other kids, babies like Zella, and it hit me that deciding to get a vasectomy robbed her of the chance to have kids of her own. And it robbed me of the chance to give them to her." Keith ground his teeth to avoid showing too much emotion. Mal was right about his inability to let people see his vulnerabilities. "She said that Angie and Corey were enough. She said she isn't sure she wants more kids." Her admission still stabbed at his heart.

Malcolm shrugged it off. "I wouldn't get all bent out of shape about that. If I remember correctly, one of her diary entries consisted of names she'd picked out for your children. She had contingency plans for between two and four kids."

Keith chuckled. "If she knew you read her diary, she'd kill you."

"She'd get over it pretty quickly." Malcolm slapped Keith's thigh. "But you're missing the big picture. You can't see the forest for the trees. This is why you have me. Trina's not hurt about any of that. She's hurt because you made a major decision without discussing it with her. She wouldn't expect you to ask permission, but the fact that you acted without consulting her is what hurts. She lives to serve you, and you made her feel irrelevant. If you wanted to surprise her, get flowers, not a vasovasectomy."

Narrowing his eyes and pressing his lips together, Keith regarded Malcolm with undisguised malice. "She told you already."

"Nope. I know you, and I know my sister. Now, what are you going to do about it?"

He exhaled hard. "Give her time. She asked for time." He hated having to give her time. It was selfish, but he wanted things back to the way they were.

Malcolm rolled his eyes and sat back in his chair. "You've always been unbelievably clueless when it comes to women."

"She was very clear about what she wanted."

"But what she needs is to know she's relevant to you. She needs to know she's the center of your world."

Keith shifted. His balls were sore, and wearing jeans for this long had been a mistake. "I can't have sex for another week."

"But you can scene with her. You can show her that she hasn't lost her place in your heart."

Scenes turned him on. It would be a punishment for him to not be able to find completion. Also, having his best friend back—fully—lightened a burden he hadn't realized he was carrying. "You're right."

"Of course I'm right."

"Women are complicated." Keith laughed. "I had this done for her. I had a paternity test done for her. I had her mend fences with the Kenyons for the benefit of her career. I want to have more kids with her. How in the world does she come away from that with the notion that she's irrelevant to me? For fuck's sake—she's the only thing that matters."

"Not to mention that you gave up a promotion for her."

He hadn't told her that he'd turned down the offer to move to Counterintelligence and work under Rafael Torres. It seemed so long ago. At first he'd put off telling her, and then with the wedding planning, this opportunity to convince a senator to nominate her for District Court, and the murders, he'd forgotten all about it.

He opened his mouth to say that it wasn't a big deal, but he noticed two women standing behind them. He swiveled to get a better look, and that's when he saw the mutinous slant of Kat's lips.

"Kat, I didn't see you come back."

Her eyebrow arched, an invitation to a fight. "You turned down the job at CI?"

Malcolm coughed. "You didn't tell her? Oh, man. You are fucked." He stood up. "Come on, Darcy. This argument doesn't need an audience."

Michele Zurlo

Chapter 14

Anger vibrated her insides so hard it hurt. Coming after the bomb he'd dropped on her last night, this was more than she could take.

"Kat, we can talk about this later."

All this time, she thought he was transitioning. Leaving WCCU meant he needed to close as many cases as he could, and she knew he was in the middle of two very large fraud investigations. He hadn't said anything to the contrary, so she'd assumed it was a done deal.

No words came to mind. For someone who spent her entire day dealing with them, words had always come easily. Right now, she couldn't even find the right word to identify her emotions. Without uttering a single sound, she turned and stalked away. The need to get away didn't need a noun to identify it.

Most of the seminar was taking place in the back of the establishment, so the front, where the lobby and locker rooms were located, was almost devoid of people. An iron hand closed around her arm, whirling her around and halting her progress. She met the flashing green steel of his ire head-on.

"Where the fuck are you going?"

"Home." Ah—a word showed up. That was progress.

"Really? I have the car keys."

She held out her hand. He could get a ride home from Dustin and Layla. They lived fairly close.

He hauled her to him, crushing her hand between them. "You're not leaving. We have guests here, guests who need to have a positive experience while they're here. Guests who need to like you a lot more than they need to like me. If you're not here, then we're losing an opportunity."

She pushed against him, but he didn't budge. "Then I'll stay. You leave."

"We're both staying. We will both attend events together. You will behave, or you will be punished."

Blinking, she almost floundered under the onslaught of words that assailed her. The dam was well and truly broken. "I'll be punished? Because I'm the one who keeps secrets in this relationship? I'm the one who makes major life decisions without discussing them with the other? I'm the one who so stubbornly insists that I need to be a judge even though I'm planning a wedding, working, parenting, and hoping a murderer doesn't send more gruesome bouquets? God, I sound like a real jackass." She inhaled sharply. "Oh, wait. I'm describing you."

"That's one, Kat." His voice was deceptively soft, velvet over iron, and it shattered her tirade.

"One what?"

"Punishment. I am your Master, and you cannot speak to me like that. I'll make an allowance for the fact that you're surprised and upset, but that won't get you out of being punished."

She fought his hold, not caring that doing so would leave handprint bruises on her arms. "Let go of me." She pushed against his chest and clawed at his hands.

"Stop struggling. I'm stronger than you, Kitty Kat. You're going nowhere unless I say, and if you hurt yourself because you are so intent on disobeying me, you'll earn two more punishments instead of just one more."

Seething, she ceased fighting him, but that pent up energy didn't dissipate. "I feel like kicking you in the balls."

"Let's hope if it comes to that, you decide to safeword instead."

Her head shook, small movements that communicated the tenuous nature of the hold she had on her temper. "I can't believe you turned down that job. You wanted it, Keith. I know you did. I hate that you made me the reason you turned it down. My career isn't more important than yours."

"It is to me."

She met his gaze, noting his sadness, though it didn't deflate her fury. "It isn't to me."

"I know, Kat." His grip on her arms eased. "From the time you were in high school, you've wanted to be a judge. I wanted to be an FBI agent. My dream has come true—actually, more than I dared to dream has come true—but we're still working on yours. It may not seem important to you right now, but I know just how vital it is."

She wanted to stay mad at him. After all, he'd made yet another huge decision without consulting her. Yet most of her anger drained away like a balloon refusing to be tied. The place it had occupied was hollow, and it ached. Though Keith stood inches from her, it seemed like he wasn't really there.

Michele Zurlo

Her gaze fell with her temper. This was yet another thing he refused to discuss with her. In so many ways it felt like they were heading toward a divorce instead of a wedding.

"All right." Her voice came out so softly that she wasn't sure she'd spoken aloud. "I'll behave. I'll be a good submissive, and I'll make sure our guests enjoy the seminar."

Under other circumstances, Katrina would have enjoyed the demonstrations and being around people with similar kinky interests. But the harsh glare of too much heartache meant the whole thing felt pointless. She pasted a smile on her face and went through the motions, but inside part of her was dying.

Relief flowed through her at the end of the night when it was time to leave. They walked Erica and Burke partway to their car. Erica hugged Katrina. "Get some rest. We'll see you at the luncheon tomorrow."

Burke shook Keith's hand. "Thanks for inviting us. It was quite educational."

Once they headed off, Keith parked his hand on the small of her back. "Let's go home. You have two punishments waiting for you."

She couldn't summon the will to care, but the counselor in her was in the habit of arguing. "Wasn't having to stay there a punishment?"

He laughed as he opened her door. "No, Kitty Kat. It wasn't."

On the drive home, she was quiet. No thoughts nagged at her, but a general malaise had settled over her as she watched the city lights fly past.

Keith drove in silence for most of the ride, and then he started talking. "I'm happy with my job. I like what I do, and I'm good at it. Maybe going after people who embezzle money from towns and schools isn't glamorous, but it makes a difference. It makes a real difference to real people. It improves the lives of citizens and school children. I protect businesses, many of them small and locally owned, from financial threats. Sometimes I nail a violent offender, and sometimes the persons I hunt cross over into cybercrime, human trafficking, terrorism, and counterintelligence. I'm proud of the work I do. I'm proud of the man I am."

The lights lost their luster. She looked at him, noting the firm slant of his lips and the muscle ticking on the edge of his jaw. His eyes glittered hard in the reflection of light from oncoming traffic.

"I didn't want the promotion. I was flattered to be asked. Someone noticed the good work I do, and that's always nice. It would mean more pay, yes, but it would also mean longer hours. Right now my workload is manageable. I can be the best agent I know how to be, and I can still make it home most nights for dinner. I can take time to attend school events for my kids. These are my priorities—my family is the most important thing to me right now."

He kept his eyes on the road as he spoke, and the heat of his vehement tone chased away the worst of her melancholy. She watched him fall silent, but his defensive posture never changed.

"It would have been nice if you'd told me this weeks ago. I would have understood, Keith. I would have supported you in whatever decision you made."

"You've been busy. Preoccupied. You didn't ask."

Oh, he was not going to throw the blame on her. "I trusted you to tell me if your mind changed. The last conversation we had about this, you said you wanted the job, and I supported that decision. I know transitioning to a new department can take time. I figured that Lexee was having you close out most of your cases before you went to Counterintelligence."

He didn't respond as he parked his SUV in the garage. "Go inside. You have five minutes to do what you need to do in the bathroom, and then I want you to kneel at the foot of our bed with my belt in your mouth."

Katrina wasn't the kind of sub who misbehaved often. She expected him to spank her, but the addition of the belt surprised her. She wasn't the masochist in this relationship, and she did not relish being hit with his leather belt. He'd never done it before. The moment they were inside, he removed his belt and handed it to her.

Unable to summon the will to care, she took the belt upstairs. She undressed and used the facilities, and then she put her hair up in a ponytail. Kneeling, waiting for him, was a ritual that usually heightened the experience for her. This time it did nothing. She heard him enter the room, but her body failed to respond. When he touched her, she didn't have to counsel her body against swaying toward his hand.

After some time, he took the belt from where she had it clenched between her teeth. "Stand up. Bend over the side of the bed, legs spread, ass high. Rest your head and upper body on the bed, and fold your hands together behind your neck."

She got into position. It wasn't a new one for them, but when she stood like this, he usually fucked her. She knew that wasn't going to happen tonight.

"Why are you receiving this punishment?"

Michele Zurlo

"Because I spoke disrespectfully and I fought you when you tried to keep me from leaving."

"Correct. While I have you here, I am also going to warn you that if you ever walk away from me again, you may not sit for a week." The cool leather brushed across the skin of her bottom. "Do you understand, Kitty Kat?"

"Yes."

"Yes, what?"

"Yes, Keith. I understand that if I walk away from you again, you'll punish me for it."

He muttered something under his breath, but she didn't catch any of it. Then she felt the edge of the belt trace a path up one thigh and down the other. "This is going to hurt. Four for speaking disrespectfully and two for fighting me. Count them out."

The first hit seared her backside, though it wasn't nearly as bad as she'd thought it would be. If she'd been warmed up first, it might have been pleasurable. But she hadn't been warmed up, and it hurt. "One. Thank you, Keith."

She also knew it was driving him crazy that she wouldn't call him by title, but she couldn't bring herself to call him something so precious when part of her felt like he was a stranger.

The strikes came fairly close together, with him pausing long enough for her to count and thank him. Six didn't seem like much, but by the time he finished, the skin of her ass felt like it was on fire.

After the last one, she remained in place, waiting for permission to move. His cold touch skated over her heated flesh. "This is such a beautiful image. I think I might do this more often." He grabbed her ponytail and used it to pull her up. "You belong to me, Kitty Kat. You're mine." He cupped one cheek of her rear end, his fingers digging in. "This ass is mine." Then he reached around to squeeze her breast. "These are mine." Next he cupped her pussy, two fingers forcing into her dryness. "This pussy is mine." Then he forced his fingers into her mouth. "This mouth is mine."

He whirled her, the motion making her lose balance, and she fell on the bed, her sore ass catching the edge of the mattress. "You belong to me, Kat." He grasped her roughly by the arms and hauled her up so that her face was inches from his. "Body and soul, you're mine. Say it."

Shocked by his fierceness, some of her numbness faded. "I belong to you."

"Body and soul."

"All of me."

Re/Captured

He pressed his forehead to hers. "And I belong to you, Kat. All of me. I'm sorry I hurt you. I'm sorry I made big decisions without talking them through with you. You are my heart and soul, the reason I'm alive—really alive, not just going through the motions. I fucked up. I can't promise I won't fuck up again, but it'll be about different stuff."

Her insides thawed some more. She moved her hands slowly, caressing his chest and stopping when she framed his face. "I forgive you."

His lips devoured hers, an act of possession and dominance threaded together with an unbreakable ribbon of love. She melted in his embrace, her body quickening under his onslaught. His did as well, and he pressed growing evidence of his desire against her abdomen.

He broke away suddenly, grimacing as he doubled over.

"Keith? Are you okay? Did you tear your incision?" She fell to her knees and attacked the button on his pants.

He clapped his hands over hers. "Are you trying to kill me?"

"I want to check your incision site to make sure you haven't pulled a stitch. The last thing you want is for it to get infected."

"You're naked and on your knees, Kat. I'm trying to get the hard-on to go away, and everything you're doing is making it stay."

She got to her feet. "So, you're saying you find me attractive?"

He glowered. "Six smacks of the belt clearly were not enough."

"I'm not sure you could handle more."

The heat of his glare did not diminish. "In the dungeon. Now."

"Are you sure you're up for that kind of physical activity?" Words were clearly not failing her now. "You can't have sex for at least one more week, and I've never seen you in that room without an erection. You're going to hurt yourself, and then it'll be weeks and weeks before we can have sex. Don't ruin our honeymoon. It's already booked and paid for."

He straightened up, and his expression sent chills down her spine.

She pointed to the door. "I'll be in the dungeon awaiting your pleasure."

Kneeling on the thick floor pillow in the center of the dungeon, Katrina worried about Keith. Almost any activity he liked to do in this room involved a movement on the list of restrictions she'd found tucked into his medical file. He had restrictions on what he could lift, and he was supposed to be using ice on the swelling. As an addict, he wouldn't be taking painkillers stronger than Motrin, so he was bearing all that pain without the benefit of drugs.

Michele Zurlo

She took inventory of the dungeon, mentally cataloging all the things he couldn't do, and she wasn't left with much. It was taking him longer than usual to get down there, so she had time to map out all sorts of hazardous scenarios. She'd accidentally left the door open, and she realized it when she heard him coming down the stairs.

It closed, the latch catching this time, and he stopped in front of her. "Besides your safewords, the only things you're allowed to say tonight are yes, please, and Master. Got it?"

"Yes. Yellow."

"Kat, you can't safeword yet. We haven't even started."

"Yes, I can. Keith, I'm concerned about you. Please let me check to make sure you haven't pulled a stitch or worse."

"I checked. Set your mind at ease. It's fine."

"I can't help but think that you wouldn't tell me if there was a problem."

His lips pressed together. "I know. That's my fault for keeping things from you. I promised not to do that again, remember? That was about ten minutes ago."

Kneeling naked on the basement floor made it seem so much longer. "You also said you'd do different stupid things. I don't want this to be one of them."

He gripped her ponytail and forced her to meet his gaze. "I've never lied to you, Kat. When I tell you that I'm fine, trust that I'm not sugar-coating."

She accepted his reassurance. "Yes, Master."

"I've been lax with you in so many ways, and that's not good for either of us. Tonight I'm going to remind you of who you are to me. More than my friend, fiancé, lover, and mother of my children, you're my soul." He released her hair, but not her gaze. "You belong to me, and you've forgotten exactly what that means."

Her breath caught as she realized his ruthless intent.

"Get on the cross."

This was his, not hers. In all the time they'd played, he'd never tied her to the St. Andrew's Cross. As she approached the large, imposing structure, her knees trembled.

"Face me."

She turned, and he secured her arms and legs with the cuffs. Spread open, she waited for his next move.

It was a kiss. His tongue plunged into her mouth, taking over her senses and robbing her of breath. A sharp pinch on each nipple reminded her that his hands were free. She struggled against the pain as his kiss reminded her that he was in control.

When he finally broke the kiss, he pulled her nipples, stretching them past the point of comfort. A quiet squeak of protest escaped, and his sadistic grin widened. He released her nipples and went across the room to the cabinet housing all his toys. When he returned, he had nipple clamps in one hand and a velvet bag in the other. She watched the bag fearfully. It contained clothespins, and she hated the clothespins.

With her suitably distracted, she barely noticed the clamps tightening in place until he tugged on the chain connecting them. She winced, and he laughed. "I love the sounds you make, Kitty Kat."

Following the guidelines of her hard limit to the letter, he didn't put the clothespins on her breasts. He put them everywhere else. He lined them up on the soft flesh of her arms and inner thighs, and then he clipped them along the twin lines of her labia. Lastly he attached one to her clit. Her body was on fire, and she breathed against the pain. Such small things shouldn't hurt so much, but they did.

Next he produced a small flogger with few falls no more than five inches long. He lifted the chain connecting the nipple clamps and pulled until she moaned. Then he flogged her breasts, the falls landing with unerring accuracy on those tender globes. It stung. Unable to keep it inside, she cried out.

"Yes," he hissed. "I want to hear you."

She didn't know how long he tortured her breasts, but when he finished, he moved to the clothespins. Using the flogger like a whip, he hit each clothespin until he knocked it off her flesh. If she thought her body was on fire before, now it was an out-of-control blaze. He went after the ones on her arms and thighs first.

"Don't move," he warned as he took aim at the tiny vises on her labia. "The pussy is a wondrous thing."

Struggling not to wiggle—the cross didn't impede her hips from moving—she held her breath while he dislodged the clothespins there. Because she had more flesh there for them to grip, it took multiple tries even though he was good at hitting his target. When he came to the one on her clit, she cried out before he took aim.

He laughed, an evil chuckle that made her pussy weep, and let the flogger fly. The wave of pain competed with the endorphins flooding her body. She collapsed back against the cross, her chest heaving as she gulped air. He moved closer, angling his body to brush against hers and remind her that the nipple clamps were still attached.

She felt his breath on her neck as he pressed small kisses there, and then his teeth sank into her shoulder. Her hands flexed, fisting tighter to withstand the pressure. Then he kissed her shoulder and licked his way back to her ear.

"Kitty Kat, this body is my playground. It's mine to use however I want." He nipped her neck, a small pinch that definitely left a mark, and then he dropped to his knees. He spread her pussy lips wide, and then he kissed her clit. "This poor thing is in need of a workout."

He licked her cunt, moaning his enjoyment of her flavor. His tongue explored her folds, stroking the long legs of her clit from the nub to where it disappeared into her opening. She twisted her hips to give him a better angle, but he ignored the offer. This wasn't for her pleasure, but because he wanted a taste. His talented mouth licked and sucked, kissing her pussy the same way he kissed her mouth.

She was so close. "Please, Master."

He paused. "No orgasm, Kitty Kat. You're here for my pleasure, not yours." Then he sucked the tip of her clit into his mouth. An orgasm detonated in her core, and she cried out. He moaned, slurping her fluids as she came in his mouth. After her cry died away, he rocked back and stood up.

"Thank you, Master."

"That wasn't on your list of approved words, Kitty Kat, and you climaxed after I told you not to." Satisfaction blazed behind the steel in his eyes. "You've earned a punishment." He released the bindings holding her to the cross. "Go stand under the chains."

In the corner of the room, a set of chains was bolted to the main floor joist. Limping from being bound in one position while he tortured her, she made her way over.

Keith buckled leather cuffs on her wrists. "Some of this will be punishment, but all of it will be for my pleasure." He attached the snaps on the cuffs together, and then he lifted her arms over her head and attached her to a chain. It was at the perfect height because everything in here was made to fit her body.

He went to the cabinet and came back with two more items. One was a bondage collar with huge D rings sewn into it. The other was a big metal hook, a gift from Layla to Keith for his last birthday. The hook end had a bulb on the head so that it would easily penetrate her anus. He drizzled lube on the thing, and then he put it inside her ass. The metal nested between her butt cheeks, and he connected the top of the hook to the collar. Every time she moved, she would feel that thing.

The belt he'd used upstairs was back around his waist. He took it off, folded it in half, and a sinister smile tugged the corner of his mouth. "Have I told you how much I enjoy this belt?"

She wasn't gagged, and she wasn't going to make the mistake of saying something she shouldn't. She shook her head, the movement making the hook wiggle in her ass.

"Very much, Kitty Kat." He brushed a gentle kiss across her lips. Then he stepped back, lifted his arm, and brought the belt down on her thigh.

The chain left her flat-footed, and instinct had her trying to move away from the blow, but the move tugged at the hook and the belt landed a solid blow. He punished her by taking the belt to her thighs, ass, calves, and back. Her body danced on that hook. This punishment was wicked and humiliating, yet the undercurrent of sexual pleasure only grew.

When he tired of the belt, he snagged a flogger and went after her some more. Her skin was on fire, but the position and the hook kept her mind from taking flight. She writhed and cried, begging with a please-please-please mantra. So caught up in the misery, it took her a few moments to notice when he stopped.

Using his hand, he wiped tears from her cheeks. "Have you learned your lesson, Kitty Kat?"

Had she? Well, she'd learned something, but it may not have been what he'd sought to teach. "Yes, Master."

"And what was that? Tell me, Kitty Kat. For this you can use any words you want."

Her voice was raw, but she forced the words out. "I learned that I crave your ruthlessness. I learned that I need to be reminded exactly how much I belong to you."

If he was surprised, he hid it well. He stroked wisps of hair away from her face. "I love you, Kat, and I need this with you as much as you need this from me." His kiss was tender, unfurling a host of desperate emotions in her core.

He let go of her, but he didn't release her bonds. Instead he brought the high-powered wand vibrator over. She stared at the thing and considered her position. "Master, please."

Purposely misunderstanding her, he grinned. "I love when you beg." Then he set it against her clit. "You're going to have an orgasm, Kitty Kat. Actually you're going to have a few of them."

This vibrator hit her just right, and it didn't take long for her to orgasm. Keith, true to his Dominant nature, kept the vibrator in place. She fought it with a futile effort to move out of his reach, fucking the hook into her ass with every shift of her pelvis. He forced her over-stimulated pussy to a second orgasm, and then he set the wand aside.

He held her against him, stroking a hand up and down her back. Once she calmed, he unhitched the top of the hook from her collar and removed it from her ass. Her body relaxed as she waited for him to let her down. Instead of doing that, he went back to the cabinet. He returned with a tripod that had an attachment on the top to hold a dildo.

The tower of pleasure, as he called it, was another toy they'd only used once. He set it up under her. Then he lubed the dildo and slid it into her vagina. Once that was accomplished, he attached it to the stand.

He rolled the stool he used for the gynecologist table to where she stood, and he sat down. "Kitty Kat, I want to see you fuck that thing. Put on a show for me."

She didn't think, in his condition, that this was a wise move, but she'd promised to take him at his word. If he needed, he could end the scene. She'd take him upstairs and ice his balls.

Free of the hook, she moved her hips, riding the tower of pleasure like it was his cock. He powered up the wand and held it against her clit. Soon another orgasm blossomed.

"Don't stop, Kitty Kat. Keep riding. I want to see another one."

She struggled to keep moving, but she did it because he'd commanded it. The languor of satisfaction overloaded her senses, and she wasn't sure if she could climax again.

"Faster," he commanded as his hand cracked against her backside. "Move those hips." He spanked her ass, the pain blotting the serotonin enough so that she could have another orgasm.

She came in a blinding riot of frenzy, her screams echoing from the walls. Unable to stay on her feet, she collapsed, knocking over the tower of pleasure. Keith caught her, his lightening reflexes saving her shoulders from the strain. He freed her hands and scooped her in his arms. He carried her upstairs to their bathroom, and he held her while he ran a bath.

Dully she noted that he put Epsom salts in the tub and tested the temperature. He lowered her in, and she remained still while he bathed fluids from her body and massaged the muscles in her shoulders. When he pulled the plug, she stood and watched his face as he dried her body.

"Thank you."

In the midst of drying her leg, he glanced up, a pleased glint in his emerald eyes. He finished ministering aftercare, rubbing arnica into her sore muscles and the places where the clothespins had left small bruises. Then he carried her to bed. As she lay in his arms and surrendered to sleep, he kissed her forehead.

"I cherish the gift of your submission, Kitty Kat, and I love you more than words can express."

Michele Zurlo

Chapter 15

"Hi, Corey. Did you have a good night?" Katrina held her phone up so that her son had a good visual of her.

Corey hopped up and down, shaking the phone and blurring his image. "Poppa took me frog hunting. We caught a lot of them, but we had to throw them back because they were too small."

"Oh, that sounds like fun." Katrina did not recall her father doing things like that with her or her brothers. They'd been wonderful parents, but her parents had really come into their own as grandparents.

"Yeah, it was fun. But I wanted to find a big one so I could keep it as a pet. Poppa said it had to be big enough for Muppet's dog collar to fit around the neck, or we couldn't take it with us." He rambled on about frogs and other adventures. Katrina listened while she ate breakfast. Keith was upstairs getting dressed, and they had to be on the road in a half hour if they were going to make it to the senator's luncheon in time.

Angelina leaned into view. "Hi, Mommy. You look beautiful this morning. You must have finally caught up on your sleep."

After a session with Keith, she always slept like the dead. Katrina laughed at the compliment. "Thank you, sweetheart. You're also looking quite beautiful. Have you two been good for Grandma and Poppa?"

"We sure have." She took the phone from Corey and peered into it, her expression somber. "Mommy, my fitting is today."

"I know, Angelina. Layla is going to take you, and then you two are going to get a mani-pedi. It'll be fun." Katrina sincerely wished Keith had not scheduled this lunch on the other side of the state.

Keith came into the kitchen, opening the pantry next to the stove before he stopped moving.

"I know it'll be fun. Layla is crazy, so we always have a good time."

At Angelina's assessment, Keith's brow furrowed, but he finished pouring a bowl of cereal before joining her at the table.

"I'll just miss being with you. Can we have a make-up day next weekend, Mommy? Just you and me?" She looked so hopeful that Katrina hated to turn her down.

"Sorry, Angelina. Our weekends are booked solid until the wedding. How about when Daddy and I get back from our wedding trip? We can have a whole day with just us."

"And me." Corey took the phone. "I want a girl day with you, Mommy."

"We can do that too, Corey. A day for just you and me."

Angelina hissed in the background. "You can't have a girl's day with Mommy, silly. You're a boy. Are you going to get your nails done?"

"Yes." Corey's eyebrows drew together, looking for all the world like Keith when he was angry. "Daddy gets his toenails painted all the time."

Katrina squelched a giggle. Keith often painted her nails, and ever since Angelina had witnessed that happening, she'd insisted that he do her nails, and then she did his. The first time, he'd tried to protest, but one tremor of Angelina's lip had staunched his objection.

Keith took the phone from her. "Corey, you can absolutely get your nails done. Don't let anyone tell you that you can't do something just because girls do it." He often said the same thing in reverse to Angelina. Katrina was glad to see that he didn't have a double standard when it came to their son.

A loud sigh came through the phone. "Okay, but we get separate days with Mommy. I want her all to myself."

Grinning, Keith nodded. "I know the feeling."

"And with you, Daddy. You can be with Corey on our girl's day, and then we can switch." Angelina sounded very pleased with herself.

"I like that plan," Keith said.

"Daddy? I've decided that I'm going to be called Lina from now on."

Keith arched a single brow. "Oh?"

"Yes. It rhymes with Trina. We'll be Lina and Trina. Of course, you're still going to call me Angie. That's your thing only, like how you're the only one who calls Mommy Kat and Grandma Mama L. Grandma said it's a thing you do."

"Grandma knows best." Keith brought the phone around to Katrina, and he positioned the camera to capture them both. "We need to get going now. We love you two. Be good, and we'll see you tonight."

Michele Zurlo

After virtual hugs and kisses, Keith ended the call.

"Lina and Trina." Katrina shook her head. "She never ceases to amaze me."

"She wants to be just like you." He shoveled cereal into his mouth, and drops of milk fell back into the bowl. This was the sexy 'morning after' for almost-married people. "She loves when your dad tells her that something she did is just like you used to do."

Katrina took a bite of her yogurt and fruit mixture, noting that Angelina also liked to eat healthy for breakfast. It was all downhill after that. "How are your balls? Do you need ice? I could bring the cooler."

He gave her the evil eye. "They're fine."

"The aftercare directions said you have an antibiotic cream to put on the incision site." She was determined to take care of him. "And I noticed this morning that we're almost out of Motrin."

"I have a new bottle in my car. I used the cream. I do not need ice." He slurped down the remainder of milk in his bowl and smacked his lips. "I promise that I'm okay. If you really want to save me from unnecessary jostling, you can run upstairs and get our bags."

For a day trip, they'd packed a garment bag containing suits for each of them that straddled the line between professional and casual. The other bag held makeup and other fun stuff that could be used to pretty them up. She loaded them into the car, and just in case he changed his mind, she packed some freezer packs into a small cooler.

The luncheon was much larger than expected. The intimate guest list included thirty of Senator Kenyon's closest friends. Keith had booked a room at the hotel where the meal was being held, and Katrina was grateful. They arrived half an hour early, and that had given them time to change and freshen up.

Katrina held Keith's arm, much like she did when they followed protocol. This arrangement gave her courage she did not feel in the room full of strangers. She leaned closer to Keith. "How many people do you think are here because they want something?"

He scanned the room, his trained gaze seeing more than she could discern. "All of them."

"Katrina, I'm so glad you could make it." Senator Kenyon's loud voice boomed across the private banquet room. His physical body followed close behind. He shook her hand. "I know this is a busy time for you, with wedding preparations and such."

Before she could respond, he stuck his hand in Keith's direction. "Special Agent Keith Rossetti, thank you for coming and for bringing your lovely fiancé."

"My pleasure." Keith donned his most charming smile, guaranteed to draw people to him. "Thanks for inviting us."

His attention reverted to Katrina. "Counselor, there are some people I want you to meet." He lifted his hand to hail someone a few feet away, and then he took her elbow and guided her to them. She kept one hand on Keith, pulling him along because there was no way she was doing this alone.

Robert released her elbow and gestured to his friend. "Edmund, I'd like to introduce you to Katrina Legato, a brilliant prosecutor with the US Attorney's office in Detroit, and her fiancé, Special Agent Keith Rossetti. Katrina and Keith, this is one of my oldest friends, Edmund Ricci. He's the CEO of Ricci Cosmetics."

They exchanged greetings, and then Edmund threw a question at Katrina. "Ms. Legato, may I call you Katrina?" At her nod, he continued. "What do you think of the minimum sentencing requirements?"

This topic was very controversial in the legal world, and Katrina didn't know how in-depth an answer this man wanted, so she strove for something succinct. "There are great arguments on both sides of that issue, Edmund. On one hand, sentencing requirements make sure people who commit certain kinds of crimes serve an adequate amount of time. That way you don't see one person getting five years for murder while another serves 25 years for a similar crime. Of course, minimum guidelines don't allow a judge to use discretion, to take into account extenuating circumstances."

Edmund nodded. "Not every crime has minimum requirements."

"No, and that's another flaw in the system. Some serious crimes don't have a minimum, and some less serious offenses have stiffer penalties that don't fit the crime." Katrina shot a glance at Keith, inviting him into the conversation, but he only smiled.

If Edmund noticed her gesture, he didn't comment. Instead he delved into more legal topics, picking her brain on a multitude of issues. Through it all, Keith participated minimally, adding a laugh or a word of encouragement here and there. More people joined them, and the conversation flowed through the meal.

At one point, Lester Simpson, another businessman who was close friends with Senator Kenyon, asked Keith a direct question. "Agent Rossetti—"

"Keith, please." In true alpha style, he made the order sound like a friendly request.

"Keith, tell me, do you have an opinion on the lenient plea deals the Justice Department cuts with criminals after you've put so much time and effort into compiling evidence and catching them?" Simpson was one of those older men who looked like they stayed up nights worrying about things that would never happen, like an asteroid hitting the earth or gunfire penetrating the wall of his house and lodging in his spine.

Pausing to consider the question, and probably the man's motives for asking it, Keith waited before answering. He finished chewing and sipped water. "Well, Lester, it doesn't make me happy. But plea deals have a place. Sometimes our evidence is mostly circumstantial, which means that if it goes to trial, even the best attorney wouldn't be guaranteed a conviction. I'd rather see them go to jail than not, and if they're going to plead guilty or give up something bigger, I don't have an issue with shaving some time off the sentence. I do have an issue with a perp serving no time, though."

Lester challenged him, the excitement of debate making his color high. "What about when you have a solid case?"

Keith glanced at Katrina, silently urging her to field this one. Katrina favored Simpson with a generous smile. "Lester, we don't make deals unless the circumstances are right, and no judge worth their salt would accept a plea deal when the evidence is crystal clear and conclusive."

There were women at the table as well, and they fired off equally charged questions. Katrina found herself mired in debate as the senator held court at the other end of the room. If she was with all these people, then she was not impressing Robert.

"I thought you seemed familiar, and I've finally remembered where I know you from." Patricia Ephron, a woman associated with a company that manufactured car seats, shook her finger at Keith.

At his charismatic best, Keith grinned. "Oh, yeah? Where's that?"

"You arrested Gabriel Galipeau."

Keith's smile remained slightly flirty. "Was he a friend of yours?"

"Competition." Patricia's lips thinned. "He stole intellectual property from my husband's company. Your actions saved the company from going under."

"Glad I could help." Keith dismissed his accomplishment as if it was nothing, when Katrina knew nothing could be farther from the truth. She knew how hard he worked to make sure justice won.

"Oh, you." Patricia's laughter tinkled through the space. "Modest. I should have known." She winked at Katrina. "You've found yourself a good one, dear. Most men who are that good looking are not modest."

Katrina would never have described Keith as modest. He was focused on a goal, and nothing got between him and the things he wanted.

The meal passed quickly, and most people lingered afterward, each wanting five minutes with Robert. The group around her drifted away, and Katrina looked at Keith, silently imploring him to let them leave.

He did not get her message, or if he did, he ignored it. "Erica and Burke aren't here."

Katrina had not noticed. She'd been so busy that she'd completely forgotten that her friend was supposed to be there. "I hope she's feeling okay. Last night was pretty intense."

Keith chuckled. "For you more than for her." He bent down, speaking so only she could hear. "When we get back to the hotel room, I'm going to give you an erotic spanking."

She pushed at his chest. "Oh, you're bad."

Patricia approached, and Katrina fought down the heat rising to her cheeks. "Hi Patricia. How are you?"

"Please, call me Pat. All my friends do." She spoke mostly to Keith, and she slipped her arm in his. "I want to borrow this dear boy. My husband was seated at the other end of the table during dinner, and I want him to meet the man who did so much for us."

Robert joined them. "You go ahead, Keith. I want a word with Katrina."

Keith kissed her cheek. "Be right back."

How did one tell a senator that they wanted them to suggest them for a judicial appointment? Katrina did not know. "What did you need, Robert?"

He chuckled. "I needed you to do exactly what you did this afternoon. You're intelligent, sharp, witty, and easy on the eyes, if you don't mind me saying so, and you charmed most of the people here."

"Um, thanks." She didn't get the sense that he was coming on to her. If anything, his assessment of her looks was just part of the list. "What, exactly, did you need me to do?"

"Sell yourself." He clapped her on the back and looked over her shoulder. "Come with me."

She followed him out of the private banquet room. She tried to look for Keith, intending to catch his eye so he would know where she'd gone, but she couldn't find him.

The alcove off the hallway was private, a place no one would find unless they knew it was there. Robert steered her in there and around where no one who walked by would see them. "Katrina, you're aware that there are two District court openings."

"I am." In addition to the original vacancy, one had been created by Judge Osman's death.

"And I'm aware of your role in the Bouquet Murders."

She stared at the senator. Nobody had named the killer—or even determined that there was a serial killer on the loose—and she didn't like the way he'd linked her to the murders. "I don't have a role in the murders."

Robert blinked. "I phrased that badly. I'm aware that the killer has sent you flowers and that the flowers he leaves at the crime scenes are for you."

These things weren't common knowledge. The killer had sent photos and a statement to the media, but only one local news outlet had picked up the story. Not only that, but no mention of her had been made. It seemed Jordan and Rakeem had a leak they needed to plug.

She schooled her expression to remain neutral. "Where did you hear that?"

"I have sources in high places."

She scoffed at his claim. "Nothing is conclusive, and two murders does not make for a serial killer. Right now, it's two homicides."

Robert studied her, his practiced calm giving him an edge. "Katrina, if I were in your shoes, I'd be terrified. It speaks to your courage that you haven't let this threat stop you from doing your job."

"Thank you, Robert, but I'm not in danger."

"They found two more bodies. It was on the news."

She froze. Nobody had mentioned a thing about this development.

Robert's gaze fell to the floor. "You didn't know. I'm sorry. I hope this doesn't change your determination."

"No, it does not." Her mind raced. "They're going to get that bastard, and he's going to prison for the rest of his life."

"That's what I like to see." He flashed a grimace that was meant to be a smile. "Keep it up, Katrina. I have big plans for you. No promises. That wouldn't be appropriate." With that, he patted her on the arm and exited the alcove.

Stunned, Katrina sank down on the nearest bench. She had seen Jordan last night, and he hadn't said a word. Why wouldn't he keep her informed? Did Keith know?

As she gathered her wits, someone sat beside her. She turned to find Burke. He wore rust colored slacks and a stylish white button-down shirt with the top two buttons open. His red hair was windblown.

She pasted on a small smile that she did not feel. "We missed you and Erica at lunch."

"Erica isn't feeling well. She's napping in the room. I went boating with a friend. There are some great lakes in this state."

Katrina didn't laugh at his attempted joke. She got up to leave. "I'll call her later. Please tell her I'm sorry I missed her."

Burke grabbed her arm, halting her attempt at a polite escape. "Trina, wait. I saw you fighting with Keith last night. Are you okay?"

"I'm fine." She brushed off his concern as she tried to brush off his hold.

He parked a hand on each of her shoulders. "I saw the fight, Trina. I saw the way he grabbed you and the way he got in your face. You deserve better than a man who treats you like property."

Keith may refer to her as his possession, but he'd never treated her as property. People who weren't in the lifestyle didn't see the distinction. Keith saw himself as her caretaker, the person responsible for protecting and nurturing her. Possessing her gave him power, but she was the one ultimately in control of herself.

Katrina didn't want to explain the nuances to a man who had no interest in learning them. "He treats me like a princess, and you don't understand what you saw last night."

"Oh?" He moved closer, sliding his hands down her arms, his grip loose. "You like when a man gives you bruises? Huh? Do you like to struggle, Trina? Do you like it rough?"

She'd been training in self-defense from the time she was a teenager, and the Tae Kwon Do classes she was taking with Angelina had polished the rust off her skills. In one move, she dislodged his hold and knocked him back.

He stumbled, not catching himself until his ass met the bench. Mouth ajar, he glared. "Oh, honey, if you want it like that, I can accommodate." He came at her, and she landed a blow to his gut and to his nose. Blood gushed out, and she moved out of the splatter radius.

"It seems you were laboring under the delusion that I'm defenseless. I assure you that I'm not."

"Kat?" Keith's voice diffracted around the corner leading to the alcove.

"Here." She stepped backward, putting herself on the side of the alcove that was open to the hall.

Keith came to her, a frown on his face. "What's going on?"

"Nothing I can't handle."

Michele Zurlo

He came into the alcove and took in the sight of Burke with his hand over his nose and blood covering his hand, the lower half of his face, and his shirt. He pointed to Burke. "Did you do that?"

"He tried to make a move on me, and when I turned him down, he thought to press his advantage." She put a hand on Keith's chest. "I'd rather you didn't act on what you're thinking right now."

A struggle played out in the ticking of his jaw and the flashing of his eyes, but all Burke probably saw was his life flashing before his eyes. His gaze darted to the exit, but he'd have to pass her and Keith to get there.

Keith's response was limited to a curt nod. "If he tries it again, or if he tries it with any other woman, no promises." He visibly relaxed, and his fists unclenched. "Kat, I think he needs medical attention. Go to the front desk and tell them that they have a guest who suffers from nosebleeds."

Katrina moved to obey, but she stopped short. "Keith, don't make him bleed more."

"Sure, Kitty Kat. Anything you say."

She ran to the front desk, not trusting Keith's easy agreement. Her Master was seething, not only because he had an issue with men who forced unwanted attention on women, but because she belonged to him, and nobody touched what was his.

The concierge at the front desk had a sedate smile on his face. "Good afternoon, Ms. Legato. How was your luncheon?"

"My compliments to the chef. Listen, my friend, Burke Cornwall—Senator Kenyon's future son-in-law, suffers from severe nosebleeds. I'm afraid he's having one right now in the alcove off the front hall."

The concierge nodded as if she'd requested extra towels. "Does he require medical attention?"

"He'll be okay, but there's blood everywhere. He could use something to staunch the bleeding and maybe some ice."

When she made it back to the alcove, she found Burke slumped over, and Keith holding up the wall opposite him. His arms were folded casually, as if they were two guys shooting the breeze. She looked from one man to the other. Keith lifted his hands. "I did not touch him. I merely described some of the things I could do and what the pain might feel like. It's not my fault he's a wuss."

A bell boy appeared with towels and ice. He blanched at the sight of the blood. "Mr. Cornwall, do you need an ambulance?" His voice shook. There was one man who would not be going into the medical field.

"No. I'll be fine. I'm going up to my room." He took the towel and wiped off his face and hands. Dropping it to the floor, he swiped the towel full of ice from the bell boy and pushed past them.

Katrina and Keith followed him out. Erica met them in the hall. She wore silk pajamas and a robe. Her face was pale and devoid of makeup, and her nose was red.

"Oh, my God, Burke. What happened?" Her hands fluttered over his clothes, not quite touching the parts soiled with blood. "The front desk called me."

Keith inserted an answer. "He got a nosebleed. It happened suddenly. One second, he's talking, and the next second, he has his head between his knees."

Burke shot a death glare at Keith.

Erica looked from one to the other, and then she focused on Katrina. She'd been pale before, but now she was positively white. She covered her mouth with one hand.

Burke put an arm around her. "Honey, it's not that bad. It's already stopped bleeding. I just need to get cleaned up."

She winced, jerking from his hold. "Don't lie to me," she hissed. "I know exactly what happened. This is why I have no friends."

"Don't be dramatic," he cajoled. "We're in public."

Robert Kenyon came out of the banquet hall with a group of people. With one hushed word, the group disappeared. He came to them, sizing up the situation, and then he put his arm around Erica. "Sweetheart, you don't look well. Why don't you go rest in my room, and I'll take care of this."

He handed her off to an aide who shepherded her to the elevators. Then he faced Burke. "Go up to your room and don't come out."

Sent to his room without dinner, Burke scampered off.

Robert addressed Katrina next. "Do you want to press charges?"

Pursuing this matter wouldn't lead to anywhere significant. It was her word against his, and if she created trouble for the senator, he might withdraw his support. "No. It's best that this stay quiet."

Robert shot a silent question at Keith.

Keith shook his head. "She doesn't need media attention right now. While bloggers might eat up the story of a brilliant lawyer who punched a man who came on too strong, Kat doesn't want that kind of publicity."

Robert's jaw dropped. "She did that to him?"

Michele Zurlo

Before Keith could brag about how much more damage there would be if he'd been the one throwing the punches, Katrina interjected. "I can take care of myself, Robert. I'm fine. You should see to Erica. Please ask her to call me later, when she's feeling better."

They took their leave. On the way home, Katrina chewed her cuticles until Keith admonished her to stop. "You're going to make them bleed. We've had enough blood for one day."

She folded her hands in her lap. "Did we do the right thing?" She didn't have to explain that she meant how they'd handled the situation with Burke.

"There is not one right thing. If we'd pursued charges, he would have hired a high-priced lawyer to get him out of it. And the last thing you want is publicity for something like this. You want to be known for putting criminals away, not socking them in the nose." He set a hand on her thigh. "I'll make sure you're not alone with him again."

She had handled the situation, but she understood that Keith wanted to be the one who protected her. Besides, she'd never wanted to be alone with him in the first place. "Did you know that there were two more murders? They're calling it the Bouquet Murders."

"What?" His head swiveled in her direction, and the car swerved. He got his driving under control, and he kept his eyes on the road. "Where did you hear that?"

"Robert knew all about it. He said he has friends in high places." A knot of fear twisted in her stomach. "Why hasn't Jordan or Rakeem called to let me know?"

"I don't know." That muscle in his jaw ticked. "They didn't call me either." He pushed a button on the steering wheel and commanded the car to call Jordan.

"You've reached Jordan Monaghan. At the tone, leave a detailed message."

Keith waited for the beep. "Jordan, what the hell is going on? Why am I hearing about more murders from someone else?" He disconnected the call and dialed Rakeem.

"Bahu."

"Rakeem, this is Keith Rossetti."

"Keith, I was just about to call you."

"To tell me about the other two murders that you found?"

Rakeem paused. "How did you know?"

"I was at an event in Grand Rapids with Senator Kenyon, and he said something to Kat. How does he even know she's involved?"

This time, Rakeem whistled. "Senator Kenyon. Wow. He's got friends in high places, know what I mean?"

Katrina bit back a retort calling for Captain Obvious. "Rakeem, it's Trina. Was it the same as the others?"

"Pretty much, but we have new clues. They're supposed to be confidential. I'm going to have to talk to Jocelyn to make sure she's aware of the leak."

Her palms were suddenly sweaty. She rubbed them on her sweats and asked the question he hadn't answered. "How did Senator Kenyon know I was at all involved?"

"This is amazing. You know these were found this morning, right? Like, the crime scenes are still intact."

They hadn't known anything, but at least that explained why Jordan hadn't said anything to them last night. "Rakeem, how did Senator Kenyon know I was involved?"

He chuckled as if he'd honestly thought he could get a seasoned prosecutor to forget the question. "Someone called the tip line and pointed out something in the two photos the killer released. The positioning of the hand holding the bouquet has been a little odd. The caller is an expert in ASL—American Sign Language—and he pointed out that the position of the first hand was in the shape of an A, and the second one was a T. When we found these two, the hands indicated K and R. He's spelling out your name in sign language."

It also indicated that one of the bodies had been killed before the other three, and so one was old and one was new. Katrina closed her eyes and leaned her head back.

Keith said, "Was there anything else we should know?"

"Just that we're on it. We think we know who it is. Eddie Maddox had an alibi for two of the murders, and Mason Charles Norris has dropped off the grid. We found his DNA under the nails of two victims, and we're looking for evidence to link him to the other two. We've upgraded him from person of interest to suspect." Rakeem said something to someone in the background, his words garbled and unclear. Then he returned. "Look, I have to go. We're close, but keep an eye out, okay?"

"Yeah. Of course. Thanks." Keith ended the call, and then he twined his fingers with hers. "Kat, they'll catch this bastard."

Tears leaked from her eyes. "How many more people have to die first? Is he going to spell out my first name only? Last name? Middle name? I can't believe this is happening."

"Hey, it's not your fault. This guy is sick in the head. You're probably not the first person he's fixated on, and you won't be the last."

Michele Zurlo

She nailed him with a doubtful look. "It will be if Jordan and Rakeem catch him. He'll be lucky to see the light of day or a human being besides his guard ever again."

"That's the spirit. Have faith in the law."

"I want to get Corey and Angelina, hold them tight and never let go."

"Lina," he corrected. "She's rhyming with you now, remember?"

Katrina tried to smile, and it was too hard to see through the sheen of tears. "I remember."

Chapter 16

Rakeem and Jordan showed up at Katrina's desk a few days later. She saw them coming toward her, poster boys for two different kinds of tall-dark-and-handsome, and she stood, steeling herself to greet them.

"Hey, Trina." Jordan hugged her. "Is there a room open somewhere?"

"I'm sure there is." Her smile was watery and tenuous at best. "Hi, Rakeem."

He nodded. "Good morning, Trina."

Now that pleasantries had been exchanged, there was an awkward silence. Then she remembered. "Oh, the room. Follow me."

She didn't want to go, but she led them there, her gait evincing a confidence she didn't feel. Conference room six was open, and the schedule posted on the door indicated that it wasn't signed out until the afternoon. She ushered Jordan and Rakeem inside, and then she closed the door.

Both men waited for her to sit first. Jordan, she knew, did so because she was the submissive who belonged to his friend. This was his way of showing respect and taking care of her. She didn't know Rakeem so well, but he was the one who pulled out a chair for her.

"This feels a lot like you've got bad news."

Jordan tapped a hand on the table. "Not bad, but we don't have the good news you want. Updates—we found the leak."

"It's been plugged," Rakeem added. "The case is now eyes-only for me, Jordan, and Jocelyn." Jocelyn Alard was their immediate supervisor.

Katrina was less concerned about the leak than they were. Robert had blindsided her, but she'd moved on. "Okay."

"We identified the bodies and the hands." He swiped through photos on his phone, and then he set it in front of her. Thankfully the pictures were of living people. She didn't have a hankering to see dead people. "This is Ramon Hawkins. Time of death makes him the first victim. He's the one whose hand was positioned as a K."

Michele Zurlo

She stared at the image, noting his dark, wavy hair and the mischievous sparkle in his light brown eyes. He looked like the kind of man who would be the first one on the dance floor, beckoning to his friends to join him. More than that, Ramon Hawkins looked familiar. "I know him. I don't remember from where."

"You defended him your first day at Legal Aid. He pled out for probation."

A light bulb went on. "He propositioned me when I was leaving court. He didn't want to take 'no' for an answer, and I ended up speaking quite harshly to him."

Rakeem pressed his lips together. "Did he threaten you?"

"No. He just came on strong. Some men do that." She hadn't felt that she was in danger. Ramon's case was coming back to her. He'd broken into an FBI storage facility looking for seized marijuana. He'd told her that he "just wanted a little, for personal use."

Jordan swiped to the next picture. "Margaret Bergeson."

This woman also had brown eyes, but her hair was white. Katrina knew that Margaret went by Maggie. She was seventy-eight years old and more sprightly than she let on.

Bile rose in Katrina's throat, and she clapped her hand over her mouth.

"Breathe, Trina." Rakeem lifted her hair and fanned the back of her neck. "Slow inhale and exhale. I take it she looks familiar?"

Slowly the sick feeling diminished. "She lives in my neighborhood. I see her all the time. She has a little dog that she lets poop in my yard. We argued last week because she doesn't pick it up. She said she was too old and infirm, and since my kids were young, they could handle a chore. She said it builds character."

"And you disagreed?" Jordan asked.

"I was tired, and I'm afraid I wasn't very nice about it." And now she felt horrible. The pattern was clear. "Judge Osman kept assigning me to Legal Aid. I complained about the workload in public. Many places. I don't think I knew Jason Harris, the flower delivery man."

"Remember when your car was hit in a grocery store parking lot? Keith was going to file an insurance claim. He requested footage from the store where it happened, but he never followed through with the paperwork. The driver of that van was Jason Harris."

Katrina vaguely remembered the incident when she noticed her back quarterpanel. It was a small dent, but the scrape would eventually rust, which was why Keith wanted it repaired. That had happened months ago. "Wait. That's before the charges against Norris were dismissed."

Rakeem grimaced. "Now we come to the part where we hit a confidentiality wall. We shared some details with you to confirm what we suspected."

She stared, eyes wide. "Are you fucking kidding me? This guy is fixated on me, and you want to keep secrets?"

"Trina, you, of all people, know we have good reasons." Jordan rubbed a circle on her upper back, probably intending to soothe her nerves.

That didn't mean she was going to accept his refusal. She took a calculated risk. "He knew of me before I met him. Let's see—how might that happen? He probably saw me around the courthouse, possibly when he was arraigned." She stood because she thought better on her feet, and she paced the length of the table. It was a good move because she remembered a connection. "This was Keith's case. Maybe he's trying to get to Keith. But why would he kill people who have interacted with me?"

She fell silent as she considered the incident in the parking lot. Nobody at work would know about that. She'd discussed it with Keith, and she'd talked with the insurance adjuster on her phone. Patting her pocket, she considered the idea of her phone. It might not take much for someone to hack it and listen in. Phones weren't exactly secure portals.

Jordan and Rakeem exchanged a look, and then they got to their feet. Jordan coughed. "In the meantime, we've put surveillance back on you."

Great. More of being watched. "Do you really think he'll come after me? It seems the people I meet casually are in more danger than I am."

"We know." Rakeem set a reassuring hand on her shoulder. "We're tracking him down. There isn't a rock he can hide under that we won't find."

After that reassuring meeting, she called Keith to see if he wanted to meet for lunch. He had some time, so she met him in his office at the McNamara building.

"I brought grinders." She set the nine inch, toasted sub sandwich on his desk, and she tossed hers down across from his. Just being in the same room as him calmed her nerves and made all problems surmountable.

He kissed her hello. "It's always a great day when I close the books on an international fraud case, and I get to have lunch with the most beautiful woman in the world."

Michele Zurlo

"Congratulations," she said. "How many arrests?"

"Two hundred and twenty-one. Three countries."

"That's fantastic." She unwrapped her grinder while he stared at his.

After a minute, he took out a pad of paper and began writing. "What's amazing is the paperwork involved. I have to create reports for each individual charged."

She knew that wasn't true, but she understood the value of continuing the conversation. "I got you turkey and extra cheese."

"And onions. It's a good thing I already kissed you." He slid the paper to her, and she read it while he tapped out an email on his computer.

On the paper wrapper for his grinder, she'd written that she suspected that she'd been bugged.

He'd written back that the building was shielded, but he wanted to search her just in case something got past their countermeasures. He locked the door to his office and lowered the blinds to the three windows—one facing outside and two facing inside.

"I got onions too, so more kissing can happen after we eat. I'm famished." She took a bite of her grinder, also turkey.

Keith started with her cell phone. He opened the back and searched the component parts. As they chatted about mundane things, he systematically went through everything in her purse. Then he had her strip naked so he could search her clothes. When he finished, she dressed, and there was a knock at the door.

"That's a buddy of mine. He's been wanting to meet you." Keith opened the door, and ushered in an agent Katrina hadn't met. Dressed in a black suit, he looked like the average, hot FBI agent. Katrina estimated his age at a little north of forty.

"Kat, this is Madden McCauley. Mad, this is my fiancée, Katrina Legato. You can call her Trina."

Katrina found herself engulfed in the arms of a stranger. Though he didn't come into physical contact, his hands roamed her body. Shocked, she gaped at Keith. This was not okay.

He held up a hand, cautioning her to not say a word. "Madden is new to the FBI he used to be a technology teacher in Illinois. He was recruited when he built this really cool scanner that can fit in the palm of your hand."

Now that she knew what was going on, she relaxed, and she noticed the bands on the backs of Madden's hands that held the device to him. Keith hadn't found anything, but he wasn't going to dismiss her concern that easily.

"I miss corn fields," Madden said. "Alfalfa. Wheat. Beans. But mostly corn. I once had a kid do a whole project on the technology involved in improving corn production." He swept the objects on Keith's desk that had been in her purse. A light flashed when he got to her cell phone.

He nodded at the phone, and Keith frowned. "Kat, is that beep I heard from your cell phone? Did you forget to charge it again? My charger is in my car. Why don't you power it down, and I'll go grab my charger for you?"

"Sure." She turned the phone off and handed it to Madden.

He opened the back and removed the battery. "It was great to meet you, Trina. I have some work to do, so I'll see you around." He left, taking her cell phone with him.

Katrina faced Keith. "How did a bug get into my cell phone? I always have it with me."

Keith's office phone rang, and he picked up. "Rossetti." He listened intently, occasionally offering a sound of agreement. "I understand. I will." He replaced the handset and sighed. "Let's have lunch, Kat."

"Seriously? Who was that?"

"Rakeem. They're not going to deactivate the bug. Instead they're going to piggyback on it, see if they can trace it to the receiver." He sat down and dug into his grinder. "It's only active when it's on, so anything you say on there is being overheard. Be careful about what you say, and you can't power down more often than you normally do. In the meantime, I'll get you a secure phone for emergencies."

She stewed as she ate. "Why didn't they think of the bug? It's their job to think of these things."

"The working profile on Norris indicates that he'd want to watch you himself, not use a listening device. When laundering money, he was very careful to cover his digital footprint. I had a hell of a time identifying him, much less finding hard evidence." He wiped his lips with a paper napkin and took another bite. "I hit the jackpot when a search of his property turned up a false floor in the utility room that contained his books—all handwritten."

There was a ton she didn't know about the Bouquet Murders, and so she couldn't fully put herself in Jordan or Rakeem's shoes, but it rankled that a listening device was her first thought and their last.

"They need to find out where Norris first saw me and why he fixated on me. I wonder if it has to do with you, since you built the case against him and arrested him."

He sat back. "You think he's using you to get back at me?"

Michele Zurlo

"I wouldn't know how his mind works. I have not seen his profile or all the evidence in this case. I only know what they tell me, and the rest is supposition." Katrina took the top piece of bread off her grinder so she could eat more without filling up on bread. "Only I'm not sure that's a good theory."

She shared details of Jordan and Rakeem's morning visit to her office.

Keith balled up the wrapper from his lunch and chucked it into the trash. "You're right. It makes no sense for him to kill people who've somehow wronged you in order to get back at me."

"None," she agreed. "But maybe you should tell Jordan about what happened Sunday. If killing people who've been mean to me is the M.O., then Burke Cornwall is in danger."

"Right. I'll take care of it. What does your afternoon look like?"

"Research, filing motions, writing briefs—the usual. I have court tomorrow and Friday." She disposed of the remains of her lunch. "I can pick up Angelina—Lina—and Corey."

Angelina had followed through with her insistence that everyone address her by a new nickname, and she refused to answer to anything else, except when Keith called her 'Angie.'

Senator Kenyon called that evening on Keith's phone—which had been cleared by the FBI—instead of hers. Not wanting her privacy invaded, she'd put it in the upstairs bathroom and prayed that Corey would drop it in the toilet. He'd already managed to do that with tiny action figures, a stuffed animal, and sundry mystery objects that were MIA. Anyone listening in would hear his gasp of glee—she was fairly certain that he was fascinated with watching things go down that particular drain.

Katrina was in the midst of trying desperately to lose at Candyland when Keith handed her the phone. "It's Robert Kenyon," he mouthed.

"Hi, Robert. How are you?"

"I guess that depends on how you look at it. Am I happy to be rid of a no-good, potential son-in-law? Yes. Am I happy that my daughter's heart is broken? No."

Katrina motioned for Keith to take her place in the game, and she went into the next room. "They broke up? Is Erica okay?"

"Much to my chagrin, they did not break up. Burke Cornwall's body was found this morning in a hotel room, dead."

Lightheaded and dizzy, Katrina sank into a chair at the kitchen table. "Was it...Was it..." She couldn't bring herself to finish the thought. Though she had a very low opinion of Burke, she hadn't wished him dead.

"I'm in D.C. right now, trying to get a flight out. I have not seen crime scene photos, but from what the hotel manager told me, his right hand was severed, and there were flowers."

"Oh, my God. Does the FBI know?"

"I'm sure they do. I was calling to see if you knew anything more, but I can hear from your voice that you're surprised. I'm sorry to be the one to tell you this news. But if you hear anything, please let me know. This has become personal." The call disconnected.

Katrina set the phone down and stared into the middle distance. She'd suspected that Norris would go after Burke, but she'd thought the body guards the senator had hired would protect him.

She floated through the rest of the week, always wondering if and how she was being watched, and she was terrified that every stranger with whom she interacted might end up a victim of this serial killer. She wanted to destroy her cell phone, but Jordan had impressed upon her the importance of using it as she normally would so that Norris wouldn't know they were onto him.

Keith did his best to raise her spirits, but not only was he equally worried, there was nothing he could do to fix the problem. Any involvement he had with the case would taint the evidence, and Jordan and Rakeem regularly assured them that they were making progress. On Saturday, they raided a home where they'd traced the signal to find the elderly owner dead. Norris had left in a hurry, meaning they'd recovered a partial print from the hand that had been positioned to indicate N.

One letter left in her first name, and then would things stop? Or would Norris continue with six more to pay homage to her last name?

Monday she took the day off to go to Keith's doctor appointment with him. It was the one piece of normal she needed right now, so Keith didn't argue with her.

She waited on the uncomfortable chair in the room while Keith stripped down to his birthday suit and donned one of those paper gowns he liked to rip off her when they played gynecologist scenes.

"You're very sexy in that gown," she said. "Not everyone can pull of the paper look, but you—wow. You're freaking hot. I'm getting ideas."

With one look, he shot a warning. The dominant part of his personality did not ask her to behave. He commanded it.

And yet, Katrina did not feel an urgent need to heed him. "Okay, when you look at me like that, I'm getting more than ideas. I have visuals, naughty visuals."

Michele Zurlo

He pressed his lips together and got on the exam table.

"I see you have the same problem."

"Kat, be good. I know you're still upset that I had this done, but that's no reason for me to tolerate bratty behavior."

She tilted her head and said nothing.

He narrowed his eyes. "What are you doing?"

"From this angle, I can see under your gown." She bent down a little more. "Hi, boys. It's been a while. How are you holding up?"

A knock on the door announced the arrival of the doctor. It opened, and an attractive woman came inside. She had sleek black hair that spilled all the way to her ass and a petite figure that managed to still have impressive curves. Her skin was darker than Katrina's, owing to Indian ancestry, and she was every bit as pretty.

Her eyes shone with joy, and another woman, a nurse, followed her into the room. The nurse was also pretty, but she paled in comparison to the doctor. The doctor zeroed in on Keith. "Good morning, Keith. How are we today?"

Sitting in a paper gown with three women in the room did not seem to faze Keith. He shrugged. "Everything feels fine. Healed."

Katrina smothered a laugh at the fact that Keith was basically ordering the doctor and his body to comply with his wishes.

The doctor turned to her. "And who have we brought with us?"

Katrina stood and extended her hand. "I'm Katrina, Keith's fiancée."

"It's nice to meet you. I'm Doctor Kumar."

Katrina didn't let her get away so fast. "You did the surgery?"

"I did."

"Wow. You have one hell of a job. I want to ask you so many inappropriate things."

"Kat." Keith's warning also included promise of punishment. "Behave."

Doctor Kumar laughed, a tinkling sound that filled the room. "It's okay. I field a lot of inappropriate questions. It's in the job description." She washed her hands while the nurse took Keith's vitals. When the nurse finished, Doctor Kumar said, "Go ahead and put your feet in the stirrups."

Katrina's chair was in the perfect position to see the peepshow, but the nurse blocked her view.

Doctor Kumar put gloves on and sat on the stool between Keith's legs. She pushed the gown out of the way. "My hands may be a little cold. I apologize for that. Okay, incision looks great. No swelling. Can you shine that light a little to the left? Okay. Nope. Looks good."

She pushed back with her feet, rolling the stool away as she took off her latex gloves, and stood up. "Congratulations, Keith, you're healed. Go ahead and get dressed. I'll come back in a few minutes, and we can talk about next steps." She washed her hands again, and the pair left.

"That was quick."

Keith took off the gown and stood before her wearing nothing but black socks. He attacked his clothes, sliding into his briefs first. "Why did I have to take all my clothes off? Completely unnecessary. And her hands were like ice. My balls shriveled up and tried to crawl into my spine."

Giggling, Katrina shook her head. "Maybe she forgot to do the breast exam?"

"I'll show you a breast exam," he grumbled, and then he perked up. "Did you hear that? I got the all-clear. Tonight I'm going to make up for lost time."

She snorted. "You're going to wait until tonight? I took the whole day off for a reason, and you put naughty thoughts in my head."

He grinned as he finished dressing. "I thought you wanted me to take you to lunch."

"You can do that too." Eager to get her hands on him, she helped him with his tie. "I bought condoms to use until I can get back on birth control. I have an appointment next week to see my doctor."

A knock on the door announced the return of the doctor. This time, she came alone, and she got right to business. "Okay, now that this part is done, I recommend taking it easy for another week or two. By easy, I mean that you should avoid rough sexual activity. Bruising the scrotum at this point could undo all my hard work."

Keith crossed his arms. "Would normal activity, which hasn't caused bruising in the past, cause bruising now?"

"It's possible. The incision has healed, but you don't want to take the chance you'd rupture anything important, like the vas deferens that was just reattached." Tired of looking up at Keith, she indicated the chair, and she parked herself on the rolling stool. "It's going to take four to six months for sperm to reappear. You should notice a difference in the consistency of ejaculate once they do."

Katrina slid onto the exam table. "Doctor Kumar, are you saying that right now, even though you replumbed his lines, he won't be producing sperm?"

"Anything is possible, but it generally takes time for sperm count to establish. It'll be very low at first, but it should gradually increase over time. About 43% of patients who undergo a vasovasectomy are able to impregnate their partner in between four-to-twelve months. The odds shoot up to about 60% if your partner is under 35. If there's a problem after that time, you might consider harvesting sperm and trying insemination. But that's way down the road."

Keith nodded. "We're not looking to get pregnant right away."

Katrina didn't comment because she had not come around to the idea of having more children. "So, back to the sex thing—how do we know when it's okay to resume the rough stuff? Our wedding is coming up, and we have plans."

If Doctor Kumar was shocked, she hid it well. "He should be good to go in two weeks. If not, there's something wrong, and he needs to come back. Any more questions? No? Okay, I'll need to see you back in four months. We'll do a motility test and a sperm count at that time."

They held hands in the parking lot, and Keith opened her door. Before she got in the car, he pressed a hard kiss to her lips. She giggled. "Wow, you really want to get laid."

"I'm going to fuck every hole in your body at least once today." Another kiss, and he got into the driver's side. "Where would you like to go for lunch? Pick something good because it's the last decision you'll be making for a while."

She thought about it. "You know, we have leftover lasagna at home." Her mother had surprised them yesterday afternoon with a pan of her special lasagna.

With a sly slant to his lips, he smiled. "Perfect."

Getting home didn't take long, and Keith attacked her the moment they were in the door. His lips devoured her, and she realized how much he'd held back for the past two weeks. Subsumed by his will, she melted in his embrace. In the front hallway, he reached under her skirt and divested her of panties.

Lips never leaving her body, he walked her to the sofa in the living room. Knowing he needed her now, she opened his pants. They fell down his thighs, and he sat heavily on the sofa.

He took his cock in hand, stroking it softly. "Lift your skirt, Kitty Kat. Show me that greedy cunt."

Due to recent events, she'd put curtains on every window, and she kept them closed, so she didn't worry that the neighbors who could see through the huge picture window were going to get a show. She lifted her skirt and spread her legs. Then she peeled back the lips of her labia so he could see how wet she was for him.

He crooked a finger, and she straddled him. He traced the sensitive crown of his cock through her wetness, and when she felt him at her entrance, she sank down with a contented sigh.

"You feel so good, Master. I've missed having you inside me."

"I've missed being inside you. This is going to be quick and dirty."

She didn't expect anything but to serve him, so she concentrated on his pleasure. She clenched her pussy around his cock.

He gasped and clutched her hips. "Fuck. Kitty Kat, I'm not going to last."

"That's okay, Master. Let me give to you." She set a fast pace, squeezing his cock every time he thrust home because he liked that edge of pain. He didn't hold back, and in less than a minute, his orgasm bathed her insides. She silenced the alarm bells in her head. Not only was she not at a fertile time of the month, but he was most likely still shooting blanks.

His head lolled against the back of the sofa. She kissed his slack lips. "I'll go heat up lunch, and when you're ready, you can join me."

When she would have got up, he stayed her with a hand on her arm. "I want to see you come." He lifted her off his softening cock, positioning her over him. "Like this. Touch yourself, Kitty Kat."

His fluids mixed with hers, running down her inner thigh. She dragged a finger through the stickiness, rubbing it over her clit. He watched, his eyes barely slits, as she brought herself to orgasm under the power of her hand and his gaze. Her body stiffened as waves of pleasure washed through her system, and he held her when she slumped forward.

He stroked her back. "Next time will be slower."

"And naked. We should be naked so I can kiss every inch of your body." She previewed upcoming events by nipping at his neck. "Let's eat because I'm starving."

They heated leftovers and ate them in the midst of intimate touches and laughter. All the stress and worry of the outside world ceased to exist, and it was just the two of them, lovers intent on making love.

After lunch, they left their plates on the table. He put his arms around her and kissed her tenderly. They slowly made their way toward the stairs. She removed his tie, and he unbuttoned her shirt. In the distance a phone rang. His movements stuttered.

"No," she said. "Let this be someone else's emergency."

"It's Angie's school's ringtone." He broke away. "Hopefully it's something stupid, like a notice that I need to put money in her lunch account."

She followed him back to the kitchen.

"Rossetti." His politely inquisitive demeanor vanished, and blood drained from his face. "What? How long? Have you called the police?"

That got Katrina's attention.

"I'll be there in five minutes. Do not let anyone leave the building." He ended the call. "Angie is missing, and so is Kyle S."

"What do you mean, she's missing? What the hell does that mean? How do you lose a kid?" Katrina freaked out. "Did they look for her? Did they search every classroom? The playground? Did she get in trouble and is hiding?"

"They searched the school and grounds. They're in lockdown right now, and they've notified the police. You are going to call Jordan and tell him what happened, and I am going to the school." He grabbed his badge and keys.

"I'm going with you." She wasn't going to wait here while her baby was out there, lost and scared. Angelina wasn't the kind of kid who hid. She faced her fears, kicking and screaming.

"You have to stay here, Kat. What if she ran away from school and is coming home? Someone has to be here. Call Jordan. I'll call you as soon as I know anything." He hugged her to him. "We'll find her. I promise that we'll find her."

With that, he was gone. She called Jordan on her cell phone, the one with the bug in it because that's what Keith wanted. "Jordan? Angelina is missing. Her school called. No one can find her or her friend Kyle Smith." As soon as he answered, the words tumbled out. "Keith is on his way there. We're at home today, so he'll be there in under ten minutes. He told me to stay here."

"Rakeem and I are on the way too. It'll take me about twenty minutes to get there. I'm going to dispatch agents to your place. In the meantime, call your family and get them there with you. Got it?" Garbled sounds came through, Rakeem or the radio talking.

"I got it." He meant she should call Malcolm, which she did, but she also called her parents—they had Corey—and M.J. Within an hour, her house swarmed with family and FBI agents. Jordan had also dispatched agents to the Smith house to cover the bases on the missing Kyle.

Katrina tried to stay strong because Angelina needed her to be. Her mother sat her on the sofa and put an arm around her shoulders. "Honey, don't hold it in. It's okay to cry."

She wasn't going to cry until Angelina was home. "She's so little for her age. So trusting. We've talked about strangers, so I don't think she'd go off with anyone, and she knows better than to leave school." Alert and ready to flee at a moment's notice, Katrina watched the front door.

After a while, Layla replaced Donna. She held Katrina's hand. "I put your panties in the laundry."

The statement took a moment to make sense. Katrina tore her gaze from the door and questioned Layla. "What?"

"Your panties were in the hallway. I assume that since you and Keith both took the day off, you were staying home to have sex. I also put his tie in the wash."

Katrina blinked, and then she thought about the fifteen people traipsing through her house, walking past a pair of panties and a tie on the front hall floor. She laughed, a bubbly giggle that turned manic.

Layla hugged her. "Sweetie, they're going to find her."

Her cell phone rang, an unfamiliar number. "Lexee!" It was all hands on deck for the missing daughter of an agent, and more people were there than were being paid to be there.

Lexee ran into the room, motioning to the agents with the recording and signal triangulation devices. "Keep him talking as long as you can."

The last two unknown callers had been telemarketers, though they'd traced those signals just to be sure.

She answered. "Hello?"

"Trina." He breathed heavily. She didn't recognize his voice, but she was willing to bet it was Mason Charles Norris. "Your daughter and son are fine. I knew you'd be worried."

"Mason?"

"Ah, you know my name. I like how it sounds on your tongue. Say it again."

"Mason, where are you guys?"

He laughed. "I only called to tell you that the kids are fine. They've had dinner and are getting ready for bed. I'll call back later, after you get rid of the FBI." The call ended.

She stared at the phone as fear morphed into a slow-burning rage.

Michele Zurlo

Chapter 17

Under the watchful eye of the FBI, the school was being slowly drained of students. Each classroom was questioned by an agent with a degree in child psychology, and every inch of the place was systematically searched. As frantic parents came to pick up their children—news spread like wildfire through the community—they were vetted by the FBI before being allowed in the building. Even then, parents were shown directly to the office and were required to wait for their child to be escorted to the front door.

Rakeem and Jordan were there. Keith found himself on the playground with Mrs. Glyss, the principal, and the aide, Mrs. Collins, who had been in charge of recess. The aide, the mother of a couple of other students at the school, wrung her hands.

"They were there the whole time. I swear it." Mrs. Collins. "They go off to right here and play every single day."

Crime scene specialists combed the area for clues.

Mrs. Glyss sighed. "They're not supposed to interact. I told you that."

Tears gushed from Mrs. Collins' eyes. "I know, but they're never any trouble. There's no drama or fighting. If anything, when they play together, the other kids are nice to Kyle. That poor boy gets picked on something awful." She sniffled into a tissue.

Rakeem cleared his throat. "Mrs. Collins, I assure you—it has no bearing on this case. I need you to take me through every detail, no matter how small or seemingly insignificant. Walk me through your day."

Mrs. Collins set about doing exactly what Rakeem had described. She related every thought, action, and interaction. The kids had fallen off her radar when another student skinned her knee.

Mrs. Glyss chimed in. "Their teacher, Ms. Tully, noticed their absence when she went to take attendance after lunch. We've searched the building."

"And you have no security cameras?" Rakeem already knew the answer to that question, but as a good agent should, he asked the same question multiple times.

Keith scanned the area. The school was on a main thoroughfare at the far end of a neighborhood. The parking lot was on the street side, as was the bus pickup area, and a narrow stand of trees separated the school from the adjacent subdivision. Agents and volunteers were already canvassing the area, and if the children didn't turn up, they'd visit again in the evening when most people were home from work.

Because the houses were so close, the walkway that went alongside the building turned into a blacktop path that led through the trees. It met up with a sidewalk in the neighborhood, and it provided easy access to the yard, which was not fenced.

On either side of the school were complexes housing office buildings. A steady stream of traffic came and went. Though each complex had a wall separating their property from the school, they were low and brick. That meant there was good access on three sides. Security in the school was adequate. Doors were locked, and entrants needed an employee badge or a picture ID. The exterior of the building was not at all secure.

Keith walked the walls on either side of the playground. Dustin, off duty but here because he cared, joined him.

"You're thinking Norris did this." His friend and former partner's observation communicated agreement. "It's likely he came through the neighborhood, since the place where Lina and Kyle were playing was near there."

Keith shared his thoughts. "The parking lots of these businesses have outdoor security cameras mounted to the light posts."

Dustin identified them and studied their placement. Then he motioned to the wall. "We need a closer look. Come on."

They hopped the wall to check the angles, and then they went to Rakeem. He got on the phone and made calls. In a half hour, the owner of each complex had agreed to make all recorded feed available, no warrant necessary.

By the time he made it home to Kat and a house full of family, friends, and agents, he had confirmed that Norris had taken the two children by force. Still images showed a progression of events that had Norris parking a delivery van for a medical supply company behind the Dumpsters. His image was captured going over the wall. A few minutes later, he was photographed returning with Kyle in his arms. He had one arm around Kyle's stomach, and his hand was clamped over the boy's mouth and nose. Angelina got into the van without a struggle. The last image shows her looking back at the playground, probably hoping that someone would notice what was going on.

Michele Zurlo

This was going to break Kat, not that the idea of losing her child hadn't already fractured her heart.

Kat sat on the sofa in the living room with Layla at her side. The two held hands, but Kat's mind was a million miles away. She didn't look up when he came in, probably because so many people were coming and going.

Papa L took one look at Keith, and all hope fell from his face. Keith had no comfort to offer anyone. Mama L came down the stairs with Corey on her hip. He held his arms out to Keith, and Keith took his little boy, holding him tight.

"Daddy, did you find Lina?" The faith and hope in Corey's voice nearly killed him.

"Not yet, but we will. Everybody is looking for her."

Corey nodded, a sagacity to his movement that no four-year-old should have. "Uncle Mal hacked a phone."

"Did he? That's fantastic." He went to Kat, kneeling in front of her to make her look at him.

Her eyes focused slowly, but her expression didn't otherwise change. "He called. He said they were fine, that they'd had dinner, and that they were getting ready for bed. Also, he thinks Kyle is Corey."

That hit Keith like a physical blow to the gut even as his brain screamed that this information hinted at motive. He wanted Kat's children, and the next move was to use them as bait to lure her to him.

Keith pulled Kat into a tight embrace that sandwiched Corey between them. She buried her face in his neck.

"We'll find them." He squeezed her tighter, noting that Layla had scooted over to give them space. "We'll bring them home."

Agents and family came and went. Mama L made them both eat a little something, and then she took Corey up to bed, promising to stay with him all night. Papa L put an air mattress on Corey's floor, and he assured them that at no point would Corey be alone.

As the hour grew later, they sent most people home. Kat insisted that Malcolm take Darcy and the kids home, and then she sent M.J. and his family home to sleep, promising to call the moment they knew something.

Layla refused to leave, though her parents did go home.

The agents that were set up to record any incoming calls made themselves at home, but even they diminished to a skeleton crew. Tech geeks, Special Agents Gibbs and Firstenfeld, remained with them. Field agents rotated tired agents out for fresh ones. Jordan and Rakeem spent much of the night following the leads Malcolm gleaned from the phone he'd hacked. He'd been able to triangulate where the call had originated using methods he wouldn't disclose. His information had narrowed it down to one square mile, which was a lot of ground to cover.

Keith rose to join the search, but Kat grabbed his wrist. "He's gone now. Don't leave. I know Norris is going to call again. He—He likes the sound of my voice."

Hours passed, during which Keith tortured himself for giving in to her plea. Somewhere out there, his Angie was being held hostage. Refusing to go up to bed, Kat had fallen asleep leaning against him on the sofa. Layla was curled up in an oversized chair across from them, and Keith may have nodded off for a few moments.

Kat's phone rang, and immediately the room swarmed with agents. Keith blinked the sleep from his eyes, and Kat leaped on the phone. "Mason? Is that you?" She nodded at the agents who were already at work on tracking the signal.

He tilted the phone so he could also hear what was being said.

"Katrina. I wondered if you'd be awake. Don't worry. The kids are still asleep. I thought I'd make eggs for breakfast. Are there allergies I should know about?"

Kat controlled her breathing the same way she did in the dungeon. "No allergies, but they like cheese slices mixed in with the scrambled eggs."

"Cheese?" They heard the sound of a refrigerator opening and closing. "Is cheddar okay?"

"Yes. If you have a little milk, you can mix that in to make it creamier." She was doing a great job keeping him on the line.

"Great. Now, listen carefully, Katrina. I'm going to text you an address. If you come there alone, I'll give you further directions. If you disobey me, then you won't see your children alive again."

The call ended, and Keith looked to the tech geeks. Agent Gibbs nodded. "We're tracking the address now." He moved away from them and called Jordan. Now that they had a location, a SWAT team would be assembled, and they'd swarm the place.

Kat tugged on his sleeve. "Keith, if I don't go alone, they're going to kill Angelina and Kyle. He's not going to deal. He's going to kill them and himself."

He knew she was right. "Give me a minute."

Firstenfeld let loose a whoop that woke Layla. "We have an address."

Gibbs came back. "SSA Monaghan says to stay here in case more information comes through."

Michele Zurlo

Kat got to her feet. "Where are they?"

"A farmhouse near Ortonville."

Her phone buzzed, notification of a text. She checked it. "That's where the first meeting place is located. I need to freshen up before I go there. Where are we meeting Jordan?"

Gibbs opened his mouth. "He said for you to stay here."

Kat looked to Keith for backup. "I'll call Jordan while you're changing." While she went upstairs, he memorized the address and set the phone down. "Gibbs, what else did Jordan say?"

"He wants to check out the location first. It may not be safe for Ms. Legato to be the one to go inside. He may just kill them all." Gibbs set a hand on Keith's shoulder. "I know this is excruciatingly difficult, especially because you're used to being on this side of the action, but let us do our jobs. We've got a hostage negotiator on the way."

Keith nodded. He knew the procedure, and he understood the call to not put more people into the line of fire. "I'm going to check on Kat."

Upstairs, he found that she'd changed into dark jeans, a long-sleeved cotton shirt, and a hoodie. She glanced at him. "You should get changed. Bring your personal piece if you want, but leave your badge behind."

He shed his shirt and pants, and Layla came in without knocking. She hugged Kat and pressed a set of keys into her hand. "I parked down the street. Go left. I'll keep them busy in the kitchen while you sneak out." She waited until he'd put on black running pants to hug him. "Don't worry about Corey. I'm not leaving, and neither are your parents."

As he closed the door behind them, careful to not make a sound, he heard Layla in the kitchen, laughing and offering to make breakfast. He and Kat ran down the street, finding Layla's car parked in front of a neighbor's house without a problem. They got in and took off.

"I brought my phone," she said. "I wasn't sure whether I should leave it behind to prevent them from tracking us, but then I didn't want to in case Norris should call again or want to send directions via text."

"Good thinking," he said. "They know where we went, and I'm okay with them tracking us as long as we stay two steps ahead. It's going to take several hours to assemble the SWAT unit and brief the negotiator on the situation." He'd left his phone on the dresser, along with his badge. His FBI-issued firearm was in the gun safe in their bedroom, and his personal piece was in his holster.

In the early morning hours, the drive to Ortonville went quickly, especially as they left the suburbs behind. Once they exited the

Re/Captured

freeway and headed in the direction of the address Norris had texted to them, fields and pastures dotted the landscape, broken by stands of trees and the occasional farmhouse.

Before they came to the address, Keith pulled the car over. "I'm getting out. You drive there, get the next instruction, and then come back for me. Take the next two lefts, and the house will be on your left. We'll meet here in twenty minutes."

The Dom part of him didn't want to let her go there alone, but the Special Agent part knew that if she didn't follow directions to the letter it could put them all in jeopardy.

The address Norris had given them was for a house in the middle of nowhere. He'd looked at the laptop screen over Firstenfeld's shoulder, and he knew that the house was empty, abandoned years before. He set off on a fast jog, going overland to approach the house from the rear. Fields like this had holes, and last year's crops had not been turned under yet, so he was careful in the placement of his feet. With the first streaks of dawn throwing some light on everything, he kept his body low in the unplanted field.

When headlights pulled into the driveway, he was in position. He whipped out his night vision binoculars and took stock of the setting. It didn't take long for him to find the surveillance camera pointed at the front door and another on the crumbling garage pointed down the road. Two more kept an eye on the road from the other direction and the front of the house. If there wasn't a trick, and the next set of directions waited inside, then Norris had shown himself to be careless. Nowhere had Keith found precautions that would prevent someone from sneaking up from the back. That didn't mean the actual location would have the same weakness, but it gave him hope that he'd found one at all.

Kat went inside. A flashlight beam bounced off windows as she searched the house. Minutes later, she emerged. She looked around, and he could tell exactly when she noticed the camera. Without much of a reaction, she hurried back to the car. Keith hot-footed it back to the rendezvous point to find her already there.

He slid into the passenger seat. "So?"

"I have another address. I programmed it into Layla's GPS while I waited for you. Where did you go?"

He pointed to the field. "This backs up to the house. I watched from the back while you went inside. He didn't have cameras pointing this way, so I think he thought the field was cover. We'll see how the next location is different. Was that all he sent—an address?"

Michele Zurlo

"Also a smiley and a thumbs-up emoticon."

His lip curled in distaste. "He's fucked up."

"Is that your clinical assessment or a professional one?"

A laugh escaped, though he wasn't at all happy. "Both." He used the computer on Layla's dashboard to switch from street view to a geographical readout.

"Should we send Jordan and Rakeem the new address?" She chewed her lip as she turned onto a northbound country road.

"I'd rather not at this point. Dustin can access the GPS of this car at any time. I expect he'll bring it up after giving us a sizeable head start."

Keith studied the map, making out what he could without real time satellite imagery. "It looks like it's a farmhouse that sits on fifty acres, give or take. I see two outbuildings, a barn and silo, and a cell tower. Driveway is long. The house actually sits toward the back third of the property."

"Keith, promise me that you'll save Angelina first."

"I plan to save them both."

"No, I mean, if something should go wrong, leave me there and get out with Angelina and Kyle, if you can."

"I can't promise that." He hated these kinds of conversations. Unless someone was hovering near death, like they were bleeding out from a gunshot wound, he didn't entertain these kinds of scenarios. Expecting a bad outcome often led to bad outcomes.

"I couldn't live knowing I failed her." Kat's voice was quiet, and pain permeated her words.

He gave her a hard look, hoping to imbue her with some of his strength. "That's probably the most selfish, cowardly thing I've heard you say the whole time I've known you. Kat, I wouldn't like to live knowing I failed either one of you, but you don't see me making doomsday predictions. We're going in there. We're going to get them, and we're going to get out. We're going to have to think on our feet and take chances, but this is happening. We're bringing our baby girl and her friend home." He didn't add that it was unlikely everyone would survive this encounter. He had no plans to let Norris walk out of there.

"I value my daughter's life more than my own, and that's selfish?" Of course, she seized on that.

"Deciding that I should value her life more than yours is selfish." If any sacrifices needed to be made, he'd be the one making them.

She rolled her eyes, but at least her defeatist attitude was gone. "You're impossible."

"Oh, Kitty Kat. I'm very possible, but only for you."

She reached over and squeezed his knee. "I love you."

"I love you too."

"We're getting close. Do you want me to let you out around back like last time?"

If this was where Norris was holed up with the kids, he wanted to do reconnaissance. "We're going to check out the place first. I'll sneak up from the back and report back to you. Then we can come up with a plan."

Snorting, she disagreed. "We're going together."

"Kat, I don't think that's the best plan."

"I'll agree if you can give me one good reason why not."

He couldn't think of any except that he wanted to keep her away from any hint of danger. "Stay low. Stay quiet. Do exactly what I tell you."

"I know the hand signals," she volunteered.

"The hand signals?"

She pulled off the road. As open farmland flanked the entire area, there was nowhere to hide the vehicle. "You know, the ones for stop, look, listen, two guards over there. Like that. Mal likes to point them out when we watch movies or TV shows with sneaky commando types."

He knew this, but in the midst of everything else, he'd forgotten. "Sure. I'll use those."

She stuck the keys in her pocket, and they left the vehicle. Withered plants stuck up from the ground, the skeletons of cornstalks that had been cut down during harvest. They picked their way across the spiky terrain, heading for the scant cover the line of trees separating this field from the next would provide.

When they got that far, he used his binoculars to check the layout. The farmhouse was in sight. He handed the binoculars so Katrina could look. "Go around to the south side, approach from behind the shed." That way, if he was keeping the kids in there, they could get them out and get away without engaging Norris. The FBI could take his ass out without worrying about hostages.

They followed the tree line as far as they could, but it didn't exist on the south side of the house. He made sure they approached from an angle that would put them in a blind spot from the house, plus they were down the hill, so the ground would actually prove to be a barrier. The sun had risen enough so that they'd be seen if they didn't take precautions.

Michele Zurlo

Kat kept low, and she didn't inadvertently stick her ass in the air like so many untrained recruits. He headed for a patch of tall grass that hadn't been mowed. He picked through it carefully, reasoning that this had probably been a dumping ground for old equipment that was no doubt tangled in the weeds and brush.

They were nearly through the patch, perhaps ten feet from the protected side of the shed, when the ground beneath him gave way. He didn't cry out, but Kat let loose a yelp of surprise. He landed hard.

"Kat?"

"I'm okay."

His eyes adjusted to the dimmer light, and he made out their surroundings. It looked like they'd fallen into a pit that at one time had stored hay and other farming items.

"Oh." Her whisper carried to him. "We fell through an old barn floor. That's why it wasn't mowed."

This made no sense to him. He'd been under the impression hay was stored in a loft. "Come again?"

"On a field trip once, we went to a farm that had storage under the barn floor. There was probably an access that came out on the side of the hill at one point." She looked around. "They would have sealed it off."

He looked through the hole above them. Jagged edges of wood surrounded it, marking the weak spot. "They should have filled it in."

"We're going to have to climb out."

He jumped, aiming for the edges of the planks. It was only a few inches out of his reach. "Okay. We can do this. I'll boost you up, and then I'll climb out. Once you're up there, spread out like you're on thin ice, and move out of the weeds."

"Sure."

He wove his fingers together. She put her foot there and jumped, easily catching the edges of the hole. He pushed her feet up, providing support until she was out. Then he grabbed for the edges. Slivers impaled his hands. He ignored the discomfort and pulled himself up through the hole.

Halfway out, he was met with the business end of a Glock 43. Mason Norris wasn't a man who would stand out in a crowd. Medium height, medium build, wavy brown hair—he fit the image of the Average White Male. The only thing about him that stood out was the deadness in his eyes. Behind Norris, Kat lay on the ground, wrists and ankles wrapped with duct tape, and there was a line of it over her mouth. He lifted his gaze to impale the man behind the gun. "You went with a subcompact? I had the opportunity to test out one of those recently. It has a great grip."

Norris ignored his comment. "I knew you'd try something sneaky. I was thinking you'd tell the FBI, they'd call in a big SWAT team, and then I'd have to kill the kids and myself. But this is much better." He backed up in an arc, motioning for Keith to move forward. "Toss her over your shoulder and carry her inside."

Keith went to Kat, moving slowly so that Norris didn't freak out. He peeled her gag away. "Are you hurt?"

"Just my pride. I didn't even know he was there until he put his hand over my mouth and threatened the kids." Her lips were too tremulous to attempt a smile.

"Okay, you two. No talking. Pick her up or I'll shoot you."

Keith helped her to her feet, providing the balance she needed, and then he scooped her up in his arms.

"To the house." Norris demanded.

Keith went quietly. If Norris was alone, then this was going to be a matter of looking for an opportunity to knock him out.

The back porch consisted of two stairs leading to a narrow landing. Keith opened the door without dropping Kat, and he took her inside. The back door led directly to a utility room. He went through there and into the kitchen. Light streamed through the windows, and Keith took in the red, white, and black décor. The wallpaper had roosters in the design. The crockery was all rooster-shaped. He made out salt-and-pepper shakers, a sugar bowl, cookie jar, and other items that might just be there for decoration.

Kat snickered. "You like roosters?"

"This isn't my house."

"Relative?"

"Don't know. Don't care."

Keith pressed his lips together. "Aren't you afraid they'll come home to find you here?"

Norris grunted. "They're dead. I have not had the time to cut off their hands or position them in an A and L."

The house was tidy, well-kept and homey. Keith noted pictures of people, children and grandchildren, competing with roosters for space in the curio cabinets and on the shelves. Following Norris's directions, he set Kat down on the sofa in the living room.

"So, Mason. Where are the kids?" Kat sat forward, her hands on her lap and her feet together like she meant to have them that way. He loved that she was so calm and poised. Having an active role in rescuing Angie and Kyle made a difference.

Norris tossed a roll of duct tape to him. "Bind your ankles and wrists."

Keith wrapped the duct tape around his ankles.

"Nice and tight," Norris observed. "I like that you're taking this seriously."

When it came to his wrists, he unrolled a long strip. He held the end in one hand and swung the roll in a circle to bind his wrists. Norris came over, wound it around a few more times, and then he ripped away the roll.

"Mason?" Kat tried again. "The kids? Are they all right?"

"They're still asleep. I ground up a sleeping pill and put it in their juice. They'll be out for a little while yet."

Alarmed, Keith leaned forward. "They're little kids. How do you know you didn't kill them?"

Norris glared. "I just checked them—that's when I saw you two coming around the back. They're breathing just fine. The boy wet himself, which won't kill him."

"I don't understand why you did this," Kat said. "You killed people for me before we even met."

A clock crowed seven, greeting the morning with a full throated cock-a-doodle-doo. Norris shot the thing a withering stare. "Who the fuck gets a cuckoo clock with a rooster? Doesn't that defeat the whole purpose?"

"Mason?"

Keith liked that Kat kept using Mason's first name. That technique worked to familiarize their relationship and create empathy.

Norris jerked his attention back to Kat. His face softened with a smile. "That? Well, I didn't originally set out to seduce you. I wanted him."

Keith was utterly comfortable with another dude having a crush on him. He objected to being the target of desire for a serial killer, much as Kat had. He arched a brow. "Me? I arrested you."

Norris fanned himself. "Hottest moment of my life, I'm sure."

"So why switch to me?" Kat kept her tone on the compassionate side of neutral.

"I was kidding." Norris aimed the gun at Keith's chest. Keith wasn't sure whether he didn't prefer for Norris to have a crush on him. "I wanted to kill him, so I researched him. There's nothing else to do in prison. When I stumbled on a picture of you, I knew the perfect way to get back at him—make you fall for me."

Kat handled it well. "So those were romantic gestures—the flowers? Getting rid of people who'd done some kind of injury to me?"

"He didn't do anything." Smirking, Norris waved the gun, adjusting the aim to point at Keith's groin. "Someone manhandles you, and he does nothing."

"She broke his nose," Keith said. "There was nothing left to do." He did not want to draw attention to the fact that Kat knew self-defense. Leaving the element of surprise gave her an advantage, and he was going to allow for every advantage possible.

"A real man would have made sure it could never happen again."

"Is that why you did it?" Kat asked. "You wanted to protect me?"

Keith was impressed by her ability to remain soft and unassuming. He shouldn't have been surprised—Kat was very intelligent and accomplished—but he was. His fiancée performed very well under pressure. Pride elbowed aside any doubt he felt.

Norris came closer. He touched her cheek, and she didn't flinch away. "Katrina Legato, you are the type of girl who deserves flowers every single day."

"Aww." She brought her hands to her heart. "That's so very sweet. Tell me how you engineered it so that we would meet."

He laughed, and he put more distance between them. "You figured that out? Damn, you're good. I mean, I knew you were good, but you're damn good." He positioned himself behind the occasional chair covered with rooster print fabric. "Jerry Osman and I go way back. I provided some cleaning services for him when he came into a windfall from a grateful defendant. I used my influence to persuade him to get you as my attorney. You don't work as a defense attorney, so this is literally the only way I could have you. He assigned you to Legal Aid, and he suggested to Brooks—the boss man there—that you'd do well with my case." He ended the telling of his genius with everything but a rooster crow.

"Wow." Keith was impressed. "Did you also arrange for the chain of evidence logs to disappear? We keep those electronically, so that's quite a feat."

"Jerry took care of that." He faced Kat. "Katrina, you were every bit as magnificent as I knew you would be. It took you all of two minutes to find that they were missing. My last attorney never noticed. I thought I'd have to wait for an appeal to get the case thrown out. But this way, Jerry made sure the logs had been permanently erased, and then he dismissed the charges."

Michele Zurlo

The whole picture came together. Keith wondered how much of this Jordan and Rakeem knew and how much they hadn't been able to discern. Knowing them, they'd figured it out, but this was the sort of thing that needed to be kept confidential. It threw into doubt every decision that had ever come in front of Judge Osman, opening the door for endless appeals and retrials. If anything it was the criminals who went free—after paying off Osman—that needed new trials. Unfortunately the justice system did not work that way. Once someone was found not guilty, they couldn't be tried for the same crime again.

Before this came out, the US Attorney's office would need to comb through every case, looking for improprieties. The FBI could assist by tracing the sources of bribes.

Katrina coughed. "Mason, can I have some water? My throat is parched. And, if you can find a glass without a rooster, that would be great."

"I'll get you water, but while I'm gone, I want you to think about one thing. You need to choose, Katrina. You can be with Agent Rossetti here, or you can be with me." He took two steps before turning back. "Oh, I almost forgot. Only one of those options include being with your kids. I've always wanted to be a father, so I've decided to keep them. We're moving out in ten minutes."

He left, and Kat looked at Keith. Wordlessly, she raised her arms above her head and drew them down sharply, separating them to tear the duct tape. Then she stood up and squatted down, tearing the tape on her ankles. Keith did the same thing. Duct tape was a stupid choice for tying up anyone who had taken a basic self-defense class.

The other stupid thing Norris had done was not search Keith. His gun was tucked in his ankle holster. He grabbed it out, motioned for Kat to get out of the way, and he followed Norris into the kitchen.

There wasn't a plan to take him alive. Keith had no reason to warn him or seek his surrender. This man had kidnapped his child and her friend, and then he'd held Keith and Kat captive. He was justified in shooting first and asking questions later.

The sound of the tap shut off as Keith stepped into the kitchen. Norris turned, his brown eyes widening in shock, and he raised his gun. Keith fired two shots, both hitting Norris in the chest. The glass dropped to the floor, shattering an instant before Norris crumpled. Keith went toward the man. He used the toe of his shoe to slide the gun out of reach.

Nudging Norris with his foot, Keith said, "Do you want an ambulance?"

No answer.

With the bottom of his foot on Norris's shoulder, he pushed the criminal onto his back. Norris stared up at him with wide, lifeless eyes.

"Kat, let's find the kids."

"Already did." Her voice came from upstairs, so he hurried in that direction.

The first bedroom had the door closed. He peeked inside to confirm his suspicion. Both homeowners were inside, their bodies thrown carelessly on the floor. He wanted to reposition them, to give them dignity in the midst of this senseless violence, but he knew better than to touch the bodies. He closed the door.

The room at the end of the hall had the door open. He found Kat in there, unwinding the duct tape from Angie's motionless body.

"They're breathing," she said. "I tried to wake them up, but they fall right back asleep. It's a blessing, I think, that they slept through so much."

"Yeah," he agreed. "I'm going to call Jordan. Do you have your cell?"

"Lost it when we fell. They have a land line. I saw a phone in the living room."

He picked up Angie's slumbering form and hugged her to him. Then he kissed her forehead. "I'll be right back."

Jordan was already on his way when he called. Dustin had used the GPS locator on his car to find where they'd parked it, just as Keith knew he would.

"Norris is dead, but he drugged the kids. Bring two ambulances, okay?"

"Consider it done. I'll see you in about twenty minutes."

He went back upstairs and helped Kat finish untying Kyle's arms and legs. Then they carried the kids downstairs and held them until Jordan, Rakeem, and the team arrived.

Michele Zurlo

# Chapter 18

"I keep waiting for her to move the wedding back again."

Katrina paused in the kitchen. The window above the sink was open, and Keith's voice carried in from outside. He and Malcolm were sitting on the patio enjoying the pitcher of iced tea she'd made.

Their wedding was four days away. She'd come home early from work to confirm some of the details and get started on the gift bags for the guests.

"Why would she postpone it?" Malcolm scoffed.

"She has every reason. I'd understand if she didn't want to leave Angie and Corey for a week."

A cup clinked on the glass top of the patio table. "That's a reason to cancel the honeymoon, not postpone the wedding. Stop beating yourself up. I told you, if she didn't want to marry you, she wouldn't."

Katrina marched to the back door and opened it up. "Why are you waiting for me to move the wedding date back? Are you getting cold feet?"

He stood up. "Kat, I didn't know you were coming home early."

"Obviously. Now tell me why you don't want to marry me."

"I want to marry you."

Malcolm got to his feet. "It's time for me to go. Call me later if you're not dead." He pushed in his chair and kissed Katrina on the cheek.

"You don't have to go," Keith said.

Mal paused at the back door. "You really need to talk to Trina about this. It's been bugging you for a while. Time to get it off your chest." He half-waved, half-saluted, and then he was gone.

Katrina crossed her arms and faced Keith. "What's been bugging you?"

There was no way out of this now. He prepared for her wrath. "I'm not sure you're marrying me for the right reasons."

She sputtered. Her hands went wide, waving like they could land on the right words in the air and swat them toward him. She paced, spinning as she fought for words. Then she faced him, hand on hip. "What, exactly, are the right reasons?"

"You should do it because it's what you truly want."

"It's what I want, Keith. You didn't hold a gun to my head and force me to make a choice. If you'll recall, even with a gun pointed at my head, I still chose you."

"The gun was mostly pointed at my dick." His jaw snapped shut. "Nope. Wrong thing to say."

"No shit. Tell me why, after all this time—after I begged you to train me, I moved into your house, I adopted two kids with you, and I agreed to marry you—tell me why you still doubt my sincerity. Are you having second thoughts?"

"You wouldn't let me propose for a year." His normally implacable temper slipped, and he shouted. "Do you know how hard that was for me? I never knew if you were in this for the long haul or not."

The weight of his admission settled in her heart and threw the depth of his torment into sharp relief. She inhaled sharply. "Do you know why I wouldn't let you propose for a year?"

He pressed his lips together and turned away. "The same reason you wouldn't let me tell anyone we were together until Malcolm caught us."

"What? No." She'd dreaded the impact knowledge of their relationship would have had on Keith's friendship with her brother. "I did that because Malcolm had just forgiven you for almost getting Darcy shot. I didn't want him to have yet another reason to cut you out of his life."

He whirled at the reminder, and his volume rose again. "His stupidity got him shot. If he'd listened to me, he and Darcy would have been fine."

"I love that you still think logic is a factor." Rounding the table, she tugged on his wrists, pulling him closer. He only cooperated to a point, leaving at least two feet between them. "I made you wait because I wanted you to be sure."

"I was sure I was going to marry you from the moment you told me that I couldn't ejaculate on your face, and I've told you that a few times."

Their first morning together, he'd ended a blowjob by pulling out of her mouth and climaxing on her face. She'd read him the riot act and forbidden a repeat performance. No matter how hard he tried, it would never be a romantic memory for her.

She growled. "From the moment they accepted us being together, everyone expected us to get married—my parents, my brothers, our friends, even your parents. Despite your hard-ass persona, you're the kind of man who does the right thing. Marrying me was expected because why else would you take a chance with the sister of your best friend and the daughter of your adopted parents? I didn't want you to ask me to marry you because it was expected. I wanted you to want to it. And so I made you wait until all the outside pressure dissipated, because it would shatter me to find out that you didn't actually love me, and that you were only marrying me because you didn't have a choice."

He frowned. His entire visage darkened. "That's ludicrous. Your entire chain of reasoning is completely out there. If I didn't want to spend the rest of my life with you, nothing could have induced me to propose."

"Really? Because earlier you indicated that you thought I might have accepted for the same reason."

Usually Keith was very reasonable, but right now he dug in. "I've heard your mother go after you, Kat, on multiple occasions. I've listened to her ask over and over when you planned to accept my proposal. I've heard her badger you about not letting me get away, how you'll regret it for the rest of your life if you lose me, and how any number of women would be fortunate to have what you have. And that's just when I was around. I can only imagine how blunt she got when I wasn't there. Add to that the veiled and not-so-veiled hints, and I'm surprised you never blew up at her."

The way he described her mother shocked Kat. Her mother's comments hadn't been harsh or mean-spirited. From the time she'd found out they were an item, she'd thrown her whole-hearted support behind them. "She wasn't that bad, and she hasn't said anything in a long time."

"Because I asked her to stop." His mouth set in a grim line. "I wanted you to want to marry me. Even after you said yes, you put off setting a date, and then you postponed twice. Our wedding is four days away, and part of me is just waiting for you to postpone it again, maybe cancel it outright."

This couldn't continue. They couldn't enter into a marriage with a cloud of doubt hanging over them. It would slowly erode their relationship, and that would destroy them both.

"Okay." She nodded. "Okay. Sure. Yeah. I get it." She released her grip on his wrists and went around him. Stopping at the table, she spread both palms on the cool, hard surface and studied the bubbles in the rough underside of the glass surface.

"You get what?"

"You're right. I didn't even realize it before now, but you're right. I did put off the wedding. I put off letting you propose." She felt his presence at her side a split second before his shadow fell over her. "Despite everything, in my heart, I still doubt that you actually want to marry me. I'm still that thunderstruck sixteen-year-old staring like an idiot at the hot guy my older brother brought home on leave. I'm still crushed because when I was eighteen, you rocked my world with a kiss and then told me it was a one-time thing. I guess deep down, I'm waiting to wake up from a dream that I know will end the moment before you say 'I do.' So maybe if I put off that moment, the dream won't end."

His arms closed around her. She found herself turned so that her cheek was against his chest, and his face was buried in her neck. His fist gripped her hair. "I love you, Kat. That's never going to change."

He'd loved her then, only it had been a different kind of love. She melted against him, but she didn't return his embrace. "Why have you never offered to collar me?" Unless it was necessary for purposes of restraint or to show ownership in public, he usually didn't bother with a collar.

A marriage certificate was a legal and social contract, and she wanted that with him, but a collar meant more. It was a commitment and a promise, a symbol of an immutable relationship. It symbolized on so many levels that she belonged to him and that he possessed her. It was his promise to love and care for her, to be her one and only Master, and it was her promise to submit to and serve him.

"Because I wasn't certain you'd accept one."

She tilted her face up. "I would." It would have allayed her fears about whether he actually wanted to marry her or if he was bowing to familial pressure, and it would have done the same for him. They both realized the truth of the matter, and he crushed her to him.

"Would it be dumb if I asked you now? I've wanted to collar you for a long, long time."

She put distance between them so she could breathe, and she met his clear, emerald gaze. "I would love if you asked now. I don't need a public ceremony. I just need to know you want me to be yours, always, in all ways."

He lifted her and carried her to the grass. "Kneel."

She got on her knees, kneeling before her Master.

"Kitty Kat, will you accept my collar?"

Tears swam in her eyes, distorting her vision. "Yes, Master. I will gladly and proudly wear your collar."

Michele Zurlo

He lifted her, and their lips met, a clash that didn't last long because she eagerly surrendered to him. When they were breathless and needy, he broke away.

"Master?"

"Yes, Kitty Kat?"

"When do I get my collar?"

"I have to buy it. Don't worry—I've had it picked out for a long time."

She touched her throat. "I feel suddenly naked."

He looked her up and down. "Not nearly naked enough. Let's go inside. I have an idea for how we can spend the next hour before we have to go pick up the kids."

All plans for knocking the gift bags from her to-do list were forgotten.

Chapter 19

The music swelled to a close, and Corey clapped as the song ended. In his black tuxedo, he looked like a miniature version of Keith. He and Keith had even cut their hair the same way, which meant Corey had shaved his soft blond waves, which used to fall past his ears, to a half inch on top and a quarter inch on the sides. "We rocked it, Mommy!"

Katrina laughed at her son's enthusiasm. "We sure did. You're quite a dancer. Where did you learn those moves?"

"I practiced with Grandpa." He held out his arms, and she bent down for a hug. "I wanted to do a good dance with you on your special day."

A few feet away on the dance floor, Keith picked up Lina and kissed her cheek. Lina's flower girl dress was patterned after Katrina's wedding dress, though it lacked a train.

He brought Lina over, and the four of them hugged. Elsewhere on the dance floor, their bridesmaids and groomsmen engaged in the traditional first dance as well. Though they'd started out together, they'd brought Lina and Corey out to join them.

"Ladies and gentlemen, please join the wedding party on the dance floor." The DJ put on a song with a faster beat, and their family and friends flooded forward.

Lina wiggled to get down. She and Corey ran off to be with their cousins. Keith set his hands on her hips, and his lips grazed against hers. "Well, Mrs. Legato-Rossetti, you did it."

Katrina had opted to hyphenate her name, and in a move that still stunned her, so had Keith. A huge smile stretched her lips. "So did you, Mr. Legato-Rossetti."

"For better or for worse," he said. "You're stuck with me."

"I wouldn't have it any other way."

The wedding had been beautiful, wrought with emotion and tears. Her mother had sobbed, and Katrina had spied a sheen wetting her father's eyes. Katrina had invited Keith's parents, but they had chosen not to attend. She felt bittersweet about that, but Keith didn't seem affected. He'd cut ties with them so long ago, when he'd chosen a sober path and they hadn't, that he hadn't expected anything different.

The reception passed in a blur of congratulatory hugs and wishes for a happy life.

Erica came with her father. She and Robert danced together, and Robert seemed to treat this as an event to talk to his constituents. She guessed that a senator's work was never done.

As the night drew to a close, they came to say goodbye. When Robert kissed her cheek, he whispered, "I've floated your name to the President. You should hear something soon. There will be a vetting process. Let's call that my wedding present."

They took their leave, and when she told Keith what Robert had said, Keith's cocky grin grew. "Tonight I'm going to sleep with a married woman, and in a few months, I'm going to curry favor with a judge through sex. Life is good."

Her parents brought Lina and Corey to them next. Her dad held Corey, who had his head resting on Mario's shoulder.

Donna hugged Katrina. "We're going to take the kids home now. They're both tired."

Katrina knelt down to hug Lina. "It's been a big day. Be good for Grandma and Poppa, and we'll call you every day."

They'd debated taking the wedding trip, but with Norris dead and her family being so supportive, they'd decided to give it a try. If Lina wanted them to come home at any time, she only had to ask.

Lina's small arms squeezed Katrina's neck. "I will, Mommy. Now that you're married, are you going to bring home a little sister? I'd really like a little sister."

Katrina pulled back to look at Lina. "Did your Daddy put you up to this?"

"Nope. It's something I've always wanted. I like Corey, but he's a boy. If you have a little girl, I can brush her hair and pick out her clothes. I'll help feed her and change diapers." Lina's lower lip came out in a pout that always worked on Keith but had a smaller success rate with Katrina.

Not quite sure how to respond, Katrina laughed. "We'll see. Maybe Grandma will take you over to see Aunt Darcy, and you can help with Zella." She kissed Lina's cheek and passed her off to Keith.

Lina had been fine since the ordeal. She hadn't wet the bed or had nightmares. Her therapist wasn't surprised at how well Lina was coping, considering what her life had been like before she came to Katrina and Keith. Kyle was another story. His parents had taken him out of school and cut off all communication with the Legato-Rossettis. Katrina didn't blame them, but she felt bad for the kids.

As for the actual experience, Lina and Kyle both maintained that Norris had been kind to them, except for when he took them and when he tied them up. Other than that, he'd played games, fed them pizza, ice cream, and juice, and he'd even put on a magic show. Neither child had a clue about the murdered couple in the master bedroom.

"Our plane leaves in the morning," Keith said to her father. "I emailed you our itinerary, and we'll have our cell phones. We'll call every day."

Mario shook his head, amusement lilting his lips. He hugged Keith. "Son, take this time to be with your new wife. Lina and Corey are in good hands."

"I know, Papa L. I know." He didn't say it, but they'd never left the kids before. This might be harder on them than it would be on the children.

After her parents left, the party kicked up a notch before coming to a screeching halt at eleven, when their rental of the hall came to a close.

Keith took her home, the back of his car full of gifts. Layla had more in Dustin's car, and she'd promised to unload everything the next day.

Coming through the door after the momentousness of the day, Katrina couldn't help but feel that this was anticlimactic. The house felt empty, like it knew it would be abandoned for the next five days. If Keith felt the same way, he showed no sign.

He tugged on her hand. "Let's go upstairs. I want to undress you."

She followed him up and took her place standing at the foot of the bed. He flipped on the light switch to their bedroom and closed the curtains. She felt him behind her. His fingertips traced the line of her shoulder, and he kissed her neck. She closed her eyes and made a small sound of contentment.

He eased the zipper down, and she felt his fingers tickling at her waist in his attempt to undo the tiny buttons and hooks that made her dress so complicated.

"You didn't say if you liked my dress."

The low timbre of his chuckle reached her. "I liked it a lot more before I realized how many doll-sized buttons are on this thing." He kissed her lower back. "It's beautiful, but to be honest, I didn't notice it much until later. When you came down the aisle, I was suddenly glad I didn't have to do any walking. You're so breathtaking, Kat, that it was all I could do to stay standing. All I could think about was that you were mine. Before you, I never thought I deserved happiness, much less that I could actually feel joy. I'd been leading a hollow existence, and I hadn't really understood what that meant, how meaningless it all was, until you showed me a whole new existence."

The fabric gave way, tumbling down her shoulders, and he got to his feet. He came around and stood in front of her.

"I love you, Kat. Before you showed me, I didn't know how to love or why I'd want to open myself to someone like this." He brushed his fingertips along her hairline. She thought he might kiss her, but he eased her dress down her body and helped her to step out of it.

Underneath, she wore white lingerie. Her lacy bra was a scrap of fabric she'd chosen with him in mind. With her small breasts, she didn't always need a bra, but he liked the way they looked on her. On her legs, she wore thigh-high, silk stockings held up by garters. She'd foregone panties.

He unbuckled the straps to her heels, and she stepped out of them. Backing up a few paces, he drank her beauty, his gaze branding every inch of her skin.

"Kneel, Kitty Kat."

She got on her knees, assuming an attentive position with her arms clasped behind her, and aimed her gaze at the floor. She heard him move around the room. She heard a clinking sound and assumed he'd removed his cuff links. A drawer opened and closed. In this pose, the calm anticipation of submitting to her Master washed over her, and she awaited his pleasure.

After a few minutes, he stood behind her, the instep of his foot barely touching her calf. She felt his touch on her bare skin, his palm cupping her throat and forcing her chin to lift.

"Kitty Kat, a few days ago, you agreed to wear my collar. Has anything changed?"

"No, Master. More than anything else, I want to wear your collar."

Something cold encircled her neck. "This collar symbolizes our loving bond, that I am your Master and you are my submissive. Wear it with pride."

"Thank you, Master." Tears leaked from her eyes. Saying her vows during the wedding hadn't choked her up this much. "I will. I promise."

Now he was in front of her, and his thumb wiped wetness from her cheeks. "This is your day collar, Kitty Kat. You will wear it at all times, except to bathe and sleep. If I'm here, I'll take it off and put it back on. If I'm not here, you will do it."

She never wanted to take it off, but she did want to touch it. "Can I see it?"

"Yes."

They didn't have a mirror in the bedroom, so she scampered off to the bathroom. It was a necklace, a thin strand of white gold with a heart pendant. The heart was encrusted with diamonds and roses, and something heavy hung on the back of her neck. She turned the necklace to find that the clasp was a lock.

Keith leaned against the door to the bathroom, his expression patiently expectant. His jacket, tie, and cummerbund were gone, and his shirt was open at the neck.

"I love it." She touched the lock, which now hung in the front. "You always choose perfectly."

"I wasn't sure about the roses on the heart, but then I though fuck it—you've always loved flowers, and I'm not going to let a psychopath ruin that for you."

She'd been wary of flowers since Norris had left the first bouquet, to the point where she questioned whether she wanted to carry a bouquet down the aisle at her wedding. She brought the pendant around so that it lay next to the lock, fingering them both. "Thank you, Master. I will always treasure my collar and what it means."

He held out his arms, and she went to him. His firm lips captured hers in a duel whose outcome was assured. She surrendered to him, melting into his embrace. He carried her to the bed and set her down gently. They kissed each other as she undressed him. His mouth and hands roamed her body, his possessive caresses sensual and sure. When he was naked, he bound her wrists to the headboard and buried his face in her pussy. With his lips, tongue, and fingers, he brought her close to orgasm, and then he sat up.

"I love this pussy. It's my pussy." His harsh emerald gaze demanded something of her.

"Yes, Master. It's yours."

His fingertip circled her anus. "This ass is mine."

"Yes, Master. It's yours."

He crawled up her body and took control of her mouth with a kiss that seared to her already hot core. "This mouth is mine."

"Yes, Master. Every part of my body is yours."

He drew himself up, kneeling over her torso. He pumped his cock in his hand. "Open up, Kitty Kat."

Michele Zurlo

She parted her lips and used her tongue to wet his length. He lifted his cock and tilted his hips so she could lick his balls. She sucked his sac gently.

"Fuck," he said. "You're going to make me come. Let go, Kitty Kat." He backed up a little and fed his cock into her mouth. With her hands bound, she was a vessel for his pleasure, and so she threw herself into making sure her Master enjoyed this.

After a few thrusts, he withdrew. He moved down her body, once again coming to rest between her thighs. His cock nudged her opening, and he surged forward. Katrina hadn't changed her mind about not wanting more children, and so last week, she had an IUD inserted. She really didn't want to use condoms with Keith, not unless they were having anal sex.

He set a fast pace, and Katrina writhed under the onslaught. She lifted her hips, meeting his frenzy with equal fervor.

"Come for me," he said. "I want to feel it." He hooked one leg with his arm, hiking it higher as he twisted his hips.

Unable to deny him, she cried out, "Master." Waves washed through her as her orgasm convulsed around his cock.

Above her, Keith's face scrunched up as he fought for control. His pace slowed, extending her orgasm and giving him what he needed to hold off.

"Again," he said. "You're going to come again.

"Yes, Master." Her pussy, extra sensitive from the orgasm, was already on the way to the next level.

He increased the pace, pounding into her tender flesh. Sounds tore from both of them, cries and moans, grunts and exclamations, until she came again. This time she wringed an orgasm from him. His hot fluids bathed her insides as his body jerked, and he collapsed on top of her.

When she regained control of her voice, she said, "Thank you, Master. Thank you for my orgasm, but mostly, thank you for this collar. I love you, and I love being yours."

Though it required much effort, he lifted his head from her shoulder and gazed into her eyes. "You're welcome, Kitty Kat. I love you, and I cherish everything you give to me."

Dear Reader,

I hope you enjoyed reading about Keith and Katrina as much as I love writing about them. These characters are close to my heart, and I hope they've winnowed their way into yours as well.

Re/Captured is the second story featuring Keith Rossetti and Katrina Legato. A lot has changed for them since they got together in Re/Paired. They've both come a long way since then.

Stay in touch. Let me know your thoughts. Email and social media are great, but your reviews and recommendations help other readers find my books. They make a difference—even if they're just a few heartfelt words. Please consider leaving an honest review on Amazon, Goodreads, iTunes, Barnes and Noble, your blog—wherever you can.

Love, Michele

Visit www.michelezurloauthor.com for information about my other titles.

Michele Zurlo

I'm Michele Zurlo, author of the Doms of the FBI and the SAFE Security series and many other stories. I write contemporary and paranormal, BDSM and mainstream—whatever it takes to give my characters the happy endings they deserve.

I'm not half as interesting as my characters. My childhood dreams tended to stretch no further than the next book in my to-be-read pile, and I aspired to be a librarian so I could read all day. I ended up teaching middle school, so that fulfilled part of my dream. Some words of wisdom from an inspiring lady had me tapping out stories on my first laptop, so in the evenings, romantic tales flow from my fingertips.

I'm pretty impulsive when it comes to big decisions, especially when it's something I've never done before. Writing is just one in a long line of impulsive decisions that turned out to showcase my great instincts. Find out more at www.michelezurloauthor.com or @MZurloAuthor.

Re/Captured

Lost Goddess Publishing

The Doms of the FBI Series
Re/Bound (Doms of the FBI 1)
Re/Paired (Doms of the FBI 2)
Re/Claimed (Doms of the FBI 3)
Re/Defined (Doms of the FBI 4)
Re/Leased (Doms of the FBI 5)
Re/Viewed (Doms of the FBI 6)
Re/Captured (Doms of the FBI 7)

The SAFE Security Series
Treasure Me (SAFE Security 1)
Switching It Up (SAFE Security 2)
Forging Love (A SAFE Security Novella)
Unlocking Temptation (A SAFE Security Short)
Drawing On Love (SAFE Security 3)

Paranormal
Dragon Kisses 1-3
Blade's Ghost

Anthologies
BDSM Anthology/Club Alegria #1-3 by Michele Zurlo and Nicoline Tiernan
New Adult Anthology/Lovin' U #1-4 by Nicoline Tiernan
Menage Anthology/Club Alegria #4-7 by Michele Zurlo and Nicoline Tiernan
Nexus #1: Tristan's Lover by Nicoline Tiernan
Discovering Desires Anthology by Michele Zurlo

Made in the USA
San Bernardino, CA
17 March 2018